## ABOUT THE AUTHOR

SJI (Susi) Holliday grew up near Edinburgh and worked
in the pharmaceutical industry for many years before
she started writing. A lifelong fan of crime and horror,
her short stories have been published in various places,
and she was shortlisted for the inaugural CWA Margery
Allingham Prize. She is the acclaimed author of eleven
novels and a novella. A film adaptation of her Trans-
Siberian-set thriller, *Violet*, is currently in development.
You can find her website, social media links and newsletter
sign-up at www.linktr.ee/susiholliday.

ALSO BY THE AUTHOR

*Writing as SJI Holliday*
Black Wood
Willow Walk
The Damselfly
The Lingering
Violet
The Deaths of December
Mr Sandman

*Writing as Susi Holliday*
The Last Resort
Substitute
The Hike
The Street

# The Party Season

## SJI Holliday

HODDER

First published in Great Britain in 2023 by Hodder & Stoughton
An Hachette UK company

This paperback edition published in 2023

1

A CIP catalogue record for this title is available from the British Library

Paperback ISBN 978 1 399 71425 9
eBook ISBN 978 1 399 71426 6

Typeset in Monotype Plantin by Manipal Technologies Limited

Printed and bound in Great Britain by Clays Ltd, Elcograf S.p.A.

Hodder & Stoughton policy is to use papers that are natural, renewable
and recyclable products and made from wood grown in sustainable forests.
The logging and manufacturing processes are expected to conform to the
environmental regulations of the country of origin.

Hodder & Stoughton Ltd
Carmelite House
50 Victoria Embankment
London EC4Y 0DZ

www.hodder.co.uk

To my nephew, Cody... Yes, this means you have to read it.

# I

# The Party Girl

It's always terrifying to walk into a room full of strangers.

Not your average room, either. The hotel lobby is probably bigger than my flat. High ceilings and ornate cornices, pillars and arches. The flooring would probably be worth a year's salary, even if it is looking a little scuffed in that way where over-shining it only makes the wear and tear more noticeable. The red velvet chairs look new though. People are milling around, criss-crossing between the various bars and suites and the toilets. The smokers bring a steady stream of cold air via the revolving doors. Classical music is being piped in through the speakers, at just the right level to blend the various chatter and clatter together. The mood is frenzied but jovial. The black and white uniformed staff look harassed but the adrenaline buzz will keep them all going through what must be one of their busiest nights of the year.

There's a giant digital-poster screen with all the names of the function suites and which parties are in them, so I take a few moments to compose myself and read down through the list.

*Amsterdam: eXperiential eVents*
*Paris: Hobbs & Parker Consultancy*
*Berlin and Vienna: Woodham NHS Trust*
*Rome: The Flat Flowers Company*
*Stockholm: Barlow & Wolfenstone LLB*

European Capitals are a bit old school when it comes to naming of rooms, I think, but it's in keeping with this hotel, which for all its lobby pomp, is no longer the place to see and be seen. It's such an eclectic mix of companies, I can only imagine what each of these rooms are like. I arrived just before nine, so I know I'm going to be playing catch-up with most of these people who have probably been here for at least two hours, and more than likely started out in the pub before that.

A couple of hairsprayed and immaculately dressed women clip clop past me on towering heels, a blend of their cloying perfumes trailing in their wake. I don't like strong perfume. I've worn Anaïs Anaïs since my mum bought me my first bottle for Christmas when I was thirteen. I made it last as long as I could, but I've had to buy my own bottle every Christmas since. I smile at them as they pass, but they don't notice me. They don't know me. Why should they care? I wait for a moment for the screen to flip to the next page again, where there is a schematic map of the location of the rooms.

This screen, and the velvet chairs, look like an attempt to keep this stuffy old place current. They need that Christmas party business. They don't want to lose it all to the fancy new hotel on the waterfront.

I take a deep breath and follow the directions to Stockholm. A place I've never been and am unlikely to visit. Not on my salary. Not that I'd have the time, even if I could afford it.

It's one of the bigger suites, according to the diagram, and thankfully the bar runs along the left side of the room, away from the white-clothed tables. I hate when you have to walk past everyone to get to where you want to be. I mean, even if no one is paying attention, it still feels like all eyes are on you, doesn't it?

I'm impressed by the classiness of this space. One of the more expensive suites, I imagine. But an LLB is a law firm, right? They can afford it. Those guys have an hourly rate that would make you weep. They work long hours too. High pressure. Male dominated. Lots of time away from their families.

My kind of people. For tonight, at least.

I have to hoist my dress up a little to climb onto the bar stool with any level of grace. I hook a stiletto heel over the chrome bar near the bottom and shimmy over into the middle of the seat. Then I fix my dress back down over my thighs, and place my blood-red clutch bag on the bar. It wouldn't usually be my kind of thing, but in these sorts of places you have to make an effort to fit in. The dress is from a charity shop, but the label says it's from Whistles. Smoky grey with a shimmering fleck. Slinky but classy. I catch a glimpse of myself in the mirror behind the bar and give my hair a little floof. It's blonde and wavy tonight, and the pair of diamond hairclips sparkle under the spotlights. A quick glance at the other women in attendance, and I think I've hit the right vibe.

There are a few excited revellers further down the bar, and the barman is making them cocktails. He's shaking and twizzling, and picking glazed, dried fruits out of a jar, but he's spotted me and he gives me a little eyebrow raise and a nod to let me know that he'll be serving me next.

3

I smile back politely, and swivel around just enough to take another look at the room. The guests. It looks like this party started early, as most of the plates have been cleared and people are in relaxed mode, chatting, laughing.

As if on cue, the music goes up and the lights go down. A disco ball spins a kaleidoscope of colours around the walls. It's a holly jolly Christmas. People are having fun.

I'm pleased for them. I am. But I'm not really a mixer. I prefer my own company, mostly. Or maybe just one or two others around me. Plus my cat, Claypole. He's always around. My constant companion. Even if he's not technically alive.

The barman comes over, white cloth tossed casually over one shoulder of his neat black shirt. He's appraising me, but trying not to give himself away. He's working. He's professional. But I can always tell when I've piqued someone's interest.

'What can I get for you?'

Strong jaw. Clear blue eyes. He's really quite a catch.

'Kir Royale, please. And a glass of still water with ice. Tap is fine.'

He places a small chrome dish of pretzels and chilli puffs in front of me, and lays down a square paper mat with the name of the hotel embossed in gold.

I'm watching him pour the Crème de Cassis into a chrome measuring cup when I sense, rather than feel, a presence to the other side of me.

*One… two… three…*

I swivel around slowly.

'Evening,' he says. His grin reveals very white teeth. Natural though, not veneers.

I smile in a way that I'm certain could be described as *demure*, having practised it many times in the mirror.

4

It's important to get this part just right. The barman returns with my drinks. He places the champagne flute and the tumbler of water on another two of his posh paper mats.

'Thank you,' I say, after a beat. I am not sure if I will have to pay or not. You assume these things have a free bar, but there have been some I've been to where it's run out by eight. Smaller companies usually. Or cheapskates.

My new companion orders himself a large gin and tonic, telling the barman to choose whatever he recommends. I'd do the same if I were ordering a G&T. There is a ridiculous variety these days.

The man beside me either reads my mind, or decides this is a decent conversation opener, and dives straight in. 'Far too many choices, right? What type of gin? What flavour of tonic? Do I want lemon or cucumber? I mean...' He shrugs theatrically.

'Or orange,' I say, nodding towards the drink that the barman has placed down on a space somewhere in between the two of us, not quite sure if we are together or not.

'Tanqueray Sevilla,' the barman says, 'and a Mediterranean tonic. Imagine yourself on a sunny Spanish beach.' He winks at me, then strides off to serve someone else.

The man looks uncertain for a moment, and I run through what I imagine he is thinking. He wonders if perhaps there is something between me and the barman. Maybe he should take his drink and go back to his table? Or should he plough on, now that he's here – getting one drink? He hasn't even offered me one, but I suppose the timing didn't quite work. Plus, he's not paying. Unless he's the CEO. But I don't think so. He's slightly too nervous for that.

I watch his throat as he takes a long swig of his drink. He places the fishbowl back down on the bar. It's mostly just ice now. I notice then that his eyes are slightly glazed.

*Too* drunk?

Perhaps he is not the one. I'll give it a bit longer and see.

'Andrew Morrison,' he says. He offers a hand, and I shake it. He has a good grip. Firm but not trying to prove anything by crushing any bones. He stands a little straighter. Re-focussed. 'Are you new? I don't think I've seen you around...'

I take a sip of my water, look him in the eye. 'To be quite honest, Andrew, I don't work here. I just walked in off the street in search of a free bar.' I wait a moment, revelling in the dead air. Then I blink.

He throws his head back and guffaws. 'Very good. You almost had me there.'

'I'm Meryl Cassidy. I'm on a temp contract... and before you say it, yes, like Meryl Streep. My mum was a massive fan of *The Bridges of Madison County*.'

'Oh, what a great film. An absolute classic. Incredible actress. Or do we say actor now, for all of them? I'm never quite sure...' He moves in closer to me. 'I love old movies, actually. So many incredible, feisty females to choose from.'

Up close, he smells a little less fragrant. A little less appealing. I want to back away, but I hold myself firm. I need to show an interest. He's not bad looking, although maybe a bit older than I'd normally go for. I should be surprised at how quickly he's attempting to move things along, but then, I suspect he has been out all afternoon. He's clearly a man with a plan. Most of them are, when it comes down to it.

I glance at my untouched champagne cocktail and consider knocking it back, then making my excuses to leave. When I look back at Andrew, his face is mostly fixed on my cleavage. He flips his head back up quickly and gives me a wide grin.

He lays a hand on my wrist.

'You know, Meryl Cassidy... I have a very nice room here for the night. Deluxe, in fact. Fully stocked mini bar. Incredible roll-top bath. Far too big for one person.' He pauses, licks his lips. 'It'd be a shame not to make full use of the room... It's nearly Christmas, isn't it? Don't you think you deserve a little luxury? I'm sure you've been very *nice* this year.' He strokes his thumb over my hand. 'Or perhaps you've been very, very naughty?'

I smile in a way that I hope confirms my acceptance of his proposal. Then I pick up my bag and slide myself off the stool. Funny, isn't it? How quickly they drop the small talk and resort to their blatant pick-up chat. I'm sure he's not a bad man. He's just conforming to his own stereotype.

It's almost a shame that I have to kill him.

# 2

# Becky

It's a frosty Friday morning in December and DS Becky Greene is the first in the office. She's got a mountain of paperwork to sort from her last few cases, and with Woodham CID under the spotlight for cuts, they can't afford to fall behind.

More importantly, for today at least, she also has to decide on the best joke for the Christmas Dip – a ridiculous idea thought up by her friend and colleague, DC Joe Dickson, who would probably have been promoted by now if he spent more time on work and less time messing around. There is a separate sweepstake going around under the desks, on whether their boss, DI Eddie Carmine, would actually contribute a joke, or just continue to rack up debt against the charity swear box.

She scans through another list of terrible jokes that would barely make it into a cheap box of crackers, then her eyes lock on an actual gem.

*What happens if you eat Christmas decorations?*

*… you get tinsel-itis.*

'That is genius,' she mutters to herself, mouth half-full of the festive fruit and nut protein bar she'd picked up from the counter when she'd paid for her petrol. Two for a pound and so far it tasted like the crumbs at the bottom of Santa's sack. She's trying not to choke, washing it down with a swig of water, when the door flies open and Miriam bustles in, mostly obscured by a huge cardboard box. She drops it next to her desk in the corner, and turns to Becky, hands on hips.

'Wait until you see what I've got in *here*.'

Becky rolls her eyes, then tosses the rest of the protein bar in the bin. This was her attempt at being healthy – trying to avoid the temptations of a sausage and egg McMuffin, or the van outside that does the best bacon rolls she's ever tasted. It was inevitable that her plan would be foiled, because now that Miriam is here, she's going to feel under pressure to nip out and get something for them both.

'Please don't say it's another tree…' Becky walks over to Miriam and holds on to the box as the other woman stabs at the taped edges with a pair of scissors.

'Nope. Even better!' Miriam unplugs her earphones from her ears and the tinny sound of 'Stay Another Day', East 17's sad non-Christmas but definitely a Christmas song leaks out before she pulls her phone out of her bag and switches the music off.

Becky glances around the room. They've got a 6ft tree in one corner, decorated with hundreds of multi-coloured baubles, a big gold star on top. Tinsel is draped around every single monitor, red and green bows are stuck to the back of all the chairs, and there is a failed attempt at stick-on snowflakes on the windows, where the boss had put his foot down and told Miriam to take them off.

Miriam is one of the longest serving civilian staff at the station. She's a big fan of kitschy, seasonal decorations, home-baking, and making sure she knows everything about everything. The latter skill comes in *very* handy at times, so it's definitely best to keep her on side.

'Ta da!'

Becky turns her attention back to the box as Miriam wrestles the last piece of tape off, and folds back the flaps, just in time for the giant inflatable snowman to pop out like a jack-in-the-box.

'Isn't he the best? They're on BOGOF in Tesco so I took one home and brought the other one in here. It's perfect, isn't it? What do you think?' She puts her hands around its neck and pulls the snowman out of the box. It wobbles a bit before righting itself and fixing Becky with its dead, black eyes.

'It's—'

'Oh my *god*, that is amazing!' The door swings open again, bringing in DC Joe Dickson. He grins at them both before yanking open his coat with a flourish, revealing a navy blue jumper with a flashing Christmas tree on the front. 'Almost as cool as this little number,' he says, giving Becky a wink. He smells like a cinnamon swirl.

Becky's mouth drops open. 'That. Is. Something,' she says. 'I really hope you didn't get me one this year.'

Joe sticks out his bottom lip. 'I wanted to, but you were so ungrateful last time...'

Miriam is tying a scarf around the snowman's neck. 'Where should I put him? Next to the tree, or—'

Becky raises her eyebrows.

'Eddie's office?' Miriam suggests, innocently.

'Oh, I think he'll *love* it.' Joe hangs his coat on one of the hooks by the door, then picks up the snowman and carries it across the open-plan space to DI Carmine's office in the far corner.

Becky feels a bit mean. Eddie hates Christmas. It was bad enough already, for reasons that he's never fully disclosed, but six years ago they'd had a serial killer running rings around them, adding his own particular brand of festivities. The Photographer case had been the first that she and Eddie had worked on together, and the intensity of that had cemented them as a team pretty quickly. But no one really liked to remember it, which is why no one in their right mind would dare bring an advent calendar into the office.

But the snowman is just a bit of fun, and she'll take the flak if he kicks off.

A flurry of other officers has started to drift into the office now, and she's missed her chance to nip out for a breakfast roll for just her and Miriam. There's no way she's going now, or she'll end up having to get stuff for everyone. She fishes the protein bar back out of her bin and takes a nibble.

'Wow,' Joe says, plonking himself down on the seat next to her desk and snatching the bar from her hand. 'You're in before anyone else *and* you're eating weird health food. From the bin.' He wrinkles his nose. 'Who are you and what have you done with Becky?'

She grabs the snack back from him and throws it on her desk. 'Come on, let's go for coffees.' Becky heads off out of the room, knowing Joe will follow her. They started around the same time and they hit it off immediately, an easy banter between them that made him feel like a brother rather than a colleague. She hasn't spent much time with him recently though, mainly because since she got promoted, he's distanced himself from her a bit. It's something they need to talk about at some point, but both of them clearly feel awkward about it.

She's heading towards the kitchen area, but he grabs her elbow and hooks his arm under hers, leading her towards the stairs.

'I need a Chestnut Praline Latte.'

Becky glances at her watch. It's 8:45 a.m. How did that happen? She got in at seven, and she's barely got half of anything done. She really needs to sign off on the Stephenson case and get it off her desk. After that, she has three more sets of notes to go through, and then she's clear... until something else comes in, of course. Nothing too big though, she hopes. They could all do with a break.

'I'm not sure we've got time to nip out before the boss gets in...'

'It's nearly Christmas, Becks. Let your hair down.'

Becky battles with this in her head as they make their way down the stairs, finally convincing herself to relent. They're on their way out of the station entrance when she spots someone she'd rather not see climbing out of his shiny black Merc. DCI William Wilde – the Big Boss – closely followed by his partner, or admin assistant or whatever he really is because no one is entirely sure, DI Jonty Davis.

Joe spots them too and stops walking. 'Uh oh. Harness the mules. Wild Bill, incoming.'

They take a step back inside. Not the best time to be nipping out. Not now. Wild Bill is a stickler for timekeeping, and if he's here before nine a.m., it can only mean one thing: something big enough and ugly enough to warrant him coming here from his cushy office with the river views and the posh coffee machine.

So much for getting that paperwork finished.

The blue sky has gone, leaving a heavy canopy of grey, and a layer of melting sleet covers the cars. Becky hugs her arms around herself, trying to keep warm. She takes another step back, stopping at the perfect place where the heating blasts out from the vents just inside the glass doors.

The pair of them watch as another car shoots into the car park, slotting itself into the remaining empty space. The car door slams and a familiar figure marches across the tarmac towards the entrance. His face is not in its happy place.

'I'm kind of regretting sticking Mr Frosty in the boss's office now,' Joe mutters.

DI Eddie Carmine is right in front of them. He's flustered, his breath coming out in icy puffs, his hair sticking up in clumps. Suited, but shirt un-ironed. Becky had told him to get one of those steamer things but he hadn't listened. He wasn't meant to be in this early today. He's clearly been summoned by a phone call.

'Get upstairs, you two,' he says, pushing himself through the narrow gap between them. 'I've a feeling the DCI's about to ruin everyone's Christmas...'

Becky steals a glance at Joe as DCI Wilde starts walking towards them. He raises a hand in greeting.

Behind them, Eddie mutters, 'Fuck.'

Joe nudges her with his elbow as he turns around to address him. 'Charity swear box is active again this year, boss. Dogs for the blind.' He holds out a hand.

Becky bites her lip and tries not to laugh. 'Morning, boss,' she says. But Eddie has already legged it up the stairs.

# 3
# Harry

Most people don't really *get* what Harry does at work every
day, so it's easier just to tell them that he works in an office.
It's technically true. But it's the *type* of office that's the
interesting part – to him, anyway. He's a Document Control Manager at a small biotechnology firm. It was set up
by two brothers – science grads who wanted to make a difference. Twenty-five years on, and they've expanded from
a workforce of two, to almost eight hundred, becoming one
of the area's largest employers. Harry's been there since he
graduated six years ago. To say it's his whole life isn't really
an exaggeration. Especially since he met Heather.

Heather and Harry. It just sort of *works*. They were
friends for almost two years before it turned into some
thing more, six months ago. She hadn't gone to the
Christmas party the year she started, and Harry had
almost got himself entangled with Lorraine from the IT
Helpdesk – she'd been quite insistent that she wanted to
'provide a good service', which had been a cheesy almost
winning line, until something stopped him. Heather had
only started two weeks before, and he barely knew her,

but already he had a hunch that there might be something there worth waiting for.

Turns out he was right.

Besides, Lorraine didn't mind. Her line worked effortlessly on Harry's workmate, Luke, and they'd dated for over a year – until she'd decided it was time for an upgrade. Matthew in Finance, no less. They're still going strong, he thinks, although he's not one hundred per cent sure that Luke has given up on her yet, although he does seem quite keen on the new girl, Joanne. She's another one of those in-your-face types. Harry imagines she's the kind of girl who would quite happily throw herself at anyone who offered her a drink at a party.

Heather, it seems, is not really into parties. She refused to attend the following year too, so Harry skipped it and they camped out on his sofa watching *Scrooged* and stuffing their faces with Domino's Pizza and a Chick-n-Mix Box. They were still 'just friends' then, but he felt like something was different. Like she was starting to trust him more. It's not that she's totally buttoned up – more that she's just a bit shy. A bit wary. Harry gets the feeling that she might've had a bad experience with a bloke before, but she hasn't opened up about it so he hasn't pushed. She probably respects that.

And he definitely respects her. She is one of the funniest people he's ever met, but in that kind of under the radar, dark way. Self-deprecating and totally just... *aware*. Honestly? She is the best thing that's ever happened to him. Everyone says so. At least, he *thinks* they do.

They try to give one another space during the work day. They work in different departments, so it's mostly quite easy to do – except that sometimes he is just so desperate to see her that he goes and stands outside the glass door that separates her department from his, and watches her at work.

He knows that sounds a bit creepy. But honestly, it's not. It's awe. Fascination. She tells him little snippets about her work, when they're snuggled up on his sofa. About the molecules that her team are looking into. About the potential of what they can do. We're talking cutting edge medical research here. Possible cures for horrible diseases that most people have never even heard of. Illnesses so rare that you'd struggle to even understand what they are, but they affect the sufferers so badly that one of the things the clinical trials teams have to monitor is the suicidality risk of the patients.

This is where the documents come in. Harry's part in the process. Everything is heavily regulated – as you'd hope it would be – and he's one of the specialists who deals with the never-ending mountains of paperwork. It suits him, this kind of menial administrative work. Unlike Luke… Luke is one of the sales reps. Always out and about, trying to convince doctors to prescribe their drugs instead of the similar ones from competitors. He tries to bribe them with branded merch. But does anyone actually want beach towels emblazoned with drug names all over them? Mugs and pens though, they're fair enough. Harry's repetitively clicking one of those pens right now, as he sits in the canteen, waiting for Heather to join him for lunch.

They don't have lunch together every day – they both agreed it was important to maintain their own workplace friendships and relationships with their colleagues. But every Tuesday, they meet in the canteen at one o'clock, at a table near the back, and have the Special of the Day – which on almost every Tuesday since Harry started working here, is Steak and Ale Pie served with mash and greens, followed by a slice of lemon mousse cake.

He's been scrolling through news, mostly the local pages, but he hasn't found anything he really wants to read. Slow news day, it seems. Someone arrested after gluing themselves to the pavement outside a supermarket. A local school fundraiser. Some random found dead in a hotel room. How awful.

That's one family's Christmas ruined.

It would be simpler to waste time on his phone if he liked sports – there always seemed to be some score or result that people wanted to analyse – but it had never really been his thing. He opens up the NME website to see if there's anything of interest there. He hasn't been to any gigs lately, and he'd heard a rumour that Foster The People might be touring. Heather likes the band too. He introduced her to them via 'Jumped Up Kicks', on a Spotify mix-tape playlist, and they've already become a firm favourite. He glances up at the clock above the serving counter and notices it's been draped in green tinsel. It's ten past one. He's dimly aware of the radio playing that cheesy Shakin' Stevens Christmas song.

She's late.

Most people come down at twelve, when the lunch service starts, and they leave about now. As if on cue, chairs start to scrape and there's the clatter of cutlery and crockery and trays being emptied at the clear-up station. No one has come to join him, or even to chat to him, because they're all engrossed in their own little routines, and that's fine.

Heather is rarely late.

He's about to ping her a message when the doors swing open and in she comes – a blast of fresh air. He grins, as she marches right over to his table. He jumps up out of his seat, ready to lean in for a quick hug. They don't really do PDAs at work, but they agreed that brief hugs in the canteen were acceptable.

'I'm so sorry,' she says, sitting down hard on the bench seat that he's left free for her. Her face is pink, beads of sweat along her hairline. 'I was going to text to say I couldn't make it, but I thought I might as well still come because I need to eat…but I can't eat here.' She pushes her hands through her hair, puffs out a long breath. 'I'm just going to grab a sandwich. We're right in the middle of something in the lab, and—'

'Just stop, will you?' He sits down beside her and takes her hands in his. 'It's fine. Look, you sit here and have a glass of water. Get your breath back. I'll go and get you something, and you can take it back with you.'

She nods, then pulls her hands away and leans over to grab a water glass. 'Thank you,' she says, pouring in water from the jug, sloshing some over the side. She gulps some down, then pulls her phone out of her pocket.

He leaves her to it and heads over to the cold counter to pick her up a sandwich and some fruit. She's got her head down, when he glances back over his shoulder at her. She's scrolling through her phone, her face pinched. She knocks back another glass of water and refills it again. The wail of someone tunelessly singing along to 'Merry Christmas, Everyone' drifts out of the kitchen.

Harry knows that Heather has these busy, stressful days, sometimes. There have actually been a few recently. But by the time he sees her again after work, she's usually calmed down, and she never wants to talk about it. He doesn't like her being stressed. There are rumours of some bullying micro-managers in that department, and he hopes this is nothing to do with that. It could be something else. Something family related. This time of year is tricky for lots of people, isn't it? Not that she's told him much about her family. In truth, Heather is a very private person, and Harry respects that. They've been dating for six months, friends for eighteen months before that and he hasn't even seen where she lives. Annoying flatmates, she says. Prefers spending time at his. Harry's lucky enough to own his own place. It's tiny, but he saved hard for that deposit. If things keep progressing with Heather, maybe he'll ask her to move in.

He sighs happily. He still can't believe his luck at bagging a girlfriend like her.

There aren't many sandwiches left, and he hesitates for a moment. Tuna and cucumber or cheese and onion? He turns back in her direction again, wondering if he might catch her attention – there are still loads of people about and he doesn't want to yell across the room like some sort of madman. But her face is still locked to her phone screen.

He decides to get both sandwiches. He'll take the other one back to his own desk. He tosses a packet of cheese and onion crisps onto his tray and picks up a slice of millionaire's shortbread for him and a chocolate brownie for her. There's a tub of Celebrations next to the till, so he helps himself to two Mars, a Snickers and a Galaxy.

It's quite annoying that Heather is so distracted today. He'd been hoping to talk to her about the Christmas party. This year it's superhero-themed and it's in a really cool venue. All of his colleagues are going, and they're all badgering him to go too. He really *wants* to go. But he doesn't want to go on his own, like some saddo. Everyone knows he's with Heather, and if he goes alone, it will only set the gossipy tongues wagging.

So he's done something a bit cheeky. He's booked two tickets. And he's ordered them both a costume. Ant Man for him and Poison Ivy for her. He knows she's not really into superheroes, or dressing up – and she's definitely not into parties – but if he plays it right, he's sure he can convince her. He really wanted to start the process today, throwing it out there for a reaction. It's just over a week away, and, well… it would be a shame to miss it.

He'll offer to cook for her tonight – his homemade carbonara that she loves. Maybe bring it up then. Hopefully she'll be a bit calmer by this evening.

He grabs another Snickers from the tub, then pays for the lunches and heads back to the table. She is still glued to her phone.

Harry has no idea what she's finding so fascinating on there.

# 4

## Eddie

Eddie disappears into his office while the rest of the team mill around trying to look busy as they wait for the DCI to find his way upstairs. Eddie knows that Wild Bill will have stopped off at the office of the Chief-Super on the floor beneath CID, the two of them being best golf buddies and all. Bill had invited Eddie to join them for a game in the summer, when he'd been assigned to Woodham on a sort of station share with Farndean. But Eddie had always despised golf, and he has a feeling that his failure to play along will work against him someday.

'Morning, Eddie!' Miriam beams at him from his open doorway, glittery-bauble earrings sparkling under the strip light. 'I'll prep the Big Room, shall I?'

Eddie grunts a greeting, mildly irritated that everyone already seems to know that something significant is about to happen, and he doesn't yet know what it is. Either Wild Bill has called ahead and the info has leaked from another department, or more likely, Miriam's radar has picked up the signals some other way. No matter how long he's been here, and how many cases he's been involved with, he still hasn't worked out how it is that Miriam knows absolutely everything before anyone else. It's a skill, that's for sure.

He's just sat down and slid his chair in towards his desk, when he spots what looks like a plastic bag that someone's stuffed underneath it. 'Who's left their crap under my desk,' he shouts, as he leans under and yanks the bag out into the open.

The giant snowman pops out and springs back to its full height, causing him to slide backwards and crash into the wall.

'For fu—'

He finishes the rest of the cursing in his head. That bastard Joe isn't getting any more money from him for that swear box this week. No doubt he's behind the surprise snowman too. Becky wouldn't dare. Would she? Miriam definitely wouldn't. Although she scurried off fast enough and he's sure he heard a snigger from her as she'd legged it back to her own desk. All three of them are off his Christmas card list, that's for sure. Not that he has one.

Bloody Christmas.

As he lets his breathing return to normal, he stares at the snowman – at its weird empty eyes – before turning it around to face the wall and throwing his jacket over the top of it, letting it fold itself over towards the floor. Now it looks like he's draped his jacket over one of those giant gym balls.

He stands up again, looking out into the open-plan to see who's in. Not many of them yet. But even from this side of the office, he can hear the sound of footsteps and voices as they travel along the corridor towards him. In a few minutes, his time will no longer be his own. He doesn't want to think about what might have brought Wild Bill and his sidekick DI Jonty Davis to the station, but it is definitely going to either ruin or make his day, depending on which way it goes. He's not going to admit this to the others, but he'd quite like a juicy pre-Christmas case to crack. He'd missed having breakfast with his son, due to being summoned in earlier than planned. Eddie had been promised a Full English on the house in the café bar where Simon was currently working, plus some much needed time with Simon. So really, this visit from Bill had better be worth it.

The door to the open-plan office flies open, and then Wild Bill is in his orbit, Jonty on his tail. He spots Eddie straight away, marching across the room to get to him. 'Eddie! Good morning! And what a lovely morning it is. Crisp frost glistening on the pavements, the distant sound of Christmas bells...' He lets his sentence trail off. Bill considers himself a bit of a poet, but he never manages to get past one or two half-baked sentences of descriptions of the weather.

Eddie stands up straighter. 'Sir.' He nods at the other man. 'DI Davis.'

The DCI smiles at him. 'A man of few words this morning, I see. Shall we get straight to it? Head straight to the briefing?'

'What's that?' Jonty points to the corner of the room. He has spotted the hidden inflatable. He pokes at it, then lifts Eddie's jacket and hangs it over the back of his chair. The snowman stands again, raising itself to its full height, bobbing and spinning around to face them all. 'Oh,' Jonty says. 'Bit creepy, actually.'

Eddie rolls his eyes.

'Come on, gents,' the DCI says. 'I believe Miriam has got everything ready.'

★★★

The room is full of bodies and stale air by the time they arrive. Bill and Jonty march straight past the pastries that have been piled up on a plate, and realising that this means they are fair game, the assembled officers make a beeline for their second breakfasts. Eddie snatches a raisin Danish from beneath someone's outstretched hand, and walks up to the front row.

Jonty takes a seat next to the giant whiteboard, legs crossed, balancing his tablet and electronic pen on his knee.

DCI Wilde claps his hands, and the pastry grabbing and chatter stops abruptly.

'Good morning, everyone.' DCI Wilde catches Eddie's eye, his gaze travelling down to his crossed-arm, closed-off stance. 'Don't look so worried, DI Carmine. It's not an exam.'

Eddie tries to look less tense, but he's not sure he's happy about whatever it is that Wild Bill is about to throw at him. He has this place running like clockwork. Good team in place, all well ahead of their targets. He doesn't like outside interference disrupting the status quo. It had taken a good while after he was promoted to inspector to shake off the ghost of his predecessor, DI Nick Keegan, and his mismanagement of the department. Nick had taken early retirement after the Photographer case six years ago, having given Eddie too much free rein. Nick was quite happy to go, and Eddie had been persuaded to push himself towards promotion – despite always saying he would never purposely move into a pen-pushing project management role that the position of DI brought with it. As it turned out, he's managed to remain hands on *and* fill in the spreadsheets. Amazing how much time you have on your hands when your wife and two of your children move out.

'OK, then!' Bill smiles a bit maniacally, which in Eddie's experience, is rarely a good sign. 'Jonty? When you're ready...' He nods over at his sidekick, who stands up quickly, and directs a pointer at the big screen. The title flashes up in giant, bold letters.

REGIONAL RESTRUCTURE STRATEGY

*Oh this is just bloody great.*

'You're shutting us down?' Eddie stands up, feeling his forearms tense as he balls his hands into fists. 'We've got a good team here. We've been through a lot, we've ticked every one of your bloody boxes, and this is how you plan to repay us?' He feels his face grow hot. He knows this isn't the way to handle it. But it's the timing that's so unbelievably unfair.

Jonty clears his throat. 'Take a breath, DI Carmine. We haven't even got to the first slide—'

'I think we can all read between the lines here,' someone calls from the back, adding a muttered, 'Sir,' as an after-thought. The sound of chairs scraping and voices murmuring increases, until there's nothing but a dull, incomprehensible racket. 'Right, that's enough,' DCI Wilde doesn't quite shout, but with his deep, booming voice raised several notches, it has the desired effect.

The room falls silent.

'Thank you,' he continues. 'Now, if you could do us the courtesy of letting DI Davis present his slides, there will be ample time to answer all of your questions at the end.' He directs his gaze to Eddie, who is now sitting on his hands. 'And Eddie... I fully accept that the timing isn't the best for you all here, but if I can just say now – absolutely nothing is set in stone. We very much appreciate all the work that you and your team have put into making this a well-functioning department. If you don't mind, I'd rather you let Jonty take us through the full details, but I want you to know that this is not confirmed, and it's not going to happen overnight, and...' There's a loud knock on the door, and Wilde lets his sentence trail off. Eddie swivels around in his seat to see two uniforms with grim expressions standing in the open doorway.

'DI Carmine?' the taller of the two says, eyes scanning the room. Eddie stands up. 'I'm here, what is it?'

'Sorry to interrupt,' the other officer says, 'but we need you.' There's a brief pause as the young man's face glows red, realising there are thirty-five faces staring at him, each one of them looking for any reason on earth to leave this awkward meeting immediately. 'Um... probably more than one of you.'

'Sorry, sir,' Eddie addresses DCI Wilde with a shrug. He scans the room for the other person he needs, spotting her at the back. Becky, his right-hand woman, is looking at him expectantly, arms crossed, hint of a smile. He gives her a nod of acknowledgement. 'DS Greene...' He catches Joe's eager eyes as he stands next to her. 'And DC Dickson. You're up.' He doesn't wait for Wild Bill to respond. It doesn't matter what idiotic plans they've got laid out in that PowerPoint presentation about the fate of this office. He's very aware that they're not immune to the ongoing cuts. But right now, he's got a job to do.

★★★

'PC Barry Wilson, sir,' the first uniform says, once they are all safely ensconced in Eddie's office. 'We've had a call about a body in a bedroom at the Woodlands Hotel and

Conference Centre on Rickford Road. Cleaner found it an hour ago.'

'An hour? Why the delay?'

'The hotel manager wasn't sure what to do at first. He's quite new, apparently…'

'He's never had a guest die in one of his rooms before?' Eddie picks up his car keys. 'Would it not be common sense to give us a shout, anyway?' He turns to Becky. 'You're with me, OK?'

'And me, boss?' Joe says sheepishly, as he stands there looking slightly guilty next to the inflatable snowman. Eddie plans to get him back for that at some point. He just hasn't yet decided how.

'Go and find DS Fyfe. I didn't see him in the DCI's briefing. You two can meet us there.' He turns back to the uniforms. 'Right then. Is everybody ready for some pre-Christmas excitement?'

# 5

# The Party Girl

I'm exhausted today. Last night was hard work.

There was a moment, when he was lying there on the bed, looking comfortable and actually quite sweet, that I thought about not doing it. I excused myself to the bathroom – a very nice bathroom, by the way; pale marble vanity unit, shiny chrome fittings, plus that massive bath he'd mentioned. He'd wanted to jump right in there as soon as we got into the room, but I gave him some spiel about having just had a massage and my skin being coated in essential oils. He'd got kind of excited by that, muttering something about 'sliding around together under the sheets', which is when I shot off and locked myself in the bathroom with my bag. I sat on the floor for a while, taking some deep breaths, getting myself into the zone. Then I stood up and stared at myself in the mirror for a while, before I opened up my bag and started taking out what I needed, laying it all out on a soft, white flannel, which I would be sure to take away with me.

Who doesn't love a nice hotel flannel?

I was shaking. The beta-blocker I'd taken on arrival at the hotel had helped a bit, but once the adrenaline kicked in hard in the bedroom, there was nothing that was going to stop it.

I did it though. After chickening out that first time. A lucky escape for Lance Jones, the IT Analyst from Friday's party. Funnily enough, it was knowing he was a predator that had put me off last time. I'd spotted the CCTV camera at the end of the corridor, looking a bit worse-for-wear. He'd been so pleased with himself when he told me that the cameras were all duds. Boxes for show, only. The hotel used to be frequented by a lot of pay-by-the-hour clients, and none of them wanted any potential evidence getting out about their activities. He'd walked into the bedroom in front of me and I'd let the door close and legged it down the stairs. I'd checked the other cameras, floor by floor. No wires on any of them. I guess that had been my trial run. He didn't come after me. I imagine he just went back down to the bar to find another willing victim. The creep.

You'd think he would have been the perfect choice... but his swagger had spooked me. I had doubts that I could carry out my plan. He wasn't the type for teasing and tantalising. He would have grabbed me and thrown me on the bed the minute I walked into that room with him. I can't fight back against men like him. I had to make sure I chose better next time.

And I did.

Although, it didn't go exactly to plan. But with something like this, there is bound to be some trial and error. Problem was, he kind of sobered up a bit too much in the room. Not my finest work, and to be honest, I'm half-expecting to get caught quickly. Not *too* quickly though. I've got a lot to sort out first.

You're probably thinking I'm sounding a bit cold – a bit matter-of-fact about what I'm doing, but you know what? If you were me you'd be cold too. I've had to switch myself off from the human side of it. I can't think about them outside of the situation that we're in. I definitely can't spend time thinking about their families, and what losing them might mean to them.

They didn't think about that when it came to *my* family, did they?

Anyway, no rest for the wicked. I might be knackered, but I don't have time to sit about all day watching TV and eating cereal. Better that I keep myself busy. I did try, but I just wasn't in the mood to deal with work today. People are *exhausting* sometimes.

But there's one person I always have time for.

I keep my head down as I walk briskly down the corridor, but I don't pass anyone on the way. The door is ajar, as it always is. Bing Crosby's dulcet tones waft out of the radio, and I wonder if we'll have snow this Christmas. I slide the padded chair in closer to the bed. The sleighbell decorations I've tied around the sides jangle gently, and the sound throws a childhood memory of my dad hiding in the dark hallway, jingling bells outside my room on Christmas morning. My throat feels thick, and I swallow back a lump.

'Afternoon, Mum. Beautiful day out there.'

I take her hand in mine and gently stroke it. Her skin is soft and pale, marred only by the dark bruises around the cannula that brings her life-preserving fluids and pain-numbing drugs. They move it from one hand to the other, now and then, but the veins are growing tired and the bruising is not going away. I take the tube of hand cream from the side-table and squeeze a dollop into my palm. Lavender has always been her favourite. I carry on talking as I carefully rub the cream into her skin.

'You'd hardly believe it was December, with that blistering sunshine! Although it's a bit cold in the shade.'

The monitor at the other side of the bed beeps intermittently, keeping a rhythm with the hush and suck of the ventilator. 'White Christmas' has been replaced by 'Mary's Boy Child', and I think about switching to another station. But she always loved these old tracks so I try to tune them out and focus on why I'm here.

The ventilator is a new addition to the care plan. They'd all been surprised how long she'd managed without one. I know from what the nurses have told me that the residents here are quite a mixture – some very long term, some shorter. Some breathing on their own, some who'll never wake up.

Even knowing that, it's an impossible decision to make.

It's a private facility, so mostly people are allowed to keep their loved ones alive until they feel ready to have them switched off. Some people can't come to terms with it at all – especially if the person in the bed is very young.

My mum's still young, in my mind, at least. If she was awake, she'd only be forty-nine. In her prime! She was even more in her prime at thirty-six though. When they brought her in here. Only seven years older than I am now. What if I only had seven years left of being able to do what I wanted? What would I even do? I've spent most of my time since I was sixteen coming into this place and talking to a ghost.

'I'm going Christmas shopping at the weekend,' I tell her. 'Probably just to the shopping centre in town, because I don't have much to buy, really – but it's nice in there at this time of year. They usually have people handing out mince pies. And there's a mulled wine stand outside. I'll get the bus in, so I can have a couple.' I squeeze her hand. 'You used to love mulled wine. I should ask the nurses to make some here, bring it in for you to sniff. It always smells so lovely, with the ginger and cinnamon and the tang of the wine.' I finish rubbing one hand and go around to the other side of the bed, pulling that chair in close and repeating the process. 'You can get bottles of it now, you know? You just heat it up in the microwave. I'll get some cinnamon sticks too, to stir it with.' I rub the cream in small circles. 'Remember that time you caught me smoking cinnamon sticks down at the bridge? I threw them in the water and told you they were just twigs, but I knew you'd seen.

'"They're a gateway drug," you said. I'm sure you were only half joking. Anyway, they weren't, as it happens. I never took up smoking. Nor anything else for that matter.'

The hush and suck of the ventilator starts to drown out the other sounds. I'm only vaguely aware of the radio now. Someone croons about it beginning to look like Christmas, and I have to swallow back another lump of sadness.

'Once she's at this stage, there really is no hope of recovery,' the doctor told me last week, after the big scary moment where I thought I'd already lost her. He'd called me into a meeting with the care home manager and two of the nurses. Strength in numbers, for them at least. 'You might want to consider your long-term plans,' he said. He was giving me that sombre, pitying look that I hated. They all were.

'What do you mean, exactly?' I knew what he meant, I just needed him to say it.

The care home manager – Gregg Wade – dialled the pity up to boiling point. 'You might think about turning off the machines. None of us want her to suffer anymore.' He took a step towards me and for a horrible moment I thought he might try to give me a hug. Thankfully, he seemed to think better of it. Bit his lip. 'There's also the matter of the cost...'

That woke me up. 'Her bed... her care... It's fully funded! It's pre-paid, and—'

'It's fully funded as long as she is still able to breathe on her own. After that, the costs will increase considerably, I'm afraid. And the plan you have in place doesn't cover the cost of the ventilator, nor the additional staff needed to monitor your mother's condition. We will, of course, assist you with whatever you need to ensure your mother is taken care of...' He cleared his throat. '... Afterwards, but—'

I stormed out at that point. One of the nurses – Gloria – the nice one who used to spend hours sitting with Mum, talking to her, soothing her, chased after me down the corridor. Told me to take my time. There was no rush. Traitorous bitch. None of them care. Not really. It's all about money, isn't it?

*Oh, Mum... it was lack of money that got us into this mess. I'm not going to let you down again.*

I place her hand on top of the blanket, then I go back around to the bedside cabinet and take out a hairbrush. It's difficult to get in to brush her hair now, with the extra machinery. Another small thing, lost forever.

A tear runs down my cheek and I wipe it angrily away.

I must finish this. I need closure, as the therapists have bleated at me over the years. But I know better.

Because what I *need*, is to make sure that someone – anyone – pays for what they did to my mum.

And I'm not talking about money.

# 6

## Becky

The hotel lobby is much grander than she'd been expecting. Freshly painted and papered, all velvet and chandeliers. Reproduction, but tastefully done. Becky doesn't spend a lot of time in hotels. Abroad, now and then. A week in Mallorca with her sister five years ago, supposedly to spend time with their absent mother, but despite them flying over there to see her, June had continued to remain mostly absent, leaving Becky and Allie to fend for themselves. That was the last time she'd had any contact with her mum, but she knows that Allie still tries to stay in touch with her.

Becky has been so focussed on work lately that going on holiday just hasn't been on her radar. And purposely spending time in a hotel on the outskirts of her own town? Well, that's just not something that would ever cross her mind.

'Have you been in here before?' she asks Eddie, lowering her voice, feeling suddenly intimidated amidst the high, ornate ceilings and the ambient classical music.

'Years ago. It's been done up a bit since I was last here. It was mostly a budget place for business travellers, but they used to do Christmas fairs and that sort of thing. Carly dragged me along once…'

Becky let that hang. She wasn't going to bring up the fact that Eddie's ex-wife's love of Christmas markets had almost cost the woman her life.

'Then it fell into disrepair and became the go-to location for hook-ups. Massive refurb, by the looks of it,' Eddie continues, oblivious to her awkwardness. 'Looks like they've spent millions—'

'Morning, sir.' Eddie's sentence is interrupted by a grim-faced uniform who's been loitering by the reception desk. There was another at the entrance, who'd waved them through. Becky's not sure she's seen either of them before. 'PC Tim Hodges, sir,' he says. 'Do you want to go straight to the room?'

Eddie laughs. 'We're not here for a mini-break, Tim.'

The young constable blushes, and Becky pokes Eddie hard in the ribs.

'Ow,' he says, dramatically clutching his side, feigning agony like a footballer who's been tripped up on the pitch. But he's smiling.

Good. His banter is back. She needs to be a bit sensitive with him at this time of year. He acts like he doesn't care, but he does. She knows he does.

'Don't mind him,' she says.

She has that familiar buzz of excitement at the prospect of an exciting new case. She and Eddie have been working as a pretty tight team since they'd been thrown together six years ago, and she was at the point where she didn't really want to work with anyone else. Other than Joe, of course. He was the sunny antidote to Eddie's changeable moods.

The hotel is eerily quiet as they pass through the open-plan lounge areas towards the lifts that will take them to the bedrooms. The classical music is still playing, but it's quieter now, and the emptiness reminds her of that scene at the end of the movie *Titanic*, where the band play on as the ship sinks.

'Where is everyone?' Eddie says, as they reach the bank of shiny chrome lifts.

'The manager has asked the guests to stay in their rooms until we tell them otherwise,' Tim says, 'and the staff are in the function room at the back. We've told them to await further instructions.'

Eddie raises his eyebrows. 'Good work.'

Becky is pleased too. So far, so good. If they've secured the crime scene and locked the place down, they've got a chance at finding something to help them. Assuming this is, in fact, suspicious, and not just the cleaner overreacting at a natural death. People don't realise that natural death doesn't always look very pretty. Even if someone passes peacefully in their sleep, there is likely to be a mess of bodily fluids to contend with.

The bedroom is on the third floor, down a maze of corridors. They've gone for one of *The Shining* style zig-zagged carpets during their refurb, it seems.

'Not Room 237, I hope,' Eddie says.

She's glad he's got the significance at the same time. The young PC though, Tim, seems oblivious. Or maybe he's just focussed. A couple of the rooms they've passed have had TV sounds coming out of them, but mostly the eerie silence continues.

'It's here,' Tim says, stopping at an open door. Becky surveys the immediate area. They're right at the end of the corridor, close to the fire escape, she mentally notes. Coincidence? Maybe, maybe not.

Tim holds out a box of paper suits and boots before saying his goodbyes and heading back down to the lobby, and they stop at the door and wiggle themselves into the protective clothing. The mood has changed now. This is the bit that Becky hates. The anticipation. What exactly are they going to find in there?

Thankfully, they are not alone.

It's a big, rectangular room. Muted colours and clean lines. Floor to ceiling windows straight ahead, desk to the right and a door just past that, which presumably leads to the ensuite. Various technicians are going about their business, collecting evidence, and a familiar face is front and centre – Dr Maria Szczepańska, the duty pathologist – carrying out her preliminary checks.

And, of course, there's the body.

He's lying on the bed, presumably naked but partially covered with a sheet so she can't tell just yet. He's on his side, facing the door. He looks to be late forties, early fifties. Probably not bad looking, if you can see past the grey pallor and the blank, staring eyes. She imagines that's what might've spooked the cleaner, which was completely understandable. Becky takes a deep breath, looks away. Tries to see if there is anything obvious in the room that might provide them with some idea of what has gone on in here.

The pathologist looks up when they walk further into the room, steps away from the back of the body, where she'd previously been poking around with a long pair of tweezers. 'Morning, Eddie.' She grins. 'Hey, Becky.'

Becky considers Maria a good friend, the pair of them often frequenting The Wheatsheaf, a bar halfway between the hospital and the nick, after work. Maria has the most beautifully shiny dark hair, and with her fresh face and petite, yoga-fit body, looks more like she should be modelling swimwear than sticking her hands into the innards of dead humans. Although she does like to tell persistent men about her job, in gut-churningly graphic detail, when they get a bit too pushy about buying them drinks.

Becky turns to greet her, keeping her eyes on her friend and trying not to let them be drawn to the dead man. She needs a moment to prepare before moving in closer, unlike Eddie who is crouched down in front of him, peering closely at his face. In her peripheral vision, Becky notices that there is a pillow on the floor just below where the man's head lies.

'Eyes are bulbous and bloodshot,' Eddie says. 'Pillow on the floor...'

'Are we looking at smothering?' Becky says, walking over to the bed.

'Not drawing any conclusions just yet,' Maria says. 'Something feels a bit out of place. I'll tell you more later once we get him back to base. He was at a party, so there's highly likely to be an alcohol element. Maybe drugs too.'

'Can we fast-track the tox screen? I heard the labs were taking up to three weeks lately, and we could really do with getting the results this side of Christmas.'

Maria shrugs. 'Maybe if you go over there and bribe them with Selection Boxes and Baileys.'

'We got a name yet?' Eddie asks. He steps away from the body and starts his own sweep of the room. The technicians have bagged various items, including a wallet, phone and watch.

'Andrew Morrison,' Maria says. 'According to his ID. But, of course, we'll have to formally verify that later.'

'Do we know if he had any guests?' Becky picks up the bag containing the wallet and peers at it. It's been left unfolded, his driving licence on display. The small picture shows a neat haircut and a strong jawline, collar and tie just visible at the bottom of the frame.

One of the technicians holds up a bag. 'We found this down the side of the bedside cabinet.'

Becky takes it, smoothing the bag out to see it more clearly. It's a delicate silver and diamond hairclip, in the shape of a feather, curled gently at the tip. She holds it up to the light. 'This looks expensive,' she says, turning the bag over in her hands. It seems to weigh almost nothing. There is something engraved on the back, next to a number: 3499. They can get an expert to look at this, try and trace it. It looks vintage and someone might have a track of sales. Maybe. She peers closer. 'Is that…a hair?' she says, grinning.

The technician nods. 'Yep.'

'Hoping we can fast-track the DNA on that too?' Becky says. 'It'd be great if it was a match with someone we already had in the system.'

Eddie laughs. 'Sure, Becks… and Santa Claus is real.'

'Well I *have* been nice this year.'

'Course you have,' Eddie says, snapping off a glove. 'I think we've seen enough here. Let's go downstairs. We need the CCTV footage, and we need to talk to the staff.'

# 7

# Harry

He's finding it really hard to concentrate today. He's hardly seen Heather for days, and this morning she'd just sent him a really basic text saying she wasn't coming into work because she was sick.

He'd messaged back straight away, asking what was wrong, if she was OK, if she needed him to bring anything round for her at lunchtime – but the WhatsApp message still only has one grey tick – meaning it's been successfully sent, but it hasn't been delivered.

It's frustrating, because of course he's worried about what might be wrong with her. Hopefully it's nothing major, but she's not off work often and he's pretty sure she left early yesterday too. He *really* wants to ask her about the party. It's less than a week away now, and what is he meant to do with the costume if she still refuses to go?

Hopefully he can convince her to go. His whole department is going, as are all of the people he knows in the other departments that share his floor. It's on a midweek night too, which means if he doesn't go, the next day will be utterly insufferable with everyone talking about it.

He fires off another message to her, drumming his fingers on his desk as he waits. He watches and waits, but no second tick appears.

'Damn it,' he mutters. He locks his computer screen and picks up his jacket. 'I'm just popping out for lunch,' he says, already on his way. 'Won't be long.'

He squeezes the key fob hard, directing it at his car like a killer laser beam. A few moments later, and he's tearing out of the car park like a boy racer.

Thoughts are whirring inside his head as he drives across town towards her flat. What if she's properly sick, and she isn't able to go to the party even if he does manage to convince her? What if she isn't sick at all, but at a job interview for a new position in another town? Or another country? What if no matter what he says, she refuses to go to the party?

He really, *really* wants to go.

Joanne, that cute new starter, who seems to already be friends with the entire department – and every other person in the building, never mind their floor – has been prattling on about it all week. She knows one of the people on the organising committee, she'd told him the other day, draping herself halfway across his desk and making it impossible for him to avoid her cleavage in her very fitted blouse. She has no shame. Apparently this 'source' has been drip-feeding her tasty morsels about the set-up: free bar with bespoke superhero themed cocktails, a photo-booth with all the props, a gaming zone, a themed menu – basically, the whole works. There are even rumours of some actual actors coming in costume. Probably the same ex-soap and reality TV C-Listers who are in town for the panto. Seems like it's no expense spared this year, after the mini-merger and the not so mini influx of cash that had come in when they'd bought up the little biotech company with the incredibly sexy new drug. If the trials are a success, the share price will rocket even further and he'll actually be able to buy a new house – a much bigger house. A car too, maybe. It would be the making of them all, as long as it goes to plan.

Of course, the people in Heather's department are the only ones who know if it is, in fact, going to plan. There are occasional snippets of news shared at the regular 'All Hands' meetings, but he knows that most of that is commercial and marketing spin. It would be nice if Heather told him more about how things were going in the lab and the trials, but she's as cagey about that as she is about her personal life.

In fact, he really doesn't know much about her at all. But it's early days, and he hopes that, in time, she'll open up more. At the moment, he's happy not to rock the boat. Although she is quite difficult to please and rarely wants to do anything with him other than sit on his sofa watching boxsets while he cooks for her. But her job is a lot more intense than his, and he does enjoy testing out his new recipes on her.

He pulls up outside her flat and kills the engine. The curtains are drawn in the two upstairs windows. Which room is hers? He'd been full of determination when he'd jumped into his car, but now that he's here, he's a nervous wreck. After all, she hasn't invited him here, and he only knows her address because an envelope fell out of her bag one day in the canteen, and he'd glanced at it before handing it back to her.

It sounds a bit stalkerish, now that he thinks about it.

Harry gently bangs his head on the steering wheel. 'Idiot. Idiot.'

He glances back over at the flat. Well... he's here now. Before he can talk himself out of it, he's out of the car, up the path and he's got his finger on the buzzer. It's cold outside, and he shifts from foot to foot, rubbing his hands together. Should've worn gloves. There's no answer, and he thinks about leaving it, jumping back into his car and blasting the heating. Maybe picking up a battered sausage and some nice hot chips on the way back to the office. But then there's a click, and the door springs open.

No one asked who he was. Not very security conscious! He has one of those Ring doorbell cameras, and it's come in handy more than once with those awful delivery companies who say they've tried to deliver when they haven't. He steps inside. The hallway is cold, but clean. A pile of mail is neatly stacked on a small table at the bottom of the stairs. He checks the doors on the ground floor, and deduces that her flat is definitely upstairs, so he jogs up briskly, warming himself up.

The door to 4a is ajar, but on the chain. 'Hello?' he calls through the gap.

After a moment, Heather's face appears. Her eyes widen when she sees him. 'Oh,' she says. 'I thought it was my food delivery.' She disappears back inside and the door closes. He hears the rattle as she unhooks the chain.

*Well, that explains why she let him in without asking who it was.*

'I, um... what are you doing here?' Her skin is bleached white by the bright hall light, and she has dark rings under her eyes. She bites her lip, appraises him. 'How do you know where I live?'

Harry feels a flash of panic now. This was a mistake. He really is an idiot. 'Can I come in? It's freezing out here.' He smacks his hands together again, trying to emphasise his point and evade her question.

'I'm not feeling great, actually. I only got up to answer the door because I've nothing in to eat, and—'

He holds up a hand. 'I'm sorry, I just wanted to make sure you were OK. See if you needed anything. I did message you but you didn't reply.'

She sighs, but she opens the door wider and he takes that as an invitation to go in. 'I was probably asleep.'

He follows her down the hall as she leads him into a decent sized living room. It's bathed in a muted glow from a couple of table lamps, the curtains closed. There is a rumpled duvet and a pillow on the couch, the TV paused on something he doesn't recognise. She sits on the sofa and pulls the duvet over herself. A small stuffed toy that looks like a slightly squashed cat wearing a jester's hat rolls off the sofa onto the floor, and she snatches it up and shoves it under the pillow. 'You didn't answer my question.'

He knows there's no point in trying to fob her off so he decides to go with the truth. 'I saw it on an envelope that fell out of your bag. Couple of weeks ago, I think. The address was quite prominent and it just stuck in my head.' He shrugs, going for nonchalance. He doesn't need to mention that he's driven along her road before, stopping outside briefly and looking up at her flat, and wondering if he might catch a glimpse of her at the window. He'd tried to convince himself it was just curiosity, but if he was to tell anyone – especially Heather – it would only sound creepy. He has no idea why he is so obsessed with her. She isn't actually very nice to him. In fact, maybe *that* is why. He's always enjoyed a challenge. That's why he's not into that over-confident Joanne. She's far too easy.

Heather gives him an odd look. 'OK. Well, I think I might just jump in the shower. Can you listen for the buzzer? That food delivery should've been here by now.'

'Sure – unless you need someone to scrub your back?' He smiles, hoping she reads it as a sweet request and not a weird one.

She rolls her eyes. 'Does anyone actually scrub their back? I'll be quick, OK? Just need to freshen up. Help yourself to tea or whatever.' She points in the vague direction of the kitchen as she gets up and leaves the room, brushing her lips against his cheek as she passes. He catches a whiff of her sweaty, unwashed skin, the scent leaching up through her pyjama top. She's right, actually – she does need to freshen up.

He waits until he hears the door being closed and the shower running before taking the opportunity to have a quick snoop around.

*What is wrong with you, Harry?* He's annoyed with himself, but carries on anyway. He peers down the hallway and sees the open door, assumes that this is her bedroom. He has no idea if anyone else is in the flat, but he senses that they are alone. He's sure she's mentioned having a flatmate in the past, but there's no evidence of one right now.

He stares in from the doorway at her unmade double bed. There's no duvet or pillow, because they are through on the sofa – so it's definitely her room. It's all very neat, the dressing table with cosmetics propped up neatly in an organiser, only a couple of items lying loose on the surface. He glances back at the door to the bathroom. Then he walks carefully into her bedroom and has a good look around.

There's a dark red handbag under her desk. It looks a bit like crocodile skin, and has a shiny gold clasp in the shape of an 'H'. Looks a bit fancy for Heather. She's usually very casual, and she always says she doesn't like to go out anywhere. Maybe it was an unwanted gift. He hasn't bought her Christmas present yet. He's been trying to glean some clues as to what she might like, but so far he has no idea. He takes his phone out of his pocket and snaps a quick photo of the handbag. He'll do a reverse-image search. See if it's a brand, and if he can get something else to match it… But no, if he does that it might look weird. She'll wonder how he knows about her handbag.

*Hmm.*

He scans the top of the desk. There's a square, blue velvet jewellery box with the jeweller's initials in looping script embellished on the top. He tries to open it, but the catch is too tight so he stops before he breaks it. He sighs and pulls open the drawer under her desk, still looking for inspiration. Or still snooping, actually, although he's trying to tell himself he's not. Nothing much of interest in there. A couple of neatly folded face cloths. An open packet of cotton wool balls. Maybe he should buy her some fancy bath products? Does The Body Shop still exist? Or is it all about Lush these days? The smell of that place gives him a headache, but she might like it…

Or would that be too boring?

He slides the drawer back in, and then jumps as the buzzer goes. A tube of lip balm rolls off the desk, and he's bending down to pick it up when he hears that distinctive swish and rattle of a shower curtain being pulled back. The water has stopped.

*Shit!*

He tiptoes quickly out of her room and presses the button on the intercom system in the hallway. He launches himself onto the sofa and is catching his breath when he hears the knock at the front door. Then the soft click of another door closing nearby. She's in her bedroom.

Hopefully she doesn't notice that he's been in there too.

# 8

# Becky

By the time they get downstairs, Joe and DS Stuart Fyfe
are waiting in the lobby. Stuart is talking to a young woman
that Becky recognises as one of the CCTV analysts. Julia,
Julie? She feels bad that she can't remember her name, but
she's quite new to the team. Shy and quiet, but very diligent. Exactly what they need. They have another analyst
too – Jonah. Becky bites her lip. Jonah is a *lot* more memorable, and he gives Becky a slow smile when he spots her.

Eddie's phone beeps as they walk across the lobby
towards the others, and she waits with him as he stops to
check the message.

'It's the DCI,' he says. 'He's working on the investigation
plan and has formally assigned us Joe and Stuart, plus DC
Keir Jameson as an extra pair of hands.'

'Wild Bill loves Keir,' Becky says. 'Hopefully he'll make
himself useful on this. Although we don't even know what
we're dealing with yet.' They need to be fully on the ball
though, whatever it is. No fuck ups allowed on this case,
not when there might be a threat of station closure. Now,
more than ever, they need to show their worth. Not that

she has any concerns about that. Eddie has proven himself to be an excellent leader since he was promoted to DI. And even more focussed now all his family stress has subsided.

'Alright, Ed? Becks?' DS Stuart Fyfe greets them. She likes Stuart and worked one of her first major cases with him, but she's glad she's been officially partnered with Eddie since the two of them were thrown into that intense serial killer case a few years ago. 'CCTV operations are commencing,' Stuart says. 'You going to divvy up the other jobs?'

Eddie nods. Becky notes that he doesn't react to being instructed like this – they both know that Stuart is just keen to get on with it all. He'd gone for promotion alongside Eddie, and had lost out – but it's only a matter of time. The good thing is that he's not bitter about it. They've had other officers transferred out of the team when they've been arsey about not getting promoted fast enough. She glances over at Joe, who is checking his phone. He should be pushing himself for promotion too. Maybe Stuart's keen attitude will give him the shove that he needs.

'Right then,' Eddie says. 'Me and Becks are going to start with the barman from last night, assuming he's here'—he glances at his watch—'which, he may well not be. Eyes and ears of the place, good bar staff. The stories that Simon tells me sometimes...'

'Is he still working at that fancy place on the high street?' Becky says.

'Yeah,' says Eddie. 'Although he's been doing some floating shifts elsewhere. Him and his mates are in demand over the festive period. He makes silly money in tips, although I still wish he'd stick around somewhere long enough to take a management role.' Becky follows

Eddie's gaze as he scans the surroundings, clocking the multiple doors leading off from the lobby. 'We need all the staff from whichever functions were on last night. Plus those on reception, the main bar, and anyone else who might've been kicking around.' He pauses, frantically typing into the notes app on his phone and swearing under his breath at his frequent mis-types. 'And then there's the guests...' He looks up. 'We're gonna need more bodies.'

'On it, boss,' Joe says. 'I'll call in and request as many uniforms as can be spared.'

Eddie is still allocating tasks when a tall, harassed-looking man in a dark suit comes flapping towards them. His face is pink, a light sheen of sweat on his brow right up to his neatly coiffed dark hair. 'Do you know how long this is all going to take?' he says, panting slightly. 'We'll have guests coming to check in soon, for our events this evening, and—'

Eddie holds up a hand. 'Sorry, I'm going to have to stop you right there, I'm afraid. Firstly, there will be no guests leaving or arriving until we're ready, and secondly, who are you?'

The man's face falls, and Becky feels sorry for him. It's clear he hadn't taken in the implications of what's happened. Talk about terrible timing. She wonders how many parties will have to be cancelled now. How much money will be lost.

'Why don't you sit down here, Mr...?' Becky says, kindly. She gestures to one of the plump sofas.

'I'm Keith Walters, the general manager.' He slumps into the sofa. He's an average-sized man, but he looks like he suddenly weighs 400 lbs.

'You'll need to cancel the room bookings, and the events, I'm afraid. Perhaps you could get one of your assistants to help?'

Keith drops his head into his hands. He looks like he's about to burst into tears. He's new here, isn't he? Hadn't they been told that earlier? Not the best start to his tenure.

'Right, I'll go and see who else can assist,' Joe says, walking off.

'And then we can start talking to the rest of the staff.' Stuart nods at Eddie. 'I'll get that barman sent through to you. If he's still at home, we'll get him brought in.'

'Cheers,' Eddie says. Then he sits down on the sofa opposite Keith. Becky sits on the high-backed armchair at the end of the low coffee table, then, realising it's not very comfortable, takes a seat next to Eddie on the couch. Eddie pulls his notebook out of his jacket pocket.

'What?' he says, catching Becky looking. 'I'll type them up later.'

Becky smiles. They're all encouraged to add their notes straight into their phones now, but Eddie hates typing on the screen. He'd loved his police issued Blackberry and was still fuming that the company no longer existed. He still ranted about it on a semi-regular basis.

'Let's start with how many parties we had last night, how many companies, how many guests…'

Keith sighs. 'I can print out the full list for you. We insist on all attendee names for functions now. For security…'

'Well that's great,' Becky says. 'That will really speed things up.'

He sits up straighter, and his face changes. 'That was my idea, actually. Previous management had the place in a bit of a state. I'm trying to sort it out. This is going to destroy all my good work.' He shakes his head. 'But that poor man...'

'Can you tell us anything about the guest who was staying in Room 312? We have a wallet with ID suggesting this is likely to be an Andrew Morrison?'

Keith nods. 'One of the partners of the law firm Barlow & Wolfenstone. He personally introduced himself to me last night. Thanked me for sorting out their event booking. They booked quite late and I had to do quite a bit of rearranging with the function rooms to fit his party in. Most people would have their assistant deal with that sort of thing, but he said he wanted to thank his staff for a good year and it was important they got the party just right. He chose the menus, the wine... He seemed very decent.'

Becky is making notes on her phone. 'Was this an employee only thing, or were there partners there?'

'Partners. But he told me his wife wasn't able to make it.'

Becky shoots Eddie a look, and he leans forward in his seat. 'Do you think Mr Morrison might have had another plus one with him? Big bedroom. Big bed. Shame to be spending the night there alone.'

'I don't like to make assumptions on our guests' private matters,' Keith says. 'They book on a by-room basis so he could've taken all the guests from his table up there with him last night if he'd wanted to.' He sniffs. 'It's not for me to judge.'

Eddie shrugs. 'Interesting approach, given this hotel's previous rep as the town's most popular by-the-hour venue...'

Keith purses his lips. 'I told you, I came in and sorted this place out. You're right, it did have a bad reputation. That's why it was closed and refurbished, and why they brought in a whole new set of staff. We've worked hard to get it going again for the party season.'

'OK, so… you're sure the previous clientele got the memo about it no longer being a thinly disguised knocking shop?'

Becky tries hard to keep her face neutral. Eddie seems to be trying to antagonise the manager, for reasons known only to himself. She can see that Keith is out of his depth here, so she attempts to change tack.

'What we're trying to ascertain, Keith, is the likelihood of anyone not on the guest list being around last night. Is that feasible, do you think? Do you check names on the door? We've got our operatives already checking your CCTV, as you know, but this could help speed things up a bit. We just need to know what we're dealing with. At the moment, we have very little and so we can't yet rule out an accident, although it does look suspicious…'

She lets the sentence hang for a moment, watching Keith as he attempts to gather his thoughts. Eddie is tight-lipped, letting her lead.

'No,' Keith says, eventually. His face pinched and pained. 'Despite me insisting on the names, we don't actually check them off at the door. These are office parties. People sit with their colleagues. It would be pretty obvious to anyone if there was someone there who wasn't meant to be.'

Eddie frowns. 'What about the main bar area? You had several parties running at the same time, right? How many function rooms did you say you had?'

'Six. But we were only using five of them last night.'

'And everyone from those five rooms was free to come and go as they pleased? They all funnel through the lobby, the same toilets, they all have access to the main bar?'

Keith nods.

'So it's safe to say that someone could have walked in off the street, blended in, mingled around the shared areas?'

'Yes,' Keith says.

'OK then.' Eddie stands. 'I was right from the start; we need to talk to the barman.'

'You mean Connor? He was on a late last night, so he's not due in until two.'

Becky's phone pings with a message. 'Speak of the devil,' she says. 'It's Joe. They've tried calling Connor but his phone is off. He's texted me the address.'

'Excellent,' Eddie says, standing up. 'Let's pay him a visit. Tell DC Dickson to carry on interviewing the rest of the staff, then get us an update on the CCTV.'

'About that...' Keith says.

Eddie sits back down. 'Please tell us you have fully functioning CCTV throughout the hotel?'

'In the communal areas, yes. But...' He pauses, looks down at his hands. 'The cameras in the room corridors are mostly dummy. The previous owners were known for their, er, discreet approach.'

Becky waits for Eddie to swear.

He manages to hold it together. 'You didn't think that was something worth spending some of your refurb budget on then?'

'It's on the list for Phase II...'

'Thank you, Keith.' Becky stands up. 'Please don't go anywhere today – we'll need to talk to you again later.'

'Of course. Of course,' Keith says. And for the second time since they met him, the man looks like he's ready to burst into tears.

# 9

# Eddie

Eddie is driving. They have three jobs to do before they can head back to the station and brief the rest of the team. They could call in now with updates, but Eddie prefers to have a chunk of the work done before he starts sharing. As soon as the sharing starts, things get pulled off in a hundred different directions, and there is barely time to breathe. He turns the radio up and is pleased that it's still tuned into a decent station that mostly plays old rock music. Meatloaf warbles out of the speakers, singing 'Dead Ringer for Love'.

He taps his fingers on the steering wheel as he waits for the lights to change. He'd like to sing along, but suspects Becky would not appreciate it, despite her being more tolerant of his musical tastes these days. She even likes some of it. He can't say the same for hers, although he will grudgingly admit he likes that popular 'Wet Leg' song.

'What was that address again?'

Becky is fiddling with her phone. '15b Oak Lane. I've got the postcode if you want to put it in the GPS?'

'It's fine. I know where it is.' Oak Lane is off Cherry Drive, in the area of the town known as 'The Orchards', which is a nice name for a horrible place, frankly. There are various areas of Woodham that Eddie doesn't particularly like, but The Orchards has always been a hive of petty crime and general unhappiness. Technically they could send a couple of uniforms to go to the barman's house and ask him to come down to the station, or the hotel, but Eddie just wants to get the ball rolling and this is the fastest way.

'I've messaged Maria,' Becky says. 'She reckons she'll have something preliminary for us in a couple of hours.'

'Perfect,' Eddie says, turning off the main road and into a long, pot-holed street lined with a variety of ugly sixties houses and flats. 'Barman, wife, then the mortuary.'

'Sounds like fun. And here was me thinking I'd have time to go Christmas shopping after work.'

The traffic is starting to build on the ring road, cars filled with people who've taken time off work to go shopping, or to go out and meet up with friends for Christmas lunches. Eddie is sure that this stuff used to only happen in the two weeks before Christmas, but now it seems to be the whole of December. Some of it even leaches into November now, with everyone trying to cash in wherever they can. All this bloody fuss for one day? People maxing out their credit cards and raising their own blood pressure for one stupid day? Commercial nonsense. He's glad that his kids are too old to care too much about it now.

'You can just get me a voucher. I'm not picky.'

Becky laughs. 'I'm not getting you anything. You're too much of a scrooge to appreciate it.'

The Darkness's Christmas song comes on and Eddie turns the volume down. As Christmas songs go, it's one of the better ones, but he still can't be arsed with it this early in the month.

'I've got something for *you*,' he says, pretending to sound hurt.

'Sure you have,' she says. 'Is it re-gifted compacted bath salts again?'

'You'll just have to wait for Santa to find out.' He actually is going to get her something now, just to prove her wrong. He'll ask Miriam to pick up something in Tesco.

They pull up outside a low-level block of flats, brown brick with damp patches on the corners. The garden is mostly a selection of bins, and various crap that's been left outside too long. The path leading to the front door is all cracked concrete and sprouting weeds.

Becky wrinkles her nose as soon as she climbs out of the car. 'What is that *smell*?'

'Orchard breeze,' Eddie says, locking the doors. He glances up and down the street. It's quiet. Too quiet. 'Let's make this quick. This place is worse than I remembered.'

Becky presses the buzzer for Flat B. Nothing happens for a while, and she presses again, and eventually there is a buzz and a click and when she rolls her sleeve over her hand to push the door open, it swings inwards.

'Could've shoved that in with an elbow,' Eddie says. 'I'm actually surprised the buzzer even works.'

He knows the layout of these places. Two ground floor flats, two above. Flat B is to their left, and just as he lifts a hand to knock, the door is opened by a bleary eyed twenty-something male in tight black boxer shorts and not a lot else. Eddie holds up his warrant card. 'Connor Temple? I'm DI Eddie Carmine from Woodham CID, and this is my colleague, DS Becky Greene. Mind if we come in?'

Connor takes a step back. 'I've had about twenty missed calls from work. What's happened?'

They follow him inside, and he disappears into a room off the dingy main hallway and re-appears a moment later with a fluffy brown dressing gown wrapped around himself. It makes him look like a stuffed bear.

'Is someone dead?'

'What makes you say that?' Becky asks.

They follow Connor into the kitchen, where he switches the kettle on. Despite the outside of the flats looking barely habitable, the inside is clean and furnished with good quality basics. Eddie's eyes scan the kitchen into the hall and across to the open living room door, where he can just make out a barbell lying on the floor by the couch.

Connor busies himself with mugs and teabags. 'Oh, just a hunch, like. With all the calls and then you two turning up when I'm on my morning off. Tea?'

Eddie nods. 'Just milk for both of us.'

'Do you remember talking to this man last night?' Becky holds out her phone, where she's pulled up Andrew Morrison's photo from his company website. Eddie realises that this is what she was doing in the car. The body will still need a formal identification, but the man in the image is definitely the same man they saw in the bed. He's just looking a little fresher in the photo.

Connor takes the phone and peers at it. Frowns. 'I was about to say, "do you know how many people I served at the bar last night", but actually, yeah, I do remember him. He was getting flirty with one of his junior colleagues.'

Becky takes her phone back. 'Flirty how, exactly?'

'Can you tell us what she looked like?' Eddie cuts in. He doesn't mean to cut Becky off, but the sooner they can get a description of who Andrew Morrison might've been talking to, the better. They can get to the rest of it in a minute.

'Well, she was hot.' Connor pours the water into the mugs. 'Quite fancied my chances myself, actually, but she seemed interested in that fella there on the phone. Money talks, I suppose.' He gestures to the flat. 'I might look alright, but I'm hardly living in the lap of luxury here. I'll be heading off after this party season, I reckon. Maybe do a season at a ski resort or something. The hotel is alright but this town is a bit fucking grim. No offence.'

'We're going to need a bit more than that,' Becky says. 'Age, roughly? Height, hair, build…'

Connor slowly dunks the teabags and gives Becky a cheeky smile. She smiles back, and Eddie feels a sharp jab of annoyance. This prick rates himself a bit too highly. All that dark hair and perfect muscles. And what does he look like in that stupid furry robe?

'This is a murder enquiry, Mr Temple. Can we cut to the chase here?'

Connor stops dunking and the colour drains from his face. 'Oh Christ.' He runs a hand through his hair. 'I'm sorry. I wasn't thinking.' He shakes his head. 'She was late twenties. Thirty maybe. Could've passed for younger but she had a way about her that made me think she was a bit older. Wiser. That's what I liked about her. Looks wise, well… good body, blonde, incredibly sexy smile…' He trails off, and a carousel of expressions takes over his face. 'Jesus… was it him who killed her, do you think?'

Becky sighs. 'We're trying to get hold of anyone who might've seen Mr Morrison last night before he went to his room.'

'Oh wait now, what? He's the dead one? You saying that bit of hot stuff did it?'

63

'We're not saying anything of the kind, Mr Temple,' Eddie says. 'But we'd appreciate a bit more information from you. We're going over the CCTV at the moment and we're trying to piece things together, and this will help. Can I ask you to get yourself dressed and make your way over to the hotel? We have a team of officers conducting detailed interviews with all staff who were on duty last night, and anything you can do to help speed this up and let your boss get the hotel open again would be great.'

'Sure,' Connor says. 'Anything I can do to help.' He looks deflated. Confused. They've absolutely no way of knowing if Andrew Morrison was killed by a woman he met at the bar, but at the moment, it's as good a theory as any. They leave him with the three undrunk mugs of tea and head back to the car.

'Want me to drive?'

He tosses the keys to Becky and she catches them, with a small victorious cheer. The first few times he'd done this, she'd let the keys fall to the ground – confessing that she'd always been the one to lose the points in rounders – but now she was snatching them out of the air like a pro fielder.

Eddie taps his phone, logs into the case file that's been set up and pulls up Andrew Morrison's address. 'House is called Gateside Lodge. It's on Laurence Avenue. You know where that is?'

Becky pulls away from outside Connor Temple's flat. 'Polar opposite of this street, right? Over the other side of Sainsbury's, on the edge of Halcyon Park?'

'That's the one.' Eddie leans back in his seat and gazes out of the side-window. He's not looking forward to what they have to do next. He wonders what the set-up is with Andrew Morrison and his wife. Will she already be worried that he's not come home? Maybe he was meant to be going straight to work after his night in the hotel, and she's had no reason to worry yet. But maybe they're a couple who message each other regularly, or call. Just because him and Carly were barely speaking to one another for the last few years they were together, doesn't mean some couples aren't happily married and actually like to spend time together.

Eddie turns the radio up again, glad that there are no other potential Christmas songs that would fit under the indie rock classics banner. If they try to shoehorn in Wizzard he'll be forced to turn it onto Radio Three for safety, and neither of them would be happy with that.

They're both contemplative for the rest of the journey. He's got thoughts about the case whizzing around his head, and he knows Becky will be the same. They travel round the ring road, where the traffic has eased a bit now, past the big supermarket, across the train track. Halcyon Park is to their left – the grass sparkling with frost, the mature sycamores that border the sports pitches quiet and bare.

Becky slows down as they enter Laurence Avenue. One of the richest streets in the town, it is a small collection of beautiful, detached houses in individual and eclectic styles – all with huge grounds, and pretty features, and all owned by the wealthiest inhabitants of Woodham. Becky is peering out of the window, reading the names of the houses as they creep slowly past. 'Leamington Villa… Sycamore View… Harington Heights…' She pauses. 'You'd think one called that would have more storeys. Ah, I think this is it.' She stops the car outside a white tiered mansion, a row of neat cypress trees lining the drive. 'It's a wedding cake house.' She yanks on the handbrake.

'What?'

'The tiers... they're like a wedding cake so that's what they call this style.'

'What who calls them?'

Becky sighs. 'Architects. Estate agents. I don't know. Looks nice though. Custom built, I imagine. I expect the whole street is.'

Eddie unclips his seatbelt. 'We're not here to evaluate them for *Grand Designs*, Becks.'

She ignores him.

He picks up his notebook from where he'd left it balanced in the central cup holder and slips it into his pocket. He really does need to get better at typing into his phone. Maybe he'll get himself one of those little pen things.

They're halfway up the drive when the oversized front door opens and a heavily pregnant woman steps out into the porch. Her blonde hair is pulled back into a rough ponytail, and despite the expensive-looking gymwear, she looks exhausted. Dark shadows line her eyes, and her mouth is pinched into a line.

'You're late,' she says. 'I expected you at one.'

Becky shoots Eddie a glance and he gives her a small shrug. 'Mrs Morrison?'

'Gwen,' she says. 'I specifically asked the office to send you at one, because I need to go out at three and I've no idea how long you're going to need to do the full set of photographs. And you can't go into Flora's bedroom now because she's in there sleeping – I couldn't send her into school with a stomach bug, could I? Little madam. I'm not even sure she's really sick, but six is a bit young to be bunking off, isn't it?' She pauses, shakes her head. 'Bloody Andrew. We really should've rearranged but I honestly thought I could do this without him. He said he had a big

66

meeting, which seems like ridiculously bad planning, the night after their Christmas party, but—'

'Mrs Morrison…' Becky says carefully. 'Gwen? I'm DS Becky Greene, and this is my colleague, DI Eddie Carmine. I'm afraid we're not here to photograph your house.'

# 10

# The Party Girl

The house is too cold, my breath making little puffs in the air. I've got the heating on a timer because I'm not here as much as I used to be. But that might change, soon. I open the door to the airing cupboard that houses the boiler, and flick the switch on the heating unit to 'always on'. I'll just have to run it on the thermostat for a while.

The cupboard is still warmer than it is in the hall. Probably because of the insulation on the immersion heater, and the shelves filled with neatly folded sheets and towels. I lift a sheet from the top of the pile – one of those old-fashioned pastel striped ones that Mum had loved, and my granny before that. This sheet is probably older than me, but it's been washed carefully and loved, and it's still as soft as I remember it. I brush the fabric across my cheek and close my eyes, remembering my childhood bedroom, where the sheets were replaced weekly and there was always the scent of Persil washing powder and Lenor fabric conditioner in the air.

Until things changed.

Water starts to rumble through the pipes as hot water makes its way towards the radiators. The hot water has been left on since the last time I was here, when I'd had a bath and thought about sliding down under the suds and staying there. But where would that have got me? I've survived this long. I might as well see it through.

It had been a surprise that the house was all mine. I'd expected a stuffy lawyer to turn up at my foster home and tell me that I would need to take the last of my things before the house was sold off to pay the mortgage.

But it hadn't gone like that.

Yes, there was a lawyer, but it was a young man who reeled off the name of a company I'd never heard of. He wasn't stuffy at all, and in fact had seemed quite nervous as he read out a letter that said the house was paid for and it was all mine now, whenever I wanted it – the proviso being that I was looked after in the care system until I was old enough to live here alone.

My foster parents – the first lot – had been surprised too. Jane and Martin were quiet and kind, and they had two children of their own – Lucy and Tim – who had been most excited to have a new big sister. They'd expected me to sell the house, put the money in a trust for when I left school. And I *had* thought about doing that. But then everything changed again when Jane got pregnant – unexpectedly, she'd said – and they decided that they couldn't foster me anymore because they needed my room for the new baby.

By that point, I'd grown used to people letting me down.

Before my life changed – the first time – I'd had what most people would describe as a model childhood. My mum and dad were happy. They looked after me, they took me nice places, they encouraged me at school. They had friends round for parties where everyone was just *nice*.

I should've known it was too good to be true.

It had been the kind of childhood you see on those cheesy afternoon movies, the ones where the mum bakes apple pie and the dad brings her flowers and kisses her on the cheek when he comes home from work. Everyone smiles all the time and nothing bad happens, ever.

It all started to change when my dad got made redundant.

He'd worked in the same accountancy firm since he'd left school at sixteen, training himself up from nothing to partner in a relatively short time. He was the Golden Boy of the company. The star pupil. He provided well for his family, and everybody liked him. Respected him. But then a new guy started.

One with a bit of an edge.

Brendan, his name was. Brendan O'Malley. My dad said he liked to take a few risks, but that he knew what he was doing. He told my dad that he could make him rich – much richer than he'd be by just trundling along as partner until retirement. He started coming round to ours every Sunday. He'd bring my mum flowers and chocolates and tell her how pretty she was. He brought stuff for me too – comics and magazines and sweets. More expensive things on my birthday and for Christmas. For Mum too. I loved his accent. A lilting Irish sing-song that made everything sound like a wonderful adventure.

Mum was totally sucked in by him, and she always seemed to light up when he was there. And Dad...well, you'd think he'd be mad about this other man trying to woo his family, but he saw how happy Mum was. He wanted things for her and Brendan said he could get them. Up until Brendan appeared on the scene, Dad had never been greedy. 'Happy with his lot', was the phrase he liked to throw around. But there was something persuasive about Brendan, and so eventually – with Mum helping with the persuasion – Dad agreed to go along with Brendan's risky plans.

In short, fraud.

Fraud, then more fraud to cover up the mess. Throw in a bit of gambling, once things were already spiralling quickly out of control, and then – that was it.

Over.

They were caught.

Only, it was Dad who took the fall for it all. Somehow Brendan had used his wily ways to make sure that the cooked books were all under Dad's accounts. He disappeared off into the sunset, a cloud of suspicion hanging over him but nothing to stop him doing it all again, destroying someone else's life for a bit of high risk fun.

I remember the day the police came to the door. I'd been in my room doing homework, Mum was downstairs, watching TV, something cooking in the oven but with less care than usual. Mum had started to let things slide since it had all gone south at Dad's work. He'd been charged, and due to his impeccably clean life up to that point, he'd been bailed and allowed to stay at home until the trial. I often thought that if he'd been put in prison on remand, then we might not have had that early evening visit from the police.

And I might not be here now, alone, in the cold – while Mum lies in a hospital bed as good as dead.

I remember how I felt as I'd crept down the stairs at the sound of the unfamiliar voices. Heard the squawk of a radio. Watched as my mum slowly slid down to the ground, the officers leaping forward, lightning fast, trying to catch her as she fell.

My heart had thumped so hard in my chest, I thought the police might actually hear it. One of them looked up, saw me. Averted his gaze. I couldn't hide after that. I'd walked carefully down the stairs, held on to Mum's hand as she sat there on the floor, propped up against the open front door, soft and sagging like a rag doll.

'Is there anyone we can call?' one of the officers had said. One of the neighbours had arrived, then. Mrs Stephen from the house across the street. Being charitable, you could say it was nice of her to come over and help. Being mean, you could say she'd been peering through her net curtains, just waiting for a moment like this.

They'd found him on the railway tracks, close to the level crossing. They didn't go into detail, spoke mostly in hushed tones. They'd given Mum a couple of days to get used to the idea before they'd called her in to identify him – by his personal effects, that is. Not the scattered pieces of his body. He'd left his wallet, his phone and his watch on the embankment, and a note, written neatly on a piece of pale blue Basildon Bond notepaper that Mum told me later was from the pad she kept in her bedside drawer.

It's that little detail that sticks with me now. Not what the letter said. It doesn't matter what he'd written. He was gone, and he'd left us in a financial pit that there was seemingly no way out of.

Until Mum got herself a job, serving drinks to rich men at parties.

At least, that's how it started.

I close the cupboard door. The hallway is warmer now. The house feels less lonely, somehow, with just that hint of heat spreading warmth around the walls. I head into the kitchen and fill the kettle. There's no milk, because I didn't bring any, but I know I left a packet of herbal teabags last time I was here.

The kettle boils, and I make myself a cup of citrus chamomile tea, inhaling the fragrant steam before taking it through to the living room and sitting down on the couch. A light cloud of dust belches out of the cushion, and I wrinkle my nose, vowing to give the place a good clean as soon as I can. It's hard to find the time, what with visiting Mum and keeping on with the task in hand. But I *will* make the time. My mum would never live in a dirty house, and just because it's neat doesn't mean it's clean.

Mum had been obsessively house-proud until things unravelled. Then it had all fallen to me to keep the place nice. I didn't have to – I was only a kid – but it was what I was used to. A place for everything and everything in its place.

Mum isn't in *her place* though. Not the place she's meant to be in. She's supposed to be here, watching soaps and shouting at the telly when one of the characters does something stupid. She's meant to be making chicken stew with dumplings, and singing along to the radio while she irons the striped sheets.

She's not supposed to be lying in a hospital bed, in a soulless clinic, hooked up to monitors and machines, while the people responsible carry on with their vulgar little lives. Brendan is out there somewhere. I know he is.

But there are so many *Brendans*.

Taking advantage of good people. Taking what they want from us. Just because they can. But I can do something about that. I've already started.

I'll sleep here tonight. Recharge myself. And then I will carry on.

Some of us have a job to do.

# I I

# Eddie

Gwen Morrison's living room is quite different from Connor Temple's. No barbells in sight. Just an expensive-looking L-shaped leather couch, and lots of classy bric-a-brac. Floor to ceiling windows face out onto the frost covered, postcard-pretty garden, and the smell of freshly brewed coffee mingles with the scent of pine needles from the large tree in the corner, tastefully decorated with silver baubles and sprigs of holly.

'I was brewing the coffee to make the place smell nice for the estate agent,' Gwen says, carrying in a tray with a cafetière and three small, brightly coloured mugs. 'We might as well drink it.' She manages pretty well, until she lays the tray on the low glass coffee table, then her hands start to shake and the mugs rattle together, and Eddie is quickly up off the couch and taking it from her hands.

Becky guides Gwen to the other part of the couch. 'Can we call someone for you? A friend? Maybe you've got family nearby?'

Gwen's head falls forward. She cradles her stomach, and Eddie feels a hard lump forming in his throat as fat teardrops fall onto Gwen's pale blue t-shirt, leaving small, wet circles. 'I think Amira will be in. She's next door. Left side.' Her voice wobbles, and she lifts her head as Becky gets up and walks carefully out of the room to fetch the neighbour. Gwen looks straight up at Eddie. 'What's happened to him?'

Eddie sits down on the couch, diagonally opposite her, elbows on knees. Gwen Morrison had worked out quickly after they'd introduced themselves that this was not a social visit. She'd disappeared into the kitchen, telling them to head into the living room, and then re-appeared shortly afterwards with the tray. They hadn't told her anything else yet, but when your husband is not where he is meant to be, and two detectives have turned up at your house, there are not many people who would jump to the wrong conclusion. Eddie takes a breath. This is the worst part of the job, and he's hoping for just a bit longer before he has to do it.

'I'd rather you just told me, Detective Inspector Carmine,' Gwen says. She seems to have gathered herself again. Bracing. Just wanting it over with. He's seen this reaction many times before. It's either this, or the hysterics. Neither one is easier than the other.

He's just about to speak again, when he hears the front door closing softly, hushed voices in the hallway. Careful footsteps on the wooden stairs. Becky walks in, followed by a short, dark-haired woman dressed in similar workout gear to Gwen. The woman hurries straight over to her friend, and sits beside her, clutching her hands.

'This is Amira,' Becky says. 'Her daughter, Prisha, has gone upstairs to check on Flora.'

Amira speaks, soft and quick. 'What is going on, please?'

Eddie nods at Becky, and she goes over and sits on the other side of Gwen. 'I'm very sorry to tell you this, Mrs Morrison. But your husband, Andrew, was found unresponsive in his hotel room this morning by the cleaner. I'm afraid, following examination, it was determined that he was already deceased upon discovery.'

Gwen gulps down a sob, pulling her hands away from Amira and pressing the palms against her eyes.

Amira blinks, takes a breath. 'Was it his heart? He is always running too much. I have told him this many times, you know?'

Eddie writes this down. It would be easier if it was something like that, something tragic but natural. But the preliminary signs don't point that way.

'We don't have all the details yet,' Eddie says, 'but I'm afraid it does look as if there was someone else involved in Andrew's death.'

Gwen's head flips up. 'Are you saying he was murdered?'

'We're not saying that right now, no,' Eddie says. This is why the hysterical reactions are often easier to deal with. The numb, calmly questioning ones are the worst. 'We'll need to carry out a post mortem, and we'll need you to come down and see him. He had identification on him, so it's just a formality, and if you have someone else that you'd rather do it – a brother, or a parent, maybe? – that would be OK too.'

'Gwen, you need to tell them.' Amira whispers this, but Eddie hears her clearly.

Becky flashes Eddie a look. Shifts in her seat. 'Was there anything unusual going on in Andrew's life?' A pause. 'Even if you think it's something minor, it could be important to our investigation.'

Gwen takes a tissue from the packet that Amira is holding towards her, and noisily blows her nose. 'He had a one night stand. It was before he knew I was pregnant. Work conference. Too much to drink.' She coughs out a mirthless laugh. 'Said it wouldn't happen again. Such a cliché.'

'He has taken drugs also,' Amira says, addressing Eddie. 'Cocaine. Bad for his heart. I told him this.'

Eddie writes more notes. The clean cut image they'd had of Andrew Morrison is quickly disintegrating. Though the man had admitted to one sexual transgression, in Eddie's experience, it was rarely only one. Perhaps this *was* accidental? A sex game gone wrong? They'll need to share this information with Maria while she carries out her medical examination as it might be relevant.

Becky stands up. 'An officer is on her way to sit with you, Gwen. She's a Family Liaison Officer. Her name is Emma, and she will help you with whatever you need, OK? As Eddie says, we will need you to come and see Andrew, but it will be a little while before we're ready for you. Emma will let you know, OK?' She nods at Amira. 'I hope it's all right for you and Prisha to stay for a while?'

'Of course,' Amira says. 'Of course.' She shakes her head sadly. 'That man. He did not appreciate what he had here.'

Eddie and Becky are quiet as they walk to the car.

'What a mess.' Becky sighs as she clicks in her seatbelt and starts the engine.

'Funnily enough, unexplained deaths usually are.'

As Becky pulls away, Eddie starts updating his notes in the passenger seat. He likes it when Becky drives. This is a fairly new development, as he'd always hated being a passenger with previous partners, but he's in sync with her. Doesn't need to feel like he's in control by driving the car.

Becky's phone rings just as she's about to take the exit off the ring road that will take them to the hospital. She's got it connected to the car speakers, and she taps the screen quickly to answer it. The name has already flashed up: Maria.

'Hey,' Becky says. 'We're about five minutes away.'

Maria's voice is loud. 'As suspected, the coroner has requested a full post mortem but I need the ID first. You know the drill. I was just calling to tell you no rush. He's in the fridge.'

Eddie frowns. 'We've sent someone to help Mrs Morrison – she's got a young daughter at home. Joe and Stuart will be in touch to give you an ETA on the ID as soon as they've spoken with the FLO.'

'Got it. Talk soon.' Maria ends the call.

'I honestly think that woman would get on better if she wasn't so verbose,' Eddie says, not looking up.

Becky laughs. 'She's matter of fact and she gets the job done. If she didn't have to wait for the ID I'm sure we'd already have the full description of the killer by now.'

'Have you been watching *Silent Witness* again, Becks?'

'It's my guilty pleasure,' she says, 'like your love of eighties cock rock. Don't think I didn't spot you mouthing the words to that Meatloaf song earlier. That poor woman, though. Alone with a little kid, and another on the way.'

'Meatloaf is not *cock rock*, actually. You're thinking of Bon Jovi and Def Leppard.'

'Who?'

'I'll educate you one day.'

'Can't wait,' she says. 'I'm kind of hoping he had an innocent but tragic heart attack.'

'Who? I'm pretty sure all members of those particular bands are still with us.' Eddie puts his phone into his pocket. 'Anyway, I'm kind of hoping that your friend Maria gets the bodywork done soon, and the tox screen sooner.'

'You thinking this is some sex and drugs thing?'

Eddie frowns. He is kind of thinking that, but he's also thinking that if that was the case, why hadn't the woman – assuming it was a woman – called an ambulance?

He shifts in his seat. 'I'm not sure what I think yet. We need to lay out everything we've got, get updates from the others at the hotel—'

Eddie's phone pings just as Becky enters one of the many roundabouts that the town has to offer. This one is advertising Christmas trees for a tenner, via a hand-painted sign illegally stuck over one of the official billboards. *Every bloody year…*

'Wild Bill,' he says, reading the message on his phone. 'Wants us in for a briefing in twenty.'

'Lucky we're on the way then, isn't it?' Becky turns a hard right and drives around the roundabout and back on themselves. 'We can go and see Maria later.'

★★★

The traffic is horrendous, and they are late.

The big room where they'd had the early meeting with DCI Wilde has been commandeered as the briefing room, with various flipcharts and whiteboards and the smaller tables all put back together to turn it into a giant board-room layout. It looks like most of CID have crammed themselves in here, plus several of the uniforms and the relevant civvies. There's a lot of chatter when Eddie and

Becky arrive, but it soon stops when DCI Wilde walks in and does another of his famous hand claps.

'Good afternoon, everyone. Well, we got cut short this morning, and I didn't expect to be here all day, but these things happen and that's the name of the game – all that kind of thing!'

He grins and Eddie has to try hard not to shake his head. Why is the man so bloody cheerful when they're about to have a briefing on a murder enquiry? He catches Becky's eye and she replies with a tiny eyebrow raise that further cements their bond. They were 'on the same page', as Wild Bill would say... if they gave him any opportunity. Eddie notices that Jonty Davis is also still around. Sitting down at the other end of the table with his tablet ready for action. Surely he can't be doing any actual work? As far as anyone knows, he spends his time scurrying after the DCI like one of those wheely-dogs on a string.

On the plus side, any further discussion about station closures will have to wait. Wild Bill is hardly going to have time to focus on that with a murder investigation under-way. Good. Another waste of time, cost-saving, bollocks initiative stopped in its tracks. Eddie tries not to look too gleeful about this turn of events.

'Right then,' DCI Wilde continues. 'Eddie... what have you got so far?'

Eddie stands up. 'I didn't have time to prepare slides...' He shrugs, knowing he had no intention of preparing slides. He glances over at Jonty, who looks like someone has just stolen his last chip.

'At ten a.m. today we were called regarding the body of a white male, found in bed by the cleaner of his room in the Woodlands Hotel and Conference Centre—'

DC Keir Jameson quips, 'Not the first time a punter's OD'd in The Commie...'

Eddie has to try hard not to roll his eyes. 'Yes, thank you, Keir. Helpful and relevant as ever.' He pauses, seeing a few blank stares. 'For anyone not familiar with what DC Jameson is referring to, the Woodlands Hotel and Conference Centre has recently undergone a multi-million pound refit, after spending several years in disrepair. It was, our older colleagues will know, once called "The Commodore" – and it was a very popular spot with ladies and gents who liked to spend some special time together.' He frames the last few words inside air quotes.

There's some laughter, some muttered comments. Eddie has many memories of the last days of the Commie – they did make an attempt to clean it up for a bit, trying out some functions for a while, but it never shook off its reputation.

He continues. 'We subsequently identified this man to be Andrew Morrison, fifty-one, partner at Barlow & Wolfenstone LLB – one of Woodham's most prestigious law firms.' He points to the board where someone has already stuck up a photo of Andrew Morrison, smiling and in good health. 'Mr Morrison's wife, Gwen, is six months pregnant, and they have a daughter, Flora, aged six.' He points to the next item on the pinboard, silently thanking Joe for setting it up for them. It's a layout of the hotel, showing the location of all of the function rooms, and their relation to the main entrance, the lobby and the bar. 'As you can see from this diagram, although the function rooms are separate from each other, each one links to the lobby and is directly accessible from the bar...and, of course, the main entrance.'

He points to the next piece of paper.

'This is the layout of the bedrooms, and you can see here the two elevators in the hallway, and the fire exit stairs, which lead directly to the car park.'

Eddie's phone buzzes in his pocket. He's silenced it but kept it on vibrate to make sure he doesn't miss any important notifications. 'Sorry, one second.'

It's a message from Maria – Mrs Morrison ID'd the body and so she's started her examination. There's definitely an element of suffocation, but she suspects something more. He glances over at Becky and sees that she's received the message too. Hopefully this briefing won't take too long, then they can call the pathologist and get more information. The sooner they know a cause of death, the sooner they can get on with the details of the case. At the moment, everything they have is pretty basic stuff.

He also has to applaud Gwen Morrison for getting down to the hospital to ID her husband so quickly. Her stoic attitude will come in useful for her, as it all starts to sink in.

'Theories?' Eddie says, then holds up a hand to let everyone know he's not actually inviting any input yet. 'Mrs Morrison told us that her husband had trouble keeping Little Andrew in his pants.' A flurry of sniggers ripple around the room.

'Sex game gone wrong, then?' Keir says.

Eddie nods. 'Possibly. Which potentially puts us in involuntary manslaughter territory, assuming we find out who's responsible and hope that they're just running scared.' He pauses before continuing.

'Right then, team. What else have we got?'

85

# 12

# Harry

He can't face going back to work. Heather hadn't quite slung him out on his ear, but she'd been borderline hostile after he'd left her to answer the door to the food delivery driver while she was still wrapped in a towel. He hadn't thought; he'd just launched himself onto the couch to get himself as far away from her bedroom, where he'd been snooping, as possible. She'd ordered a huge pizza, and she had half-heartedly offered him some, but the atmosphere was thick with barely suppressed anger and the cloying smell of onions. He hated onions on pizza. It was worse than pineapple, and that was saying a lot. So, he made his excuses about having to get back to work, then scurried off with his tail between his legs.

So… no further forward on the party plans. He would have to wait for her to calm down. Hopefully she would be back at work tomorrow, because she didn't seem particularly unwell. Unless, of course, it was her time of the month and she was too embarrassed to say. He didn't think so though. He kept track of that in his diary. It helped him to know when to expect her to be tetchy, and when she might not be up for sex. He usually tried to steer her towards giving him oral at this time, as he'd read that some women didn't really like having full sex when they were bleeding. But she mostly avoided him when she was on her period. She obviously didn't want him to have to deal with her moods. Some women are reasonable like that.

He drives his car back home and parks it on his drive. Then he sits for a moment, texting his boss to say that he'd gone for some fresh air at lunchtime but he wasn't feeling great so he wasn't coming back in today. Luckily there were other people in today who could probably squeeze in his work that was due by the end of the day. If not, his boss would do it. As a permanent employee, he knows they are not going to question him on an afternoon's absence if he tells them he's sick. After checking that the message has been received – two blue ticks – he climbs out of the car and puts on his coat and scarf, buttoning the coat and turning up the collar. There's a proper nip in the air this afternoon, and his plant pots under the front window are already starting to frost over despite there still being a nice bit of winter sun.

Harry walks down his quiet street and out onto the main road, hurrying along as the traffic sprays slush up the kerbs. Despite his plans, he has not actually had any lunch, and his stomach is grumbling.

There is a new-ish café bar at the quiet end of the busy shopping street. Just far enough away from the crowds, armed with their multiple carrier bags and determined expressions. He walks in, and is pleased to find that the place is not too busy and that they are playing that Jonah Louie song with the trumpets. That's his favourite Christmas song. The place looks nice too, decked out with a few white tinsel covered trees and lots of fairy lights. Once

Heather calms down, he'll bring her in here for drinks and nibbles one night. It definitely feels like that kind of place. He takes a seat on one of the high leather bar stools.

'Something to eat, or just drinks?' the barman asks pleasantly, striding right over to him before he's even taken his coat off. This is a good start. Harry appreciates efficient service from hospitality staff. He checks out the barman's name badge.

'I'd like to see a menu, please... Simon.' Harry smiles. 'And whatever you recommend from your craft ales.'

Simon gestures at the beer taps. 'We've got quite a selection, actually. What sort of thing do you like? Pale... dark... hoppy... fruity?' He flips a white glass-cloth over his shoulder. 'Then there's the bottles, and the cans...'

Harry folds his coat and lays it on the stool next to him, followed by his scarf. 'Well, I...' He's not sure what to ask for. He doesn't actually know anything about craft beer. He usually just has whatever someone else has, and if he has to choose himself he just asks for an IPA and hopes for the best.

'Something to cheer you up, or chill you out? I'm sensing you're a man who needs both of those things,' Simon says.

Harry chuckles. 'You're good at this.'

'It's my superpower.' Simon takes a small glass from under the counter and fills it halfway from the tap furthest away. Then he places it in front of Harry with a nod. 'Try this one.'

Harry sniffs it, then takes a sip. It smells of grapefruit, and the foamy head tickles his nose. Around him, there's a murmur of chatter, the sound of cutlery against plates. He can smell something meaty and it makes his mouth water.

'Perfect,' he says. 'I'll take a pint.' He scans the menu as Simon goes to pour his drink. 'And I'll have a cheeseburger. Does that come with fries?'

'Best in town.' Simon places the pint in front of him, then turns to the computer screen behind him and taps in the order. 'I'll run you a tab,' he says.

Harry takes a long slow sip of his beer. It's cold and refreshing, and he's glad he came in here.

A moment later, Simon fires himself a pint of Coke into a tall glass, then comes around the other side of the bar, sliding onto the stool to Harry's right.

'Break,' he says. 'Don't worry. If you need a top up, I'll be round there before you know. I'm having a burger too. I hadn't decided between that and the mac 'n' cheese, but I had mac 'n' cheese twice last week and after smelling those last couple of burgers that came out, my mind has switched over to the meaty goodness.' He laughs. 'Some weeks I try to be a vegetarian. It doesn't last long in here.'

'I could never be a vegetarian,' Harry says. 'I don't like vegetables.' He thinks back to Heather and her pizza. 'What are your thoughts on onions on pizza?'

Simon rests his hand on his chin. Looks contemplative. 'Wrong,' he says. 'Makes the room smell like B.O.'

'Yes!' Harry slaps his hand on the bar. 'My girlfriend ordered a pizza with sweetcorn, peppers, olives and onions for lunch. No meat at all. Absolutely rank.'

'That why you're in here then?' Simon takes a sip of his Coke.

Harry takes a breath. 'Kind of. Well, I popped round to see her because she wasn't at work, and from her reaction you'd think I'd suggested strangling her dog.'

Simon laughs but he looks a bit horrified.

'Sorry, that's not a mental image anyone wants is it? She hasn't even got a dog. Closest thing to a pet she has is some threadbare fluffy toy cat.' He takes a sip of his pint. 'It's probably because where she lives isn't very nice. She did try to tell me that before. A few times, to be fair.'

'Do you not go round there much, then?'

The chef appears from the kitchen, lays the plates of burgers and chips in front of them both. The chips are in a paper-lined cup, and Harry wonders why they don't just put them on the plate and save themselves the extra washing up. He watches as Simon takes a bite of his burger. Harry shoves a couple of fries into his mouth.

'First time I'd been there, as it happens.' He chews. Shoves in a few more.

Simon looks at him, burger in his hands, meat juice dripping onto the plate. 'And you just decided that today was the day to turn up uninvited?'

Harry shrugs. He lifts the lid of his burger and removes the tomato, dropping it onto his plate. 'Girls never really say what they mean, do they? No usually means yes... or maybe, at the very least.'

'Bloody hell.' Simon wipes his mouth with a napkin and stands up. 'You might want to re-evaluate that particular line of thinking.' He picks up his plate and walks around the bar. 'Unless you're after a slap in the face.' He looks Harry in the eye. 'At the very least.'

Harry prickles with annoyance. He's trying to come up with a sharp retort, but by the time he opens his mouth to speak, Simon has disappeared into the kitchen.

'*Tosser*,' Harry mutters. He takes an angry bite of his burger, but his appetite has already gone. What does that guy know anyway? If Harry knows anything at all, it's how to treat women well.

# 13

# Becky

It's Becky's turn to speak. 'We spoke to the barman who was on last night; Connor Temple. Young, cocky, but definitely observant.' She feels her cheeks grow hot, remembering him appraising her. 'He remembers Andrew Morrison talking to a sexy blonde. She might be nothing to do with this, but it's worth following up on. He's coming down to the station to give us a full statement.'

Eddie thanks her, then nods at Jonah Abboud, their hotshot CCTV operator. 'Let's try and tie that in with the CCTV.' He glances at Becky again. 'As I mentioned before, we also spoke to Mrs Morrison. Gwen. She was distraught, as you can imagine. We're going to have to talk to her again, but I've just had word that she's been in to ID her husband, and that the PM has now commenced. We should know more soon. Becky and I will follow up.' Becky watches as Eddie's eyes scan the room, searching for who else he needs.

'Stuart? Anything useful from the staff?'

DS Stuart Fyfe taps his phone, checks his notes. 'Joe and I talked to them all. They're mostly in shock, the cleaners especially. Nothing specific to go on as yet as no one seemed to notice anything untoward. It was a busy night for them all with the multiple parties, people coming and going. The cleaners came in at six to start cleaning the function suites, before moving on to the bedrooms at nine. They got to Room 312 at nine fifteen, and the young cleaner, Alice Greenwood, freaked out. She's a student at the uni and as her course is mostly wound down for the year she's been doing some seasonal work at the hotel. She's only been there a week. She says she stayed in the room just looking at him for a while before she went to her supervisor.'

'Anything on her we need to be concerned about?' Eddie asks.

Stuart shakes his head. 'Joe checked her out. No record, no red flags. I think she just went into shock.'

Joe puts his hand up like an eager kid in a classroom.

Eddie ignores him. 'Right then. Thanks, Stuart. OK, back to you, Keir and Jonah. Let's see what we've got on CCTV.'

Becky likes Jonah. He's tagged along a few times when she's been out with Maria, and they'd both enjoyed his company. Last time, Maria had suggested she go home early, leaving Becky and Jonah alone to finish their drinks, but Becky had declined her unsubtle matchmaking attempt. She wasn't sure about mixing business with pleasure, although there was plenty of it going on. She senses that Eddie is watching her, and turns to him, but he quickly re-focusses on Jonah.

'We did find something interesting on the CCTV.' He picks up one of the electronic pointers from the desk and turns to the big screen, where Jonty had presented his slides earlier. The screen flickers, then a mirror of Jonah's laptop screen comes up. He clicks again and opens up a video of CCTV footage. 'I've spliced a few items together. You can see the detail from the timestamps, but first we have this.' The video shows the bar, people around it, the barman they'd spoken to already – Connor – moving from one end to the other. He stops there and starts to pick up various things from behind the bar, mixing cocktails. At the other end, a slim blonde woman in a dark dress. Her dress sparkles as the light hits it, as she moves a little on her stool. A man approaches the bar and after a moment, she turns to face him. At one point, the man gestures to the barman, who after finishing his cocktails and placing them on the far end of the bar, comes back and talks to the man. As Connor walks over to mix the drinks, he glances down towards the blonde, who is now in deep conversation with the man.

Jonah pauses the video. 'You can watch the rest if you like, but basically, they talk for about half an hour, they have another drink, the man goes to the toilet and then returns. At no point does the woman face the camera, but we do see her move in a way that suggests she opened her bag at some point while the man was in the toilet. The man, we're pretty certain, is Andrew Morrison.' He clicks play and they all watch the scene unfold. It's hard to see what she's doing as her arm barely moves. She could be getting a tissue, or reapplying her lipstick.

'Could she have put something in his drink?' Becky says, leaning forward. 'Can you play that part again, please?'

Jonah rewinds the footage and replays it. The woman could have been doing anything, or nothing. She barely moves, and it's impossible to see what's happening from behind her.

Eddie speaks. 'We'll ask Connor Temple to see if he can shed any light, but from this angle we really can't make any assumptions.' He turns back to face the screen. 'Carry on, Jonah.'

Becky looks across the table at Joe, who has his arms crossed in a very pissed off way. She's not sure what's wrong with him but she'll find out later, no doubt. He'd clearly wanted to say something earlier when Stuart was going through the staff interviews, but Joe was never good at interrupting without being invited. He flashes her a wide-eyed look when he notices her watching him, and she mouths 'you need to speak up'. He looks pointedly at the big screen.

'OK, so next,' Jonah says. 'We see them together heading for the elevators.' He plays the video. Andrew Morrison and the mystery blonde walk together, arm in arm, towards the lifts. She has a short-handled maroon handbag looped over the crook of her left arm, the gold clasp partly obscured by her hand. Again, at no point does the woman look at any of the cameras. Jonah shows the various angles, and she seems to be flicking her hair, looking at her shoes, doing whatever she can at just the right moments.

'She knows where all the cameras are,' Keir cuts in. 'We've got other operatives now checking the cameras from the nights leading up to this, to see if we've got her there staking the place out.'

'We showed a piece of this footage to the hotel manager,' Jonah says, turning to face the group. 'He did not recognise her.'

'Hard to recognise someone from the back. Someone in a party dress... I'm sure she wasn't wearing that when she came in to check the place out,' Becky says. 'You need to be checking the cameras for a shorter woman, in casual clothes, probably hair in a ponytail.' She shrugs. 'That's what I would wear. And you can see from the previous video that she's wearing at least six-inch heels with that dress.'

'Well observed,' Keir says. He gives Becky a cheeky wink. 'Next...'

'Next,' Jonah says, 'is nothing. Because as the very sheepish hotel manager, Mr Walters, explained, the cameras in the room corridors are duds.'

There is a collective groan from the room.

'A legacy from the old days of the by-the-hour rooms, and not deemed priority to fix during the refit.'

'He told us this earlier,' Eddie confirms. 'Not a lot we can do.'

'Do we see her leaving later on?' Becky says. 'Early hours, I—'

Joe stands up quickly, knocking into the desk and causing a plastic water bottle to wobble, then fall over, rolling away. 'Sorry,' he says, as all eyes turn towards him. 'Can I just mention something...' Becky raises an eyebrow. Finally he decides to speak up! Joe goes pink. 'It's something that Keith Walters said to me just as we were leaving. I didn't think much of it at the time, but it's been bothering me ever since—'

'Go on, Joe,' Eddie says. 'You should've said earlier if you had something important to add. There's no ceremony during a potential murder investigation.'

Joe looks panicked for a moment, then his expression slides back into neutral as he starts to read from the notes on his phone. 'He said that he'd called his boss – the big boss, the one who oversees the management of several hotels – as he had to tell him why they were closing and why they were going to have to cancel all the parties. Apparently his boss replied, "I don't know what all the fuss is about – this happens at least once every Christmas party season. It's almost as traditional as the panto"…'

The room falls silent.

DCI Wilde stands up. 'Thank you, Joe.' He addresses the room. 'Now, accidental and natural deaths *do* happen in hotels all the time, but I think perhaps we should take a look at the last few years at the local hotels. Just to rule things out.' He turns to Eddie. 'I'm sure you can organise a team to look into this, DI Carmine, as well as continuing the investigation on the current case?' His eyes scan the room and briefly come to rest on Becky before he turns back to Eddie. 'You and DS Greene have good experience of this sort of thing.'

Becky feels the hairs on the nape of her neck stand on end. Not again. Not another Christmas serial killer. A small wave of nausea hits her as she looks across at Eddie.

'Leave it with us, sir,' Eddie says.

Becky taps her hand on the table. 'Can we go back to the CCTV for a second,' she says.

The other CCTV analyst – Becky recalls now that her name is Julie Peters – takes the pointer from Jonah and clicks onto the next screen. The video is blank, apart from some static. 'As we know, we have no CCTV footage from the corridors. We do, however, have this.' The video shows someone walking out of the fire exit into the car park. They're in a dark hoodie and what looks like dark jogging trousers. Trainers. Small dark backpack. It's not clear if it's a man or a woman.

'OK,' Becky says, 'so she left a bag somewhere earlier on. This is someone who had a plan, which means this is unlikely to be a sex game gone wrong situation.'

'We need the results of the post mortem ASAP,' Eddie says, 'so Becky and I are going to see Dr Maria after this.' He nods at DCI Wilde. 'Then we'll get cracking on the search for similar cases. I'll get the full investigation plan written up, and let's all do some good work.' He pauses. 'Oh… and if anyone has any idea of a motive at this stage, I am all ears.'

The DCI does one of his claps. 'Great work, everyone. Let's keep this moving.' He addresses Eddie. 'I'm heading back to Farndean, but keep me posted, all right? I'll release the first media statement. Keep it as vague as possible for now.'

There's the sound of chairs scraping on the floor as they're pushed back from the table, and excited chatter starts up as theories start to fly. Becky waits by the door for Eddie as the others file out.

'Oh, just one more thing,' DCI Wilde says. 'Eddie? Becky? Sit down again, will you? There's something I need to run by you and this might have serendipitously turned out to be perfect timing for it.'

Intrigued, Becky sits down. Eddie sits opposite. Jonty sits at the bottom end of the table and flips open his laptop and connects it to the screen once again. He clicks through to the university website. Becky recognises the logo, although the rest of the site seems to have been revamped since she last looked at it for a case last year.

'We've been approached to work on an initiative with the university. It's for a part of their MA in Criminology, which has been attracting a lot of attention. They'd like to offer their expertise as part of a collaboration, in some capacity. Assist us but also learn from us. That sort of thing.'

'Sounds interesting,' Becky says.

'I think so,' Bill says. 'It's always good to learn, and for us to show willing with these sorts of things, right? My contact, Professor Helena Summers—'

Eddie sits up straight. 'Did you say Helena *Summers*?'

Bill laughs. 'I did, Eddie. *Summers*. Like, the opposite of winters.' He sighs. 'No winter sun for me this year, more's the pity.' He clocks Eddie glaring at him. 'Your ears playing up? You know you can get them suctioned with a little vacuum cleaner these days? Surprisingly relaxing...'

Eddie stands up. 'I think this is a ridiculous idea. I don't have time to talk to some play-a-profiler type. Come on, Becky, we've got work to do.'

Becky shrugs at the DCI's confused look. She's confused too. It's not like Eddie to react like this. He's normally quite open to collaborations and assistance. His reaction to the professor's name was also strange.

There's clearly something going on with him, and she's going to have to find out exactly what it is.

# 14

## Eddie

Eddie squeezes his hands into fists to try and stop them from shaking. Releases. Stretches his fingers. Splashes his face with cold water. It's a coincidence. Has to be. Another Helena Summers who trained in psychology and happens to live and work locally. He takes a few deep breaths, tries to calm himself down. It's been over twenty-eight years. Fuck. It's actually pretty incredible that their paths haven't crossed again before. He'd just assumed she would have moved away. Why would she have wanted to stick around here?

Becky is standing outside the gents toilets, leaning against the wall. Her face is questioning.

'You OK, boss?'

He sucks in a breath. He could tell her. He *should* tell her. Tell someone, at least. But he doesn't want to get into it right now. They're at a crucial point in the investigation and they have work to do. This will just have to wait.

'Oh you know.' He shrugs. 'Wild Bill and Jonty and their bloody initiatives.' He emphasises the last word with air quotes.

Becky looks at him like she wants to say more, but she lets it drop. He knows her though. She'll store it in that database in her head, ready to be unleashed at a later date. Well that's fine. He'll be able to deal with it then. Once he's processed it himself.

They start to walk along the corridor. 'Right,' he says. 'What's on our task list?'

'Talk to Maria, get cause of death. Start looking at other potential hotel murders over the Christmas period spanning an interminable number of years. Talk to someone about that hairclip – it looked quite unusual, so maybe a jeweller can help, or an antiques expert. Get someone to grill Connor Temple. Make sure Emma the FLO is digging around at the Morrison residence. Decide which joke you're submitting to Joe's Christmas Dip. Buy my present that you definitely lied about having already.' She pauses. 'Learn to accept that "Last Christmas" is the best seasonal song and allow it to be played at all times.'

'Is that all?'

Becky laughs. 'Yeah. Opening up the search into the potential previous is going to be fun. I'm already having flashbacks to the Photographer case.'

'Let's not even go there,' Eddie says. He would really rather not be reminded of the serial killer case from six years ago. It nearly broke them all. On the plus side, it accelerated his predecessor DI Nick Keegan's early retirement and allowed him to slide gracefully into his shoes and make a better job of running the department. 'We have a decent team. The other lot can keep on it with the CCTV and the staff. Someone must be able to identify this woman from the bar – at the very least, she might be the last person to have seen Andrew Morrison alive, and we need to eliminate her from our enquiries. We'll get the barman to help us create an image. It's not like *no one* is going to recognise her, is it?'

'Ha!' Becky says. 'Have you been on social media lately? These transformations that women do, with the contour make-up and the wigs... even the expressions. Designer dresses and handbags hired for the evening from a clothing app that even insures you in case someone spills red wine or burns you with a ciggie? Honestly, I'd struggle to pick out my own sister if she went to the lengths that some of them do.'

Eddie stops walking. 'I'm not even going to pretend to have a clue what you're talking about, but is this a potential angle? If you think that she's taken the time to alter her appearance, could we be looking at someone with expertise in this area? Beauty, make-up... stage make-up? Just a thought.'

'I'll message Joe. This is the kind of thing he's into.'

Eddie opens his mouth then closes it again. Probably best not to know.

Becky messages Maria while they're in the car, and they drive over to the hospital to meet her. She's in her office, which is down the hall from the mortuary, and has nice tea and good biscuits and no stench of death. Eddie is not one of those detectives who likes to be in the room while they cut the bodies open. What's he going to be able to add, apart from potentially his own vomit?

'Hello again,' Maria says. She's sitting at her corner desk, which is extremely neat and tidy. Pens are in a mug, notepads perfectly lined up and a row of highlighters are laid out like sentries next to a stack of sticky notes. You can read a lot into someone's mind when you look at their work desk. Eddie's generally looks like someone has broken in and ransacked it. 'Help yourselves to drinks. I've got it all ready for you.'

'Fairly quick?' Becky asks, as she flips the switch on the kettle and takes teabags from a box of Darjeeling.

'Yes.' Maria enlarges the document on the screen of her computer. The words 'Pathology Report' cover the top, in large letters. 'One of those bog standard ones that don't take much time to do but which leave me with more questions than I would like.'

Eddie sighs. 'Go on…'

'Cause of death looks like asphyxiation, based on all the usual details.' She points to the lines of text on the screen. 'You can read it all there—'

'But…' says Eddie.

Becky slides a mug of tea in front of him and sits down.

'But,' says Maria, 'I found a puncture wound between the first and second toes of his right foot. It would have been difficult to spot, but there was a little bit of bruising and a pinprick of blood. I think – but for now it's just a think – that the injection did not go in straight, hence the surrounding tissue damage that has inadvertently led me to spot it so easily.'

'Oh,' says Eddie.

Becky sits forward, reading the screen. 'So he's been injected with something? Any signs that could suggest he might have been injecting himself?'

Maria shakes her head. 'Nothing to suggest he was an addict of any sort, no. No other marks on his arms or anywhere else – obviously after we spotted the mark on his toe, we went over his whole body again, under magnification. I mean, it's not impossible that he did this himself. Maybe he was new to it, but knew that sticking it there would be easier to conceal. This could explain why the angle was off, and the bruising.' She pauses, takes a sip of the tea that Becky has made her. 'We swabbed the area around the feet too as a precaution. It might be that something leaked onto the skin.'

'Do you think this is potentially a cause of death, then?' Eddie says. He opens a packet of custard creams and takes a bite.

'Impossible to know without the tox results. Which, by the way, would also reveal if he's any sort of addict. My working theory, if you're interested?'

Eddie crunches. 'Go on.'

'Whatever was injected was meant to kill him. It didn't. So your perpetrator suffocated him to make sure.'

'Can you speed up the tox results?' Becky says. 'They've been taking weeks, lately.'

'I know. We are *massively* short-staffed in the lab. But I think this will be key information for the investigation, so I've sent them to HQ. They should be able to turn it around in days, not weeks.'

Eddie shoves another biscuit into his mouth, thinking there's no end of weird ways that people can cook up to try and kill others.

Becky stands up. 'Thank you,' she says. 'OK if I take a printout of the report?'

Maria points to a clear plastic folder on her desk. 'Two copies in there, and it's already been uploaded onto the case file.' She smiles at Becky. 'Let's catch up properly soon?'

'Definitely,' Becky says. 'Although I might be busy for a while.'

They leave via the dingy corridor of doom, past the mortuary and out the fire exit into the car park, their shoes squeaking on the slightly sticky linoleum. They don't speak until they are out in the fresh air.

It's dark now, just the sodium glow of the car park lights, and an air that's chilled with the hint of frost to come. It's been a long day, but they need a break.

'I think we should call it a night, Becks. We've got a lot to do. A fresh start in the morning will do us both good.'

'You know I'll only be searching for stuff on my phone at home, while the rest of the rabble goes on around me...'

He shakes his head. 'I know. But at least you'll get a meal cooked for you while you're doing it.' Becky has been living at home, since she split with her long-term boyfriend. Her sister is there too, taking a break from her intermittent travelling. Other young women might complain about being back with their family at her age, but Becky seems to like it. In contrast, he's going back to a dark, quiet house. Normally he pretends not to be bothered by this, but he feels lonely today. Not that he'll say anything to Becky as she'll only invite him round, and he's not lonely enough to deal with her madhouse tonight.

Eddie drops her off, and as predicted, she invites him in for dinner, but he declines and heads home. He's surprised to see a light on in the living room.

'Hello?' He takes his jacket off and hangs it on one of the pegs by the door.

His son, Simon, comes out of the living room, scrolling through his phone. He's still in his work clothes – a short sleeved black shirt and tight black trousers. There is a greying stain down the front of the shirt. 'Hey, Dad.'

'Didn't expect you to be home at this time.'

'I was on an early. Finished at seven, which is just as well as I'd just spilled a pina colada down myself.' He lifts out the bottom of his shirt. 'Looks like I had a happy accident.'

'Christ,' says Eddie. 'Who orders a pina colada in December?'

'Chavs,' he says. 'Fancy a pizza?'

'Sure, why not,' Eddie says. 'Spicy meat-feast?'

Simon groans. 'Actually, can we have something veggie? I had a proper idiot in at lunchtime who hated vegetables and women. Not necessarily in that order.'

Eddie laughs. 'Order the pizza, then tell me how those deductions came about.' He is so glad to have some company, and the chance to have some non-work conversation. He'd planned to open up the university website, LinkedIn, Facebook... and start cyber-stalking Helena. He can't do that now, not with Simon around, and that's probably a good thing. For the time being, at least, he pushes Helena to the back of his mind.

Simon taps the order through on his phone, while somehow managing to get them both beers from the fridge, and flip the caps off. Eddie sometimes wishes his son had done something more intellectually demanding than working in bars, but when he sees him in action, takes in his easy banter and obvious skills, he realises that he's just being a typical dad, and that actually the main thing his son needs is to be happy. And he *is* happy, Eddie thinks. Although neither of them talk about the events that led up to his mum and sisters moving out. It's just easier not to.

Eddie takes a long pull from his beer bottle. The ice cold lager hits the spot.

Simon tosses his phone onto the side-table, then jumps onto the couch, taking up most of the space. 'Twenty minutes,' he says. 'Yeah, so this bloke comes in for lunch and seems all right at first – then, within moments, I realise he's a prick. Made a few quips about his girlfriend that pinged off a few alarms.' Simon empties most of the beer down his throat with a couple of loud glugs, followed by a loud burp. '*Scusi*,' he says, in a bad Italian accent. A long-running family joke. 'Let's just say he had *consent issues*. Reckons all women mean *yes* when they say *no*.' Simon rolls his eyes. 'It's really no wonder that women snap, putting up with this shit for years and years. I'm sure this one thought he was one of the good guys too.'

Eddie sighs. 'You might not believe it, but I do think things are getting better. Attitudes are changing…'

'Whatever.' Simon jumps up off the couch. 'Another beer? I'm having one more, then I'm gonna wolf this pizza, then I'm going to bed. I'm doing another early tomorrow, then a late over at the Blackwood. They've double-booked their functions and they're pulling in staff from all over the town.'

Eddie finishes his beer. 'Yeah, go on.' He'd planned to have the night off, but Simon has got his brain whirring. Pissed off women. Multiple functions. People to-ing and fro-ing across town. This case suddenly feels like it might be very complicated.

# 15

# The Party Girl

Oh dear. I didn't expect it all to be on the news quite so soon.

It's all started to unravel a bit quicker than I expected.

I guess I was sloppy, wasn't I?

The Woodlands Hotel is now closed pending enquiries, and I was too wired to go into work today. There's only been a short segment on the news about it, but they're clearly keeping things out of the public domain. They want to hold back, see what happens. They say they're pursuing several lines of enquiry – that old chestnut. They used the same line on me all those years ago, after what happened to Mum. I know what it means. It means: *we don't have any leads but we're going to pretend that we do so you'll think we're doing our jobs.*

Of course they're going to have me on CCTV some-where in that place. I'm good at disguises, but I'm not a ghost. I exist. I'm memorable. That barman for a start – he'll remember me. But there's nothing to link me to any of the parties that were happening last night. I slipped out this morning in different clothes, with different hair, taking care not to show my face to any cameras. I didn't show it last night either. But… the barman. Yeah, he's a problem.

So, yes. I got sloppy. It didn't look like an accident. Or natural causes. I didn't give myself enough time to think it all through. But I don't have the luxury of time, do I? Not enough.

People die in hotels all the time. I'm sure of it. They don't all make the news.

Why did I mess up though? I need to take stock. Analyse the situation. Did I leave something behind? Did something show up on his body that made it all too obvious? I doubt they've found out what I did to him. Not yet. But something *did* go wrong. He didn't just… die. Not like I'd expected him to. So I'd finished him off with the pillow and I'm pretty sure that's what's fucked me over, but what choice did I have? We'd passed the point of no return, and he wasn't dead. He might have been on the way there, but if I'd left it to chance, who knows what might have happened?

I can only assume that they will find me, sooner rather than later. Most killers get found eventually. Most killers are not as clever as they think they are. Even me. Especially me. I didn't plan this. I didn't have an ambition to kill people. But with Mum the way she is, and with no hope in sight… something went a bit strange inside my head. It's been brewing for a while. Percolating. Taking shape. I thought it was just a fantasy. Didn't really think I would do it for real. I've hung out at many bars. Lured in many men. But then I've just fucked off and left them there, confused one minute, already scoping out another target the next. They are indiscriminate beasts.

Not me though. I'm choosing carefully. Even more carefully, next time.

Because there *will* be a next time.

I'm not sure how much longer they will keep my mother alive in that home, and in my rational moments, I'm not sure how long I really want her to be there. I've been living in hope and denial for such a long time, but there comes a point when you have to face things, right?

She is never waking up.

Even when I sit with her all day long, I'm not even sure that she knows I'm there.

I used to think she knew. I used to think that she could hear me, feel the touch of my hand when I held hers, or when I stroked her face or brushed her hair. But I'm not an idiot. I know that any movement she makes is an involuntary reflex. But as long as her care was being paid for, I was happy to let it carry on. I've always taken comfort in sitting there beside her, telling her about my life.

But maybe it's time to live my life? Maybe I need to move on?

I go through cycles of thinking like this, and then something happens – something a man says to me offhand, flippantly, not meaning to cause offence – and the rage comes back... and my murderous fantasies become real.

This hotel is not as nice as the Woodlands. It's decent enough, though. And from my earlier checks, even more lax on the cameras and other security measures. It was easy to get in the staff entrance off the car park. Easy to find somewhere to stash my bag. I've had to park a bit further away, though. It's a lot more residential around here, more of those street parking permits. More people to notice if they can't get their usual space.

Walking in to this hotel lobby was just as straightforward as all the others. Plenty of people around, rushing, unseeing. Plenty of parties happening at the same time. Just like the other night. The police don't think there's any risk though. They think that lawyer was a one off. That, at least, is still in my favour.

I reapply another coat of pale, sparkly lip gloss. Fluff up my dark curly hair. Adjust my boobs so they sit higher under this plunging neckline. I love this green dress. I picked it up in a charity shop near the posh side of town. *Rich Pickings*. What a brilliant name. It's an independent shop, and they make donations to various charities. They're currently doing an initiative for young people with cancer, and I can't think of many places I'd rather donate to. You can imagine all the designer gear that gets left in that shop. In this area? It's rife. Wealthy women wearing a thousand pound outfit once and handing it in. Doing their bit. That's not where I got my bag though. That was my mother's. I don't like to think about where she got it from, because there is no way she could ever have afforded to buy it herself. It's pure, over-the-top luxury. But you need to have *something* that makes you feel like you fit into the set, even if you couldn't be further from it.

Right then. Let's do this. I talk to myself in the mirror. 'Tonight, I am Melanie Black. I work for Mason Brothers, but I've nipped in to check out the bar at the Reeves & Rocko party. I'm so naughty, but you know, my colleagues are so dull... Melanie is a nice name? Yes it is, my mum named me after Melanie Griffith – she loved her in *Working Girl*. Wink. No... no, I'm a real professional. Don't be rude.' The door opens and a couple of pretty girls in tight dresses walk in, giggling together. I smile at them in the mirror, run my tongue over my teeth. OK. I am ready.

As ever, I don't have to wait long for the first approach.

'Hi there! I'm Zac. Who are you?'

I appraise him. Take in his neatly gelled hair and his slightly wonky grin. He's in a grey suit with a bit of a sparkly fleck running through it. A lilac shirt, open at the neck, no tie. He looks young. Too young? *We'll see.*

'Melanie,' I say. 'Mel. I only started last month. Haven't seen you around yet?'

He looks me up and down. 'I don't recall seeing you, either. I would definitely remember.' He looks down at my hands on the bar, where I am cradling my drink. It looks like a G&T. I got the barman to put it in a nice glass. But it's just tonic. 'Can I get you another? Absolute cheapskates not putting on the free bar until after the meal.'

I smile. 'The meal part is soooo boring, don't you think? Much more fun later. Are you staying over?'

He licks his lips. 'I am… but, I… I'm taking things a bit easy this evening, I think. I've got a busy day tomorrow. To be honest, I might just skip off after the dinner. I'm not a big party type.'

I lock my eyes onto his. Refuse to blink.

He looks away first, then he fishes about in his inside jacket pocket, pulls out a business card. He smiles as he hands it over. 'Email me tomorrow,' he says. 'If you like? Would be nice to grab a coffee, have a proper chat.'

Disappointed, I take his card and offer him a demure pout, before dropping the card into my bag and swivelling around in my seat, then sliding gently onto my feet.

'So nice to meet you,' he says to my back. Then, 'Barman? Could I have a half pint of Peroni Zero, please?'

I pick up my bag and walk away from him, heading to the toilets again. My cheeks burn with humiliation. This is not what is supposed to happen. I'm the one who is supposed to decide if they are spared or not. If they're *nice*. Interested, but kind. If they ask for my number but they don't expect instant results, I let them go. But if they're *naughty*, if they take the bait – if they want me there and then – well, it's their own damn fault what happens to them after that. Animals. Greedy fucking animals.

I was right with my initial assessment of Zac.

Too young.

I lock myself in a cubicle, away from a couple of chattering blondes who are reapplying lipstick and perfume, and discussing Rob from IT and whether he still has a girlfriend. I'm sitting on the toilet when my phone beeps with an incoming message.

My notifications are switched off for all but one number.

The message is brief: *She's deteriorating. Please call so we can update you further. Better still – can you come in?*

The phone falls from my hand, clattering to the floor.

'You alright in there, hun?' a high-pitched voice from outside the cubicle asks.

'Fine,' I manage, keeping my voice steady. 'Lucky I missed the pan.'

Giggles from outside, then a swish of the main door opening and closing.

I pick the phone up from the floor and drop it into my bag. Take a few long, slow breaths. Clench my hands into fists, unclench. Repeat. I close my eyes, massage my temples with my fingertips.

But it's no use. The rage is building hard and fast. I clutch my bag tight and hurry out of the cubicle, out of the bathroom, glad that no one else is there to see my face.

No one there to recognise my fury.

I spot him from ten metres away, sitting there on a bar stool. Old enough. Tousled blond hair, metallic green shirt opened just a bit too far. Legs spread wide in skin-tight trousers. I slow down, watching him as his eyes scan the room, eyeing up his prey.

Or so *he* thinks.

He spots me. A slow smile spreads across his face. His knees drop to the sides, widening his legs even more. I keep to the same pace, adding in a little hip wiggle, just to make sure my intentions are clear. His tongue pokes out the corner of his mouth as I approach, and his dilated pupils do their best job of luring me in.

*Oh, consider me lured, darling. In fact, I'm a sure thing.*

This one is going to be almost *too* easy.

# 16

## Becky

Becky is in the office early again, even earlier than last time. Long before Miriam. Long before anyone else.

Except Joe.

He'd messaged her last night asking her what time she was heading in, offering to bring her breakfast so they could spend some time together while they worked. They both have a fair bit of desk-based work to do, and although Becky quite likes having some early morning time to herself, she was never going to say no to Joe. They click when it comes to work. They bounce off each other. It's different to her relationship with Eddie – mainly because she's known Joe a lot longer, but also because they're the same age, and until her promotion, they were the same level. Despite her good relationship with DI Carmine, and those fleeting moments when she convinces herself that he is flirting with her, he is still her superior. And she has to be able to gossip about him with someone.

'So,' Joe says. 'Tell me more about Eddie's face when this *Helena* was mentioned...' He has the university website open and they are sitting with coffees, reading the page. Well, they're kind of reading the page, mostly they're looking at Helena's photograph. Her bio puts her around Eddie's age, but she looks more like forty than fifty. Clear, pale skin. Shiny, dark hair. Wide eyes and a hint of a smile on her evenly proportioned lips. It's a professional head-shot, but even so, it seems to exude something of her personality. She's beautiful. She's also clearly talented and intelligent, as a Professor of Psychology, specialising in Criminology.

'He looked completely shell-shocked,' Becky says. 'Then he looked... I don't know. Pained?' She thinks about this, and remembers something Eddie told her once about his one-that-got-away. Could it be her? After all these years? Something about that makes her feel a bit funny. A low-level feeling of something that could be jealousy, or maybe it's just a fear of her friend and mentor getting hurt. Joe is already googling her, bringing up more photos from inter-views and social media. She shifts in her seat. 'Maybe we should drop this. He'll tell us when he's ready.'

'Spoilsport.'

Joe flicks to another window, where he has been search-ing the Police National Computer for other hotel murders happening in December, in their catchment area, over the last ten years. 'I'll get on with this then, shall I?'

'Go for it. I know you're going to find something excit-ing and get all the credit.' She nudges him with her elbow. 'I'll go back to my needle in a haystack.'

She wheels her seat away from his and back to her own workstation, where she has spent the last hour searching for local pharmaceutical companies and their drug pipe-lines. Maria had texted her earlier. The swab they took of Andrew Morrison's skin around the puncture wound has come back as an unknown substance. It's produced some signals on a couple of the tests, but it doesn't quite match anything, so they're sending that, plus the blood and tissue samples, to a specialist lab for further investigation. So now Becky has a hunch. It might be nothing, but she has some time so why not. Could it be an unlicensed drug? She thinks it's worth shaking all the trees, because you just never know what might fall out. She also has an appointment with a local jeweller later on, to ask him about the hairclip. Forensics have finished processing it as evidence, so she's allowed to check it out for a few hours.

She's just opened up the website of yet another small biotech company, when her phone rings. The caller ID flashes up 'Allie' along with a photo of her sister on a beach, pulling a silly face.

Becky sighs. She hasn't really got time to talk to her sister right now. She's been back home from her latest nomadic lifestyle adventure for a few weeks, and she's hardly seen her, and yet feels like she is constantly in her face. It had been fine living at home with her dad and his latest squeeze while Allie was away, but with them all there it was a bit too much. To be honest, she'd been coasting along living there on token rent, but it was time she looked into finding herself a longer term solution. She lets the phone ring out. Starts clicking through tabs on the website she's interested in.

The phone rings again, and this time she answers with a frustrated swipe.

'I'm at work, Al. Can this wait?'

There's no reply at first, and she thinks the connection has dropped.

'Allie?'

'Becks… you have to come.' Allie's voice sounds thick, like she's been crying.

Becky feels her heart start to race. Calls from family while you're at work are not too far removed from calls in the middle of the night. 'What's happened?'

Allie sniffs. 'It's Mum,' she says. 'I've found her.'

Becky feels like she's been punched in the stomach. 'What do you mean?' She glances over at Joe, and she can tell he is listening while pretending to study his own computer screen. She lowers her voice. 'I don't understand, Allie.'

Their mum has been 'lost' for years. Figuratively, if not literally. She'd left them when they were small, and their dad had brought them up alongside his carousel of kind but fairly non-maternal girlfriends. They'd got by. Becky had joined the police, and Allie had decided to pursue a more artistic life, as she called it. She travelled the world, doing whatever work she could to pay to stay there, and came back now and then for a break and some of Dad's home cooking.

June – or *Juniper*, as she had been unofficially renamed when she decided to take off to 'find herself' – had tried to re-engage with them both a few years ago. Becky had not been interested, but Allie had. She was always the softer, more fragile of the two. She'd gone off to Spain to spend some time with Juniper in a commune she was living at, whereas Becky had asked not to be updated on her life – she'd closed off her feelings for her mum when she had abandoned her as a child, and she saw little point in trying to rekindle things as an adult. She knew she would only be let down again.

'Juniper had an accident, Becks. She came back here a few months ago, and—'

'Is that why you came back from your trip?'

'Kind of… She came back to settle down, Becks. We'd been emailing. We were hoping we could all meet. Talk properly. But then the messages stopped and I thought she'd done a runner again. I didn't tell you because you always say you don't want to know.'

'Well you're right about that part. Look, can we talk about this later? I'm in the middle of a big case, and—'

'Do you know the Ivybridge Care Home, Becks? It's up by the cricket ground. It's a long-term care facility for people with brain injuries, and some patients with dementia, and various other things like that. It's not an old people's home, it's more of a medical place…'

Allie stops talking and lets the silence hang. Becky has no idea what is going on. She's not sure she wants to know. But her heart is still thumping in her chest, and she feels that primal buzz of adrenaline coursing through her veins.

'Becks are you still there? You need to come and meet me. Mum is here, and I don't know how long she might have left.'

Becky's hands are shaking. 'I'll be there,' she says quietly. Then she bends over and vomits into the small metal bin under her desk.

'Woah, Lady!' Joe is there beside her in a flash, crouched down by her chair. 'Are you ill? What's going on?' He wrinkles his nose. 'That absolutely stinks. Get yourself to the toilets and I'll deal with this.'

Becky wipes her mouth with the back of her hand, then grabs her coat and bag. 'I need to go out. If Eddie comes in before I get back, tell him to ring me.'

'Got it,' Joe says, holding the bin in one hand and his nose with the other. 'But if you're not *actually dying* right now, you seriously owe me.'

***

A gravel drive leads up to the stone mansion house that is home to the Ivybridge Care Home, a classic architectural style with a turret and the eponymous winding ivy. The trees are bare given the time of year and the short grass is winter-green and glistening with frost. This is definitely one of the nicer care homes in the area. Some of the modern ones look as soulless as budget hotels, and Becky imagines them to be just as bad inside.

The heavy wooden outside door is open, and she steps into the tiled porch and pushes open the glass-paned inner door. Inside, a small, curved reception desk has been fitted into the alcove under the grand staircase. The hallway is bathed in light via an ornate stained glass window. Becky sucks in a breath. Aesthetically, it ticks all the boxes. But it's impossible to escape from the distinctively clinical scent of boiled vegetables and industrial-strength detergent, creating an eye-watering mix with the large bowl of pot pourri on the counter.

There's a young woman in a blue tunic standing behind the counter. Her dark hair is pulled back into a neat bun, and she's wearing minimal make-up but she has the most perfectly rose coloured lips that Becky has ever seen.

'Can I help you?'

Becky swallows. 'I think my mother might be here. June Greene?'

'Ah yes, Becky, is it? Your sister said you'd be coming in. We're so pleased that we've been able to track down

Juniper's family.' She beams at Becky, and Becky tries her best to smile back. 'Allie says you're a police officer? I hope we've caught you at a good time?'

'I'm used to juggling,' Becky says. 'I'm sure you're the same?'

'Yes! Oh god. You wouldn't believe… Let me take you along to Juniper's room. Your sister is in with her now. She'll be pleased to see you.' She takes a breath. 'Gregg… sorry, Mr Wade – the manager? He's actually just popped out but I'm sure he'll be back soon. We're so bloody short staffed today, but luckily most of the residents don't need too much entertaining.' She flushes. 'Sorry, that was a bit inappropriate.'

Becky tries not to laugh. 'I think we both work in jobs where we need some light relief now and then. Anyway, no problem about Mr Wade. I'm sure Allie will fill me in… and maybe we can chat later? Sorry, I didn't catch your name.'

The woman looks down at her chest, runs a hand over the fabric of her tunic. 'Oh that bloody name badge has fallen off again. It's Lauren. I'm the senior nurse on duty this morning.'

She takes off at a clip down the corridor, her soft shoes squeaking gently on the tiles. They pass a couple of open rooms, and Becky can't help but look inside. In one, she can't see much, just the foot of a bed and a stuffed velvet chair in one corner. The TV is blaring and she wonders briefly why they don't close the door to avoid disturbing the other residents. In a room a couple of doors down, the configuration is different and she can make out a blanketed figure on a bed, the hush-and-suck of a ventilator, just out of sight. They turn a corner and Lauren pushes open a fire door, leading them into another long, tiled corridor.

'Apart from your TV addict back there, are most of your patients, er…'

'Yes,' Lauren says. 'We're about ninety-five per cent long-term care here, for patients in various stages of comas and other disorders of consciousness. The blaring TV back there is actually a bit of an experiment, based on the family's wishes. They are convinced if we just keep making it louder, then Phyllis will wake up. Apparently she couldn't hear the TV unless it was at over seventy-five decibels. It's kind of their last ditch attempt before we talk about next steps.'

'Next steps, as in…'

Lauren stops walking, lowers her voice. 'At some point, Becky, someone has to make the decision to switch them off.'

Becky shudders. The light in this part of the building is dimmer, and away from the noise of Phyllis's TV, it's quieter. How awful to have a family member in one of these situations where it's probable that they will never wake up. Is this what was happening with her mum? Since Allie's call, she's tried her best to create some mental distance from the situation. Her standard way of protecting herself.

Light classical music creeps out of one partially opened door. 'That's Karyn in there. One of our longest long-term residents. She was breathing on her own for many years, but she's recently had to be put on a ventilator and her daughter is struggling with that. We need to talk to her about… next steps.'

'Gosh, how sad. How long has she been here?'

'Just over thirteen years,' Lauren says. 'She was attacked in her home, and she never woke up. Her daughter visits her all the time. Poor thing had to grow up having one-sided conversations with a woman who, in all likelihood, has no idea she's there.'

Becky has nothing to say to that. The horror of the situation is too unbearable.

'Right,' Lauren says, her sombre tone lifting again, 'here we are.'

Becky walks into the room behind Lauren, where a middle-aged woman lies on a bed, her long, pink-tinted hair fanned out on the pillow. The sheet is pulled up to her chest, but her arms are outside the covers. Her nails are painted in rainbow colours. Next to the bed, Becky's sister is sitting straight-backed, holding a hairbrush and looking incredibly tense. There's another chair next to Allie, a plush velvet number like the one Becky had spotted in the other room. This place is clearly expensive, and walks a strangely thin line between hotel and long-term care facility. Question is – who's been paying for it?

'Allie?' Becky says. A lump sticks in her throat as she looks down at the woman in the bed. Her mother. She might have given birth to her, but other than that, she's a stranger.

Allie's shoulders slump. 'Thank you for coming. I know you're busy.' She lays the hairbrush onto the bedside cabinet, next to a water jug and mug with the same red and yellow logo of a brand that Becky doesn't recognise.

Becky shrugs. 'I came for you.' She sits down on the vacant chair. 'What's wrong with her?'

Allie flicks her eyes towards Lauren. 'She woke up earlier. She opened her eyes, and she spoke to me. It was just me that was here with her.' She sighs. 'She looked scared.'

'OK...' Becky says, still not understanding.

'It was quite hard to make out what she was saying. I held her hand, and I pulled the emergency cord. I wanted someone else to hear it. She kept trying to say things, and she was getting agitated...'

'She had a small seizure,' Lauren says. 'It's quite normal in this situation, if there are signs of things "firing up" again. I think that's the best way to put it. She calmed down after that and has been peaceful since.'

Allie nods. 'I've been brushing her hair.'

'But what's wrong with her?' Becky says, getting exasperated. 'What is she doing here? How did she even get here?' Becky digs her fingernails into her palms. 'Why is she not in hospital? Who is paying for her to stay here?'

'She was in an accident,' Allie says. 'We think she slipped on ice. Hit her head. She had no ID on her, so it took them a while to find me. She was in hospital, but then this funded place came up.' Allie shrugs, looks away.

'There's a local firm that provides a couple of free spaces. They run some of the clinical trials here, and we use some of their products too.' She gestures at the water jug and mug. 'That's them, if you're interested. They manufacture drugs for the long-term sick, among other things. You can look them up. Anyway, your mum here was lucky to qualify for a free space, and we're delighted to have her here.'

Becky wants to scream. She can't deal with this right now. Her mum was no longer part of her life, and now, here she is. Back, and in need of help. Her dad always said she was selfish. Becky bites the inside of her lip, tries to draw blood. She needs something to help release the pressure building inside her head. Both Allie and the nurse are looking at her. 'Is she... Will she wake up?'

Lauren looks at her sadly. 'We don't think so, my love. Not to any reasonable state. She's suffered a catastrophic brain injury—'

'But she woke earlier,' Allie says, desperate now.

'Just a seizure,' Lauren says. 'I can get the doctor back in for you, if you like? Get him to explain it all again to both of you? She's breathing on her own, and while she's like that, we'll give her the best care possible. You have as much time as you need, and… well, I shouldn't say this, but sometimes miracles do happen. We've seen it before. We had a patient just recently who'd been asleep for almost six years show signs of lucidity. Lovely young woman. Used to be a weather-girl, you know?' She smiles at them both, and despite her kind face, Becky has a sudden urge to slap her. 'I'll leave you both to it,' Lauren says, as though sensing Becky's mood. She backs slowly out of the room.

Becky glares at her sister. Mutters, 'what the *fuck*, Allie?' Then she bursts into tears.

# 17

# Eddie

Eddie is feeling rested and recharged after his night in with Simon. They'd had a chat about the various types that hang around in the bars he works in, and it had got Eddie thinking. He has a few theories now on the Andrew Morrison case – his front runner is that there is a disgruntled mistress out there who is regretting making a life-changing decision. They're going to have to question the grieving widow again, or maybe even her neighbour who had come round to assist – he has a feeling that woman knew a lot about the ins and outs of the Morrison household. In fact, he's actually looking forward to this morning's briefing. He's also doubly pleased with himself that he successfully managed to not think about Helena Summers all night, *and* resisted the urge to look up her profile online. It's all going swimmingly until the call comes in as he's driving to the station.

Another hotel, another body.

Absolutely bloody great.

He doesn't even know where the rest of the team has got to yet with finding any links to previous cases, but now that they have two bodies in a week, in what sounds like similar circumstances, it's a strong possibility that they are connected. Which means, of course, that Wild Bill will get his way, and Helena will be brought in to assist them with the 'profiling'. He's yet to be convinced that criminal profiling is anything other than basic policework with a fancy name, but that is the least of his worries right now.

*Fuck.*

Does he need to tell the DCI that he knows Helena? Yes, she was the love of his life once, but that was a long time ago. So much water under the bridge. And people have different memories of things from the past, don't they? As far as he knows, their time together holds no significance to her at all.

He diverts his route and slides into the shopping centre traffic. That bloke with the Christmas trees in the middle of the roundabout is still there, but he has fewer trees now. He calls Becky, hands-free, on the way to the hotel, but there's no answer. He leaves a message telling her to meet him at the scene as soon as possible.

It's the Coronation Inn this time. Another venue that will have to shut down over the party season. He imagines that Wild Bill is already under pressure from his superiors to get this nailed down as quickly as possible. The report on the news last night had been vague, but it wouldn't be long before people got wind of it and would start cancelling parties elsewhere. If they didn't nip this in the bud soon, they'd end up being to blame for the inevitable crash of the local hospitality industry, and press like that would be another reason to push Woodham nick higher up the shutdown list.

*Fuck*, he thinks again. He only swears when he's on his own, these days, and even then it's mostly inside his head.

Bloody Joe and his swear box. He tells his phone to dial Becky again. Still no answer, so he leaves another message.

'Becks, I don't know where you are but you need to get yourself to the Coronation Inn ASAP before I have to give your job to Joe, and leave you stuck with Stuart and the CCTV sifters.'

Stuart and Joe are already at the hotel when Eddie arrives, suited and booted and ready to go – or maybe they've already been to the scene. Either way, he's too late – no sense in him trampling all over it now if the forensic team is already in place and the investigators are finished. 'Morning,' he says, trying not to sound as pissed off as he feels. Why didn't they call him earlier? The overtime ban shouldn't apply when they're in the middle of a big case, and yet is still does.

Stuart raises an eyebrow at the look on Eddie's face. 'Sorry, Ed. I just happened to be on an early.'

'Fine,' Eddie says. He can't be bothered to make a fuss. 'I'm waiting for DS Greene anyway. Thought she was doing earlies but she's not answering the phone.'

'She's gone up to the Ivybridge Care Home,' Joe says, peeling off shoe covers and shoving them into a plastic bag. 'An urgent call from her sister.'

Eddie can't hide his surprise. So urgent that she didn't even have time to text him about it? He's nearly-half annoyed that she's disappeared off during working hours, and more than half worried about what she's gone there for. 'Right,' he says. 'Well I'm sure she'll fill me in when she gets back.' He eyes Joe with suspicion. 'How come you saw her? Don't tell me you've started the early-earlies too?'

'I have, actually.' Joe crosses his arms. 'We agreed to go in together. We had a very interesting chat, as it happens.' He smirks, keeping his eyes fixed on Eddie.

Eddie has a feeling he was the subject of the early morning coffee gossip, but decides not to poke that particular bear. He'll grill Becky later, and she'll feign ignorance for about thirty seconds before telling him everything. He'd always said one hint of anything resembling torture and she'd give up the King's secrets in a flash.

'Why don't you give DI Carmine some of the actual information you were in early looking into, DC Dickson?' DS Stuart Fyfe has just the right level of authority in his voice to make Joe squirm. Good.

'I was looking up other hotel murders.' He unzips his protective suit and pushes it into the same bag as the shoe covers, then he peels off his gloves and adds them too, before sealing the bag. 'There are a few contenders, it seems. I've got a list for the briefing.'

'Great,' Eddie says. 'So there are clear connections, then?'

'We don't know yet,' Stuart says. 'But signs may be pointing that way.'

Eddie nods towards the hotel. 'What's going on in there then?'

'Same as before. We've got the place on lockdown, staff being questioned, CCTV being analysed—'

'And the body?'

Stuart unzips his protective suit and reads from his phone. 'Another white male. Driving licence identifies him as Steve Bell, forty-five. He was a partner in a construction firm called Glenfield Building Company. Dr Maria Szczepańska is the attending pathologist. Preliminary thought is that he was injected with a toxic substance, she checked—'

'Between his toes,' Eddie says. 'Well there we go. She was right about Andrew Morrison so knew what to look for with this one.'

Stuart nods. 'She's fast-tracking the tox screen to the same specialist lab as the Morrison sample. Hopefully we'll get something soon.'

'Right,' Eddie says. 'See you back at base, then.'

He texts Becky as he walks back to the car. *See you back at the station for the mid-morning briefing. Also, are you ok??* The message changes status to 'read' and he shoves his phone into his pocket and climbs into the car.

He wonders if Wild Bill has brought in Helena.

*Fuck, and double fuck.*

★★★

Becky is already in the briefing room when he arrives, her laptop on the table in front of her. She looks pale, and a bit shaky. 'Hey,' she says. 'Sorry I missed all the action. I've had a bit of a morning.'

'Ivybridge?' Eddie says, sitting down beside her. 'Joe told me.'

Her eyes fill with tears, and she blinks them away. 'I'll tell you properly later, but... it's my mum. She's in a coma.'

Eddie feels like she's slapped him with a shoe. Her mum? He thought she'd been estranged from her for years.

'Jesus... I'm sorry,' he says.

Between the two of them, it's been a week of surprises, that's for sure.

Other officers and some of the support staff start to file into the room, chattering and taking seats either side of Eddie and Becky. She closes her laptop.

He leans in closer to her. 'Do you need some time off?'

She shakes her head. 'I just want to work. We'll talk later, OK?'

He takes his cue and stands up to start the briefing, but then sits down again when he realises that the DCI is back, and he's not alone.

Helena is here and standing next to the DCI at the front of the room.

Tall. Strong jaw, wide smile. Sleek copper hair, still worn long. She's wearing a neatly fitted grey suit with an emerald pussy-bow blouse underneath, that even from the other end of the room brings out the colourful flecks in her eyes. He'd always loved those eyes. He takes an involuntary sharp breath, just as those eyes scan the room, finding him. The corner of her mouth lifts, just the tiniest amount, then she looks away.

Wild Bill is grinning like that cat that got the cream. 'I'd like you all to welcome Professor Helena Summers, from the University of Woodham's Psychology Department. As you may know, we have agreed to partner with Professor Summers on a new criminology initiative, that we believe will be mutually beneficial.' He gestures to her with an open palm. 'Professor Summers?'

'It's Helena, please,' she says, smiling. 'I'm delighted to be working with you all. I have the case notes, and I'm ready to get stuck right in.'

Multiple murmurs ripple around the room. Eddie can only hear fragments, but he can guess what's being said. By the men, at least. Probably some of the women too.

Becky is trying to catch his eye, but he refuses to look at her. Keeps staring ahead, at the front of the room.

At Helena. His first love.

The one who got away.

# 18

# The Party Girl

It's still dark, the sun just an orangey blur slowly diffusing into the atmosphere, as if someone is tweaking the dimmer switch. I've considered not going into work again but I know this will lead to a flurry of concerned messages and I just don't want to have to deal with that. My little project might be coming to an end soon, but I have to try and keep up the pretence of being a law-abiding citizen for just a little longer. It won't matter soon. Besides, I need to pick up a few things from work, and there's no way to do that unless I'm officially signed into the building.

But first I have to get home. Get myself cleaned up and warmed up.

Last night took it out of me. I thought things were meant to get easier with practice? I realise now that the first was just beginners luck. I really had no idea if I'd given him enough of the drug, but it seems like my experimental solution might have done the trick after all. The drugs cupboard in that place is far too easily accessible, and Mum's mortar and pestle worked a treat to grind up the pills. I'd thought about just adding the pills to a drink – champagne would be a good option, with the bubbles – as things get absorbed faster when they're fizzy. But I thought it might be easier to trace them that way, so I'd come up with the great idea of crushing the pills, mixing them with a saline solution, and injecting it somewhere discreet. I'd watched the nurses often enough, as they'd injected things into my mum. Most things go through the cannula, just a switch of the solution and there you go…but sometimes they had to do something into her muscle, to stop the spasms, and that's the one that made me think that I could do it. Injecting into a vein can be tricky, and risky. But stabbing something into a muscle – not so hard, right?

I decided on somewhere in between. I thought that injecting between the toes was something that wouldn't be noticed so quickly. But it's harder than it looks, especially getting the angle right.

One thing I did learn after the first time was that it was hard to drive afterwards, with all the buzz of what I had done. So I slept in my car last night. I packed an old sleeping bag and a pillow in the boot. A couple of blankets. I made myself a flask of hot tea, thick with sugar. I parked somewhere inconspicuous, and now here I am, wrapped up warm, sipping tea. I thought the sleep from the adrenaline crash would only last a few hours, and then I would drive home afterwards, numb. Climb into bed and toss and turn until it was time to get up. But I slept through the night. The sleep of the dead, or the sleep of the guilty?

I'm aching from being scrunched up in the seat.

I unzip the sleeping bag and roll it up, tossing it into the back seat before trying my best to stretch out my limbs. The windows are all steamed up inside from my breathing, and I turn on the heating with the fans at full blast to try and clear it. Thankfully, it has not been the coldest of nights and there is no frost on the outside of the windows to deal with.

There is barely any traffic on the roads as I drive back towards Mum's house, and I stay within the speed limit, taking care not to do anything to draw attention to myself. There are so many roundabouts on the ring road, and I slow at every one, even though it's clear there are no cars coming from the right. Nothing much in front either, and a quick glance in the rear view mirror reveals nothing close behind.

So it's a bit of a surprise when flashing lights fill my car with intermittent blue. I look in the mirror again, and sees a police car right behind me. My heart skips a beat. Where did it come from? Then I remember there's one of those little ramps, where they hide out and look for speeding motorists. There have been posters up about it, dotted around. They're clamping down on drink drivers. Trying to catch them out early – the morning after the night before.

*Shit.*

I take a breath. Ease my foot off the accelerator. I have not been drinking. I have nothing to worry about. But the siren *whoops*, just the once, and I know they want me to stop.

So I stop.

I steal a quick glance behind, spot a uniformed officer stepping out of the car. He disappears from view at the back of my car. My eyes are drawn to the rolled up sleeping bag behind the seat, and I shove it down further, making sure the flask is hidden beneath it. When I twist back round to face front, he is already outside my window. He's making a winding gesture with one hand, even though no cars have had winding windows for many years. Not even this one, and the VW Polo I'm driving is ancient by most people's standards. It's also filthy. Cleaning the car has been the last thing on my mind lately, and the frequent days of sleet-spray and salt covered roads have not helped. I press the button and the window slides down with a slight judder.

'Morning,' the officer says. 'Early start for you today, miss?'

He's a fair bit older than me, but I can't quite put an age on him. I give him my best friendly worker smile. 'I'm on the pre-dawn catch-ups all the way to Christmas. So much to do and I really don't want to stay late.'

He nods, bending down a little to peer into my car. It might be my imagination, but it seems like he has a little sniff of the air around me. Does he think I'm smoking weed in here or something? It might smell a bit stale but that's hardly a crime.

He straightens again. 'Where's that then?'

I think quickly. Where does everyone work in the run up to Christmas? 'The retail park?' I pause. 'Over by the football stadium?'

His mouth curves into the tiniest of smiles. 'Oh I don't envy you that, love. The missus is going shopping today. Says it's already chocka and there are still two weeks to go.'

'People start in October these days,' I say, playing along, 'it's peak shopping madness at the moment.'

A crackly voice says something on his radio and he steps away briefly. I think I've got away with any further questioning, but then he comes back. He's still clutching the radio in one hand.

'Do you know why I've pulled you over today, miss?'

My face falls. 'No, I—'

'Your right rear side-light is out.' He holds up a dirty finger. 'I thought it was just dirt at first, which, incidentally, is still an offence. Obscured is as bad as it not working at all. You'll need that fixed as soon as you can. I could give you a ticket, but I'm going to err on the side of Christmas spirit and ask you to get the light fixed and the car cleaned. I am taking a note of your registration, so we may do another check in the future. Be aware of that. OK?'

'Thank you, officer,' I say. 'I'll get it sorted right after my shift; I promise.'

'Make sure you do.' He pats the top of the car, then walks off, the radio crackling again.

I close the window and sit still for a few moments until my heart rate returns to normal. Then I smack a hand on the steering wheel. *Idiot!* He didn't ask me for any ID, but he might look up the registration plate. Thankfully, I didn't tell him where I really work. I'm going to hope that this is too minor for him to bother checking up on, but if they happen to be running the plates on cars seen in the vicinity of the hotels where the two latest bodies have been found, then I could be in trouble.

I've tried to be careful. Parking far enough away. Making sure I don't look the same when I leave the buildings as when I go in. It's been simple enough to hide my bag with my change of clothes up till now, but they're going to be looking for me now. For *someone*, at least. I'm going to have to rethink my plans.

I'm going to have to get rid of this bloody car.

It was bought for cash in a private sale last year, but I'd still had to update the registration document. There is a paper trail. I have no idea how to buy a car without that.

I'm not a master criminal. I just needed something to get me from A to B.

The police car has disappeared now; it must've driven past when I was attempting to pull myself together.

I think about it as I drive. There is a patch of wasteland just past the street where my mum's house is. An old industrial estate that is part-boarded up but with plenty of access for the local hooligans and drug dealers to do their business. It's the kind of place where people dump things, and no one does anything about it.

The kind of place where a burnt out car wouldn't draw too much attention. I laugh out loud at this. What had happened to me? I'm a murderer and a soon-to-be arsonist. Would my mum be proud me?

I will never know.

Which brings me right back to why I am doing this.

There's a piece of missing fence at one side and I drive through carefully, then head around the back of the old warehouse building. There are piles of fly-tipped junk dotted around the place, peppered amongst rotting crates and pallets. I drive past these, behind a smaller outbuilding, then I kill the engine.

The sky is brighter now, an opaque grey with a citrus tinge. I take the sleeping bag and the old blankets and drape them across the back seat. From the boot, I take a small plastic jerry can from the side where it has been clipped into place with a bracket. This had been an unusual find when I'd bought the car, the owner telling me he'd had a fear of running out of petrol since it had happened to him as a kid, leaving him and his mum stranded for hours on a lonely back road with no means to call for help. I've never used it, but I know there is enough petrol in there to get me to the nearest garage, should I ever run out.

I pour the petrol over the sleeping bag, holding my breath to avoid inhaling the fumes. The car might not have winding windows, but it is old enough to still have a cigarette lighter in the central console. I turn the engine on and open all the windows, then push the lighter into its slot. Wait. I take a few deep breaths, away from the car. Away from the cloying fumes.

My handbag and my rucksack are in the passenger seat footwell, and I grab them, just as the lighter pops with an audible click. I snatch it out, check the glowing red coils inside, then I switch off the engine and take a few steps back.

A little voice in my head tries to ask me what the fuck I am doing, but I'm not listening to that. I stopped listening to that a long time ago. Torching my own car is far from the worst thing I have done.

I toss the lighter through the open back window and hurry away through the scattered detritus of the yard. From somewhere behind, a small *whoomph* is closely followed by a bang. It's done, I think.

But I don't look back to check.

# 19

# Harry

After the minor – OK, *major* – disaster of turning up at Heather's flat unannounced, Harry has been trying to keep a low profile. He'd sensed her backing off, and when he'd spoken to Luke about it, his friend had said, 'Birds don't like it when you're too needy,' which Harry had thought was a sexist and particularly out of date way of thinking. But then, Luke didn't seem to have any problem getting and keeping girlfriends, so maybe he was right. OK, so Lorraine had dumped him for a flash git, but that was mostly because Luke actually was a bit of a shit.

Harry has a feeling he maybe is not enough of a shit, despite refusing to believe that's what women want. Why would they want to be treated badly? If it is true, then he is more naïve than he thought. Problem is, he doesn't want to be a shit. He has always been attentive and keen. Being a nice guy does often get him friend-zoned fairly sharpish, but he would rather that than act like a bastard. He doesn't have it in him. He'd toyed with the idea of flirting a bit with Joanne then backing off, just to test out Luke's theories, but then she'd been off sick, like half of the office, and he'd decided against that particularly stupid plan. He wasn't interested in Joanne. She was far too *available*.

When Harry told Luke what he *was* planning next, his friend had rolled his eyes and slapped him on the shoulder, proclaiming him 'a lost cause'.

Right. *We'll see about that, shall we?*

He's left work early to get everything prepared. He's gone for the carbonara, because she does love it so why take the risk with something else and get it wrong? And he can't afford to get anything wrong right now. She may have been increasingly distant, but he is still confident he can pull things back. He knows they're good together, and he's sure she thinks the same, but she has such a stressful job and that clearly affects how she deals with the rest of her life. He knows she likes to just chill rather than go out and do stuff, but maybe in time that might change. Luke has suggested – more than once, actually – that maybe she's got another boyfriend. But what does Luke know? He is naturally suspicious of people because he is, himself, untrustworthy. He has cheated on most of his girlfriends, so he assumes they do the same – although to be fair, he doesn't like it when that turns out to be the case.

But Heather is different. Heather is not like that. When she tells Harry about her work, and the incredible things that the compounds they're developing can do, Harry listens in awe. He knows a little about these things, but Heather has a doctorate in biology and chemistry from King's College London. Harry doesn't have a degree of any sort – he's worked his way into this job via an unconventional route of temp jobs, and he's proud of what he's achieved. He hopes to start a part-time degree next year in scientific document management. He's just waiting for his boss to approve the funding, and the time off he'll need to study. Heather says she'll help him with it as well. So she can't be planning to dump him, can she? And she can't have another boyfriend or how would she find the time for all of that?

Luke is wrong. Plain and simple.

He's prepared the garlic bread just how she likes it. Fresh garlic mixed with butter, smeared on sliced ciabatta from the local bakery. A simple mixed salad on the side, to be tossed with olive oil and a light balsamic vinegar just before he serves it. He's laid the table with nice mats and rolled napkins, put out his best glasses and cutlery. He glances up at the kitchen clock, worrying that she might be late but knowing she won't be. She is never late. If she isn't coming, she makes sure to let him know in plenty of time. She told him last night when she replied to his reminder text that she was looking forward to tonight. She didn't say anything else though, despite him asking her several questions.

She is clearly stressed.

He's going to fix all that. He has a gift for her, as well as the tickets to the Christmas party, and of course he has the costume – hanging up outside the wardrobe door, ready for her to try on. It will fit though, he's sure of that.

The oven clock clicks over to 7:25 p.m. and he shoves the tray of ready-sliced garlic bread into the oven just as the doorbell rings. Three minutes max, or it'll burn. He smiles, admiring the dinner table and all of his preparations. He'll ask if she wants a neck and shoulder massage when she sits down. He learned how to do it by watching a YouTube video and she's told him how good he is at it, so he always offers. Or, actually, maybe he can do that later... before bed.

He wipes his hands on a tea towel and hurries along the hallway to open the door. He sees her shape silhouetted through the smoked glass panes. He's so excited about tonight. So keen to get everything back on track so they can enjoy their first Christmas together as a couple.

As soon as he opens the door he can tell that she's been crying. She is smiling, but her eyes are shiny and red-rimmed.

'It's so cold,' she says, stepping in towards him. She slides her arms around his back and buries her head into his chest. She's actually freezing and he wonders how she got so cold coming here from her car. She normally parks just outside.

He peers over her head, into the street. 'Where's your car?'

'Oh, I took it to the garage. There was smoke coming out of the bonnet and I didn't want to take the risk with it.'

'But... how did you get here?' It's miles to Heather's flat from here, and he's never thought of her as much of a walker. Or a fan of public transport, come to think of it.

'Believe it or not, I walked,' she says. 'The cold air really helped clear my head.'

He leans in to kiss her, and her lips are cold. 'You've finally lost it! I would've come and picked you up, you know.' He takes a step back, holds her by the shoulders. 'You go and get yourself warmed up in the lounge. That soft blanket you like has just been washed and dinner's almost ready. I just need to go and take the garlic bread out.'

'Actually, I'd like to lie down for five minutes, if that's OK? I'll go through to the bedroom and keep out from under your feet.' She wanders off down the hall, pulling off her scarf and her coat as she goes.

He can smell the garlic bread. 'Hang on—'

She can't go into his bedroom. Her costume is in there. This is not how he wants her to find out about it. He has to ease her into the idea, carefully convince her about going to the Christmas party. But she's already flicked on the bedroom light and disappeared inside.

The garlic bread is burning.

He rushes after her, tries to grab her but he's too late. 'Heather, wait—'

They're both in the bedroom now. She's standing next to the wardrobe, holding out the tiny skirt part of the Poison Ivy costume, and her face is tight with fury.

'What the fuck is this?'

He feels like his heart is in his throat. He can't believe how badly this has gone wrong. The stench of acrid smoke drifts into the room.

'It was meant to be a surprise.'

She grabs the costume and tosses it onto the bed. 'You seriously thought I was going to wear this? You seriously thought you could just buy this and give it to me, and think I'd just go along with your plans? Despite me telling you several times, *very* clearly, that I am *not* going to that stupid fucking party?'

'Heather…'

She shakes her head and shoves past him, almost knocking him over with a shoulder, just as the smoke alarm starts to screech.

# 20

# Becky

Professor Helena Summers stands at the front of the room, directing the pointer at the screen as she speaks. Everyone around the table is staring at her intently. Even Eddie. *Especially* Eddie. Helena looks utterly confident and at ease, and Becky feels a flutter of something she can't quite identify. Envy, perhaps?

'So, as you can see, I've started a preliminary analysis of the two new cases, versus the ones that DC Dickson has identified as potentially of interest—'

'Sorry, just to clarify...' Becky raises a hand but starts talking anyway, directing her question towards DCI Wilde. 'Are these cases being re-opened, sir? I wasn't clear on the focus.' Helena smiles patiently and clasps her hands in front of herself, waiting for Wild Bill to answer.

'Good question, DS Greene. Apologies if I was unclear on this before. We are not re-opening these cases... *yet* – with a big emphasis on the yet. For now, the plan is to re-examine the case files, see if there is any cause for doubt on these. We certainly don't want to suggest that any of these deaths have been misclassified, and were anything other than what they were recorded to be – which was accidental – but, in light of the current cases, it's definitely an angle we want to pursue.' He pauses, clears his throat. 'While our upmost focus must be on finding who may have murdered Andrew Morrison and Steve Bell – if, in fact, it is the same perpetrator – we must also consider that this is something that may have been going on for some time, and the reason we're only uncovering this now is that our killer has become, to use a non-technical term, *sloppy*.' He turns to Helena and gestures for her to continue.

Becky glances over at Eddie, who is now less rapt and more stony faced. She knows what he is thinking. This is Eddie's case. Two murders, potential links. He has his own theories to share, and so far the DCI is hogging the lime-light with his little project. He looks over at her and rolls his eyes. Yep. She drops her head, trying to hide her smirk. He's going to flip out after this. She'd like it if he did. She could do with the distraction.

'Right,' Helena says, clicking to her next slide. 'And this is exactly where I come in.'

Becky tries to re-focus her attention as the screen is filled with a series of names, dates, locations and photographs. She shifts in her seat, leaning forward to get a better view.

Kevin Peters – 45/Project Manager – Garden Suites Lodge – 12-Dec-2013 – cardiac arrest
Lance Jones – 34/Analyst – The Grand Plaza – 10-Dec-2014 – cardiac arrest
Mark Whitely – 38/Teacher – The Grosvenor – 9-Dec-2015 – cardiac arrest
Ian McCall – 41/Financial Advisor – Claymont Hotel – 8-Dec-2016 – cardiac arrest

*Roger Luss – 49/Traffic Warden – Hillcroft Hotel – 13-Dec-2016 – cardiac arrest*

At first glance, there is nothing in particular to link these men. Their ages range from thirty-four to forty-nine. They differ in looks from bald to blond to dark, chiselled jaw to soft jowl. There are several different hotels, and the deaths span three years, four if you include the current two victims. The one thing that does link them all though is the cause of death: cardiac arrest.

Helena clicks to the next slide. 'The reason that these deaths have been identified from among others in hotels over the same time periods – December over the past five years – is that they are male and that they all, according to the post mortems, had no prior health conditions.' She pauses, letting the implications land. 'But unexplained causes of cardiac arrest do happen on a regular basis, and all were fully examined, and because no one would ever have thought to look for a pattern before, no one has found one.' She clicks to the next slide, which shows close-up images of two sets of feet. In both, she has circled the space between the first and second toes on the left foot. 'As you can see, with our two current cases, we have visible puncture wounds between the toes.'

'Do we have the tox results back yet?' Stuart Fyfe directs his question towards Eddie.

'Maria says she'll call as soon as they're in, so in short, no. They have gone to a specialist lab though. Do we still have samples from these previous cases? Can we get them re-run? See if there's a match with anything from the new ones?'

Wild Bill nods. 'Good idea, Eddie. Talk to Abby Glengarry – assuming she's still heading up forensics?'

'Boss.' Eddie glances over at Becky, gives her another tiny eye roll and Becky gives him another tiny smirk in return. He has previous with Abby Glengarry, but they'd managed to work together reasonably well since their serial killer case, so no doubt the two of them will manage to be professional this time around too.

She knows that Maria will be happy to assist them with this too. She loves getting involved in the mysterious and interesting and has said on multiple occasions that so much of her job is really quite mundane. Becky can't imagine that dissecting bodies and trying to work out what's happened to them is anything like mundane, but like any job, the more you do it, the less you really notice what it is you're doing and why. She doesn't want to become one of those people who don't love their jobs anymore. But in Maria's case, she's pretty sure that this level of detachment is the best mechanism for getting through what is actually a very macabre set of circumstances.

Jonty, who is still hovering, trying to appear important, is handing out a set of printouts, and a pile slides across the table towards her. Becky picks one up and hands the others along. It's the list that Helena has shown on her slide – the names and details of the potential other cases, with some additional details for each one. Becky knows that Eddie has already spent hours on the investigation plan, divvying up tasks among the team. She's not entirely convinced of what Professor Summers will be bringing to the party.

'Sir...' she addresses DCI Wilde. 'Do we have enough resource for this?' She glances around the room. 'We've got two concrete cases to investigate here – Andrew Morrison and Steve Bell. There are still hours of CCTV to wade through, more witness statements to take. Various leads to follow. We've got so little… and now we're pushing towards this theory of something much, much bigger.' She feels all the eyes of the room on her now, and she pauses, takes a breath. 'Perhaps we should be focussing on trying to prevent any further incidents, instead of trying to find pine needles in thick pile carpets.' She smiles, pleased with her festive analogy. A few officers groan.

Eddie speaks up. 'She's right, sir. If you recall what happened on the Photographer case…'

More groans, a few muttered jibes.

Becky and Eddie have had to take a fair bit of flak since that Christmas, six years ago. With their festive sounding name partnership and all the drama of that big case, they're seen as the resident experts, but no one actually believes that something like that was ever likely to happen again because everyone knows the stats on the number of serial killers is incredibly low. And after the batshit set-up of the advent calendar murders, she's reluctant to go down that whole route again.

Eddie stands up to continue. 'I think we should focus on the links between these two current cases, and look at preventing another one. We need to be looking hard at the local hotels, and what they've got planned events-wise in the next couple of weeks. If we *are* going with the assumption that this is the same person – most likely a woman – who's murdered Andrew Morrison and Steve Bell, then we need to be asking ourselves who she might target next, and where—'

'If I may?' Professor Summers raises her eyebrows at Eddie, then clicks onto her next slide. 'As your colleague pointed out, you and your team are very busy plotting out a course of action. I'm sure you'll continue to progress things in the usual way, but if I could just finish my presentation, you might all find it useful. Then perhaps we can chat afterwards about any concerns?'

Becky shoots a side-glance at Eddie. His face is flushed, and he's breathing heavily. She watches his hands as he slowly makes and releases fists, his knuckles glowing white.

He must feel her stare, but he won't look at her.

Becky turns her attention back to the woman at the front of the room, who has managed to rile the DI quite considerably in a very short time. She pays close attention as Helena goes through the slides, which summarise her assumptions on the type of person they might be looking for.

'Firstly,' Helena says, 'we have the hairclip.'

Becky mutters, 'S*hit.*' She was meant to be talking to a jeweller about that. She would have to call back and apologise, hopefully reschedule.

'We don't know for sure that this was left by our suspect,' Helena says, 'but given where it was found, down the side of the bedside cabinet, we can assume that it was not there before Andrew Morrison checked in.' She clicks the pointer and an image of it pops up on the screen. Ornate and unusual, and hopefully, traceable. 'We also have the hair, which brings me to my first point.' Helena clicks again and a fresh slide pops up.

The first bullet point says: *Sloppy/Impulsive*

Becky taps this into a Notes doc on her phone.

Helena clicks again.

*Intelligent.*

Click.

*Chaotic?*

'Would you like to elaborate, please?' Eddie says, arms crossed.

'These last two are linked to the CCTV,' Helena says. 'In the first location, the cameras were dummies on the bedroom floors. She found this out and she used it. But her execution is not fully thought out. She's already left potential clues, and the hair is a massive forensic blunder.'

'Except she's not on any database,' Eddie says, 'and it's circumstantial.'

'For now,' Helena concedes. She clicks again.

*Access to drugs.*

'We don't know what it is yet,' Eddie says. 'Technically everyone has access to drugs. A leftover heavy-duty pain-killer prescription... a combination of flu meds and rat poison. Toilet cleaner and anti-histamines.'

Helena raises an eyebrow. 'O... K...'

Eddie shrugs. 'I'm just saying, this stuff isn't anything we haven't thought of.'

Helena puts the pointer down. 'I get that, Eddie. But if you'd let me get to my conclusions, I'm still hoping to convince you that I might be of some use to you.'

Becky tries to read Helena's expression as she says this, but she can't work it out. It does, however, have the desired effect. Eddie slumps, and there is an almost collective sigh, as if the entire room has been sitting at Centre Court, watching a tense Wimbledon final.

'Please,' he says. 'Go ahead.'

Helena takes a breath and clicks to her next slide. 'I know there have been some theories on who might be doing this. Pissed off mistress... disgruntled sex worker... angry colleague... But with no clear links between these current cases, or any of the older ones – which, yes, I will say again, are not currently under any new investigation – I think you need to think deeper about motive.' She pauses. 'We are almost certainly looking for a woman, for all the reasons we've looked into already. I think we're looking at someone who has suffered some deep personal trauma. Something that would drive her to kill men specifically. Men who are strangers to her. Why might that be?'

'Sex worker,' Keir says, from the far end of the table. 'It's pretty obvious, is it not? Dig a little deeper and we'll find that these two lads have availed themselves of her services. I'll bet on the other cases too. Whether they were accidental or not.'

Eddie shakes his head. 'I'm not buying it.'

Becky glances around at the faces in the room. Some, she knows, have already agreed with Keir's basic theory. And sure, that's the theory of Occam's Razor, isn't it? The most likely explanation is the simplest one. But Becky is not convinced at all. Most of the women working in the sex trade in and around Woodham are desperate – they do the work to make ends meet, to feed their children or their addictions. They don't have the wily skills to lure men to bedrooms in hotels and kill them in mysterious ways. For kicks.

Her gut is telling her it is something more than that. There's no evidence that the men have been robbed. There are no links between them to suggest they were specifically targeted. It feels random, but also planned. The woman in the first hotel brought a disguise with her and left wearing it. Presumably they will uncover the same in the second hotel, but they haven't found her on CCTV yet.

Helena finishes her presentation and sits down.

Eddie nods. Tells the room that they are dismissed.

Becky has a sudden urge for a cheeseburger. But it will have to wait. She wants to finish what she started looking into with Joe, before she got called away to the care home.

She absolutely does not want to think about what is happening in the care home.

And she wants to grab Eddie and have a proper conversation. Because she really wants to know what prompted that verbal tennis match with Professor Helena Summers.

# 21

# Eddie

Eddie watches Helena and Wild Bill as they continue their conversation in hushed tones, down at the foot of the long table. He picks up his copy of the printout and files out of the room along with the others, holding back to avoid Becky. He'd noticed her staring at him during the meeting. Of course he had. And he wasn't ready to explain himself yet.

Becky is sitting beside Joe, the pair of them deep in animated conversation. He tries not to look at her, but he senses her gaze again. She wants to know about Helena. Becky is not stupid. That's why he likes her. But sometimes her finely honed instincts are a bloody pain in the arse. He also needs to ask her more about her mum, but it will have to wait.

He disappears into his office. He will camp out in there for a while, and then get back to the task in hand. This second murder is incredibly good timing, as things go. Wild Bill's announcement about closures has been completely trumped by a potential serial killer linked to cold cases, plus a sexy criminologist from the university to help assure the public that the Woodham police station is very much in demand. Who on earth would think about closing it now?

And yes, he had just thought-referred to Professor Summers as 'sexy'. She was sexy thirty years ago and she definitely still is now.

*'Fucking fucking fuck.'*

He says this under his breath and glances over to see if Joe has noticed, but he's busy pointing at something on his screen with a pencil, while Becky nods her head.

He sits down at his desk, wishing he had closed the door. But since he took over this office, he's insisted on an open-door policy at all times – literally as well as figuratively. He does not want to be one of those bosses who rules from afar. He's regretting it now though because he could really use a few quiet minutes to collect his thoughts.

The inflatable snowman bobs out from the corner by the window, and he resists the urge to stick a pin into it. He has work to do. There was already a huge list in his nicely formatted spreadsheet, and of course he's meant to be following up with Abby about the cold case tox samples now too. Actually, he could ask one of the DCs to do this. Joe would be all over it. But he decides to deal with the initial enquiry himself. He scans the laminated list of internal phone numbers pinned to the partition wall beside his desk, and finds the number he needs.

She picks up after two rings. 'Eddie,' Abby says. 'To what do I owe this pleasure?'

'I need to know how soon you can re-run some cold case tox screens.'

'Straight to the point. You mean how long will it take to retrieve them and get them sent to the relevant lab, decide what they need to be run against, fast track the result, and match them with something current, yes?' He can hear her keys clicking on her keyboard as she speaks. Abby has always been a very good multi-tasker.

'That's about the size of it. I'll email you the case numbers. This has come from the top, so if you can let that guide your finger to the "extremely urgent" check box on your many forms, it would be much appreciated and I would probably owe you.'

'You can't bribe me with your lure of unrequited sexual promises anymore, sunshine. I'm spoken for. And besides, I can't make the backlog any shorter. We're talking weeks, here, not days. Definitely not hours. Even for a charmer such as yourself.'

Eddie sighs. 'Can you talk to Dr Maria? There's a specialist lab involved in there somewhere too.'

She laughs. 'Of course there is. Well done, Eddie. You just added another fortnight onto your request. Minimum.'

'Thanks...' he says. She's still laughing when she hangs up.

He had a feeling this would be the case. The worrying finding about these two victims is this puncture wound between their toes, and the possible implications of what might have been injected there. It could, of course, show up quickly in a regular screen at the usual lab. But Eddie knows how these things work, and they are rarely simple. At the moment, though, he has no real idea where to start.

Everything about the new cases and the old potential linked ones are stored on the police national computer, a new entry set-up with links to them all so that everything can be accessed easily. He starts reading through the notes on file so far, the witness statements, the observations from each of the team members. He even goes through the

CCTV snippets that have already been processed, to see if there is anything else to go on. Somewhere to start, even. One thing leads to another, and he's down the rabbit hole, engrossed, scribbling notes on his desk pad as he goes.

He blocks out the noise of chatter from the team outside his door, absorbed in the task of searching, hoping that something will come to him and give him a clue. Finally, as he's about to give up all hope, he spots something. A burgundy handbag. Not his area of expertise by any means, and it may be the case that this bag is common as a Tesco Bag for Life, but he's pretty sure that the handbag with the sparkly gold clasp that the woman in the first hotel is carrying is similar, if not identical to the one that's popped up in the stills from the second murder scene.

He needs Becky for this. He taps out a message to her and lets out a long, slow sigh of relief. *Something*, he thinks. *This might be something.*

***

It takes a while before he realises that he hasn't moved out of his seat for hours. He drops his pen on the desk, leans back to stretch his arms out to the sides, loosening his chest. He tilts his head from side to side, releasing a series of cricks in his neck. Then he pushes himself back in his chair and stretches his arms out in front. As he slides back towards his desk, he notices that there is something sticking out of the gap between the desk and the top of the drawer underneath. He pulls it out.

It's an envelope.

He sighs. It's one from the small pile that he's been storing at the bottom of his desk drawer for the last few years.

It has the same, familiar markings and the return address is HMP Coldfield. He's certain it's another letter from the Photographer... and it is still sealed, like all the others.

One every December since the killer was put behind bars.

Outside, the winter sun has dipped low, leaving the last remnants of daylight. He can see his reflection in the dark window. He looks spectral. He blows out a long breath, and before he can stop himself, he's slid his finger under the seal, opening the envelope. He pulls out the single sheet of lined A4 paper.

*Dear Detective Carmine,*

*Merry Christmas, Eddie (again). I have enclosed another visiting order. Please, I just want to talk. All I want is for someone to follow up on our last conversation before they brought me here. I'm not asking for anything other than to clear my name for one crime. One victim. You know I was telling you the truth about that one. I could see it in your eyes. I don't think I am ever getting out of here, so the very least you can do is grant me this one request...*

'You OK, boss?'

Eddie flinches, drops the letter into his lap. He looks up to find Becky standing in the doorway, with her hand on her hip, her head tilted in that questioning, faux confused manner that she carries off well.

'You ready for some dinner?' Becky says. 'I don't think you've left your seat since we finished the briefing. Have you even drunk anything today? Your piss must be like stewed tea.'

'Quite the mental image, Becks. How long have you and Joe been sitting out there cooking that one up?'

She huffs. 'Don't give him any credit. Anyway, he's gone for a kebab on his way home. I waited for you because I was worried if I didn't come over you would actually solidify into stone, or something. Seriously, you haven't moved… and I've been craving a bacon double cheeseburger and fries since this morning. I think I gave myself health food overload with that cereal bar I had the other day.'

'OK,' he says, 'you've convinced me. McDonald's it is, although you know I'm mainly a connoisseur of the breakfast menu. You can choose what I'm having because you're paying.' He waits until she's turned away before he stuffs the letter into his drawer with the others.

'Fine,' she says. 'Can we go now?'

'In a minute,' he says. 'I think I might have found something…'

'Oh?'

'I assume you know stuff about handbags?'

Becky rolls her eyes. 'I'm familiar with the concept.'

He swivels his monitor towards her. 'Take a look at these. The first one is zoomed in on our lady who escorted Andrew Morrison to his room. The second, is taken from the bar where Steve Bell took his last drink. See it there?'

Becky zooms the image in. 'Even without enhancing it, I say you're spot on. Is this image newly uploaded?'

Eddie nods. 'Came up earlier as I was dredging through the files.'

'Blood red,' Becky says, raising an eyebrow. 'And that H-shaped clasp is pretty distinctive. It's *Hermès*. Possibly a fake, given the eye-watering cost of a real one, but even as a fake, probably not that common. Might be available on one of those clothing apps where you can hire things. I can do some searches. I mean, plenty of women have fake handbags, but I do think this one is a bit unusual and definitely worth flagging.'

'That's great,' Eddie says. 'Wild Bill is making a statement to the press to go out on the nine o'clock news. Might be something worth releasing. See if it triggers anyone's memory.'

Becky frowns. 'Don't you have to be there?'

'Don't,' Eddie says. 'Political bullshit. He wants his face out there. I'm happy to let him, while the rest of us do the actual work.' He picks up his desk phone and calls the DCI's office on loudspeaker.

'I hope it's something good, Eddie – I'm just about to head down to the PR suite.'

Eddie gives Becky a look, and she smirks. They both know the PR suite is nothing more than a glorified cupboard with decent acoustics.

'I'm sending you over two images, sir. We've noticed that the same handbag has shown up in the CCTV from both the Andrew Morrison and Steve Bell cases. Might be a useful carrot, if you want some media interest.'

They can hear the sound of Wild Bill clapping his hands. 'Excellent, Eddie. I knew you'd come up trumps.'

The DCI hangs up and Eddie shrugs. 'Just as well I'm not one of those coppers who likes to keep the glory for themselves.' He picks up his jacket.

'Full disclosure,' Becky says, as they walk together along the corridor. 'I'm not inviting you for dinner to talk shop. I'm taking you because I need a distraction tonight, after my early morning visit to Ivybridge – which I *will* tell you about but not right now.' She pauses. Grins. 'I'm actually taking you to dinner because I want to know what your history is with the sexy Ms Summers.'

He knew this was coming. He's ready for it now. '*Professor* Summers,' he says. 'Although I just knew her as Helena, back when she broke my heart and let me bind myself into a marriage of convenience with a woman I would never love.'

'Woah,' Becky says. 'I owe Joe a tenner. He reckoned she was an epic shag from times of yore.'

'And what did you think?'

She shrugs. 'I thought she might've been someone who bullied you at school.'

He laughs, and follows her out into the car park, his breath making little white puffs in the freezing night air. He'll let Becky have her comfort food and some light relief. But he's not going to tell her anything else about Helena. Not tonight.

# 22

# The Party Girl

After ditching the car, I'd curled up in my narrow childhood bed hoping to find some comfort, but sleep didn't come. There's been a few concerned messages from work colleagues. I've played the part of the quiet, diligent employee for such a long time; genuinely interested in my work and not afraid to put in the hours when needed. But recently things have started to slip. Shorter hours, too many unexplained absences. They're sure something is going on and they want to help. But I'm beyond help. I know I am. It's always a mistake, getting too close to people. I gave up on sleep in the end, and walked up to the care home.

I've been here since six a.m., just sitting beside Mum's bed, holding her hand. Dozing on and off. At some point, someone must have covered me with a blanket and switched off the room lights, leaving just the small lamp on in the corner. One of the nurses. It's not as if my mum could have done it. I close my eyes and think back to those times long before, when I was safe and secure, with a mum and dad who loved me. Two parents to tuck me in at night and tell me they would always be there to look after me.

Lies.

Too hot now, I wriggle out of the blanket and fold it up on my lap. Mum is lying still, as always. Nothing but the machines and the tubes and that horrible artificial breathing sound as the ventilator pushes air into her lungs. They've said that there's no hope of Mum breathing on her own again. Miracles do happen, but this isn't going to be one of them. She's in a *permanent vegetative state*. That's the actual terminology. I don't know why they can't come up with something a bit more clinical sounding than 'vegetative', but I don't make the rules.

I need to stretch my legs. Picking up the folded blanket, I walk quietly out of the room and into the corridor. Overhead strip lights on a sensor spring into action, bathing everything in a too-bright sodium glow, and it takes a moment for my eyes to adjust. The whole place is in silence, most of the bedroom doors closed. This is not the kind of care facility to be plagued by incessant noise, especially at this hour. I know that most of the residents here are just like my mum. Silent, still husks being kept alive by desperate relatives clinging on to hope, spending their savings hoping for those rare moments of good news that allow everyone to justify what's happening. I'm not criticising anyone's choices though. I've made the same choices myself.

There's a large linen closet at the end of the corridor. Deep, slatted-wood shelves stuffed full of sheets and towels, blankets and pillows. The blankets are mostly used by visitors, who spend endless hours sitting at bedsides, waiting. Having one-sided conversations.

It gets cold sometimes, being alone.

I find a space on the shelf for the blanket and leave it there. It's as I'm closing the door to the closet that I hear voices. Male – one close by, one more that sounds slightly further away. Distant, a bit tinny. I check the time on my phone 7:30 a.m. now. Not so early, but early for this place. I walk along the corridor a bit further, away from Mum's room, towards the other end where the fire door separates these rooms from the longer corridor that leads to reception.

There's an office on the right. I've spent a fair bit of time in there, with Mr Wade the manager, discussing my mum's care. Being placated with the good tea and the best biscuits. I wonder if he would still be so kind if he knew I was stealing drugs from his supply. I'm sure he doesn't care. Despite what they say about their ethics, I'm sure the company running the clinical trial are incentivising it – and I don't just mean their branded water jugs, mugs and pens. How ironic that as an employee I have to do mandatory bribery and corruption training.

The door to the office is partially open, and now that I'm closer, I recognise the voice of Gregg Wade. I stop walking, stand still a few doors away. Something about the conversation going on inside that room has made my ears prick up.

'… I'm thinking another week, that's all. Maybe less—'

A tinny voice cuts in. 'Can't you make it less? You know I'm good for the money, but honestly, it's all just a ridiculous waste, now. Besides, wouldn't you want to be putting that machine to use elsewhere?'

Laughter. 'Don't try pretending you're all moralistic now...'

Tinny voice again. It sounds as if Mr Wade is talking to someone on speakerphone. 'You've some cheek. I've been paying for her care for over thirteen years, have I not?'

Something about the voice on the phone sounds familiar, the accent soft, Irish. Why do I recognise it? I take a few more steps towards the office.

'And we both know why that is, don't we? Karyn has been unconscious since 2010. Your payments have been for the daughter, not her. She could never have afforded to keep her mum alive in a place like this for all these years. It's me you're talking to, Brendan...'

I suck in a breath. They're discussing my mum.

*The daughter...*

They're discussing *me*.

Gregg Wade is talking to someone called Brendan, but no. It can't be the same one... My dad's old colleague? The one who set him up?

What is he talking about? Saying he's been paying for my mum's care?

As far as I've been told – by the social workers and foster carers over the years, and by this *actual* care home manager too, when I was old enough to start asking questions – there was some sort of life insurance pay-out from my dad's work to cover all of this, one which still kicked in, even after the redundancy. Some sort of death benefit fund, to look after me and Mum.

The tinny voice speaks again. 'Just sort it, Gregg. Switch the bleedin' thing off. If you don't do it, I'll just have to pay Mrs Latimer a visit myself. It'd be lovely to see her again after all this time. She was always a good looking woman. I'll bet she's barely aged a day.'

His laughter sounds almost robotic through the speaker. I grit my teeth, listening to their disrespect.

Mr Wade sighs. 'Brendan, please. If you can just be patient a little longer, then I'll make sure that the daughter does the decent thing and switches the machines off. Karyn Latimer will be gone and you won't need to pay another penny towards her care. It'll be over. You'll be able to move on. We all will.'

'Move on? Jesus. This has been an inconvenient financial arrangement, that's all. I've let it go on all this time, but the extra cash you're asking for is just ridiculous. There's a cost of living crisis going on, in case you hadn't realised… and that woman is barely living at all. I've done my bit. I'll admit I set up the payments out of guilt, but the daughter doesn't need the help anymore, she's all grown up. I'm doing her a favour. She can get herself away from all this hanging around a care home and live her life properly. Besides, I'm away on my holidays soon and I'd rather be spending the money on myself, to be honest.' More laughter down the phone. Deep and booming, but with a little high-pitched lilt at the end.

I recognise that laugh.

It *is* him.

Brendan O'Malley.

Why the fuck has Brendan O'Malley been paying for my mother's care? And why has Gregg Wade kept this information from me for all this time? Maybe when I was under eighteen it was fair enough. Under twenty-one, even… but all this time since? Surely I have a right to know who is paying for all this, and more importantly: *why*? Something about this is very, very wrong.

The conversation has switched to football scores now, and I zone them out. Too much is whirring around my head as I walk back towards Mum's room. I step inside, watching her as she lies there on that bed. Her muscles wasted away, despite the daily actions of the nurses who spend endless futile hours looking after her.

I think back to that snake Wade's words. *I'll make sure that the daughter does the decent thing.*

Well.

I'll be doing something, that's for sure.

# 23
# Becky

There is something strangely comforting about sitting in McDonald's of an evening. It's a combination of the too-bright lighting, the smells of cooked processed food, and the Zyklon B inspired disinfectant they spray over the tables, sometimes while people are still eating. There's also the constant chatter of shouty teens, and the occasional ranting from one of the homeless frequent fliers. The sheer rabble of it makes it the perfect place to remove yourself mentally from anything else that might be going on. That's something that Becky needs more than ever right now. She's had multiple messages from her sister, and has ignored them all. She'll deal with it, but not right now.

Becky uses the touch screen to order her food – bacon double cheeseburger and fries, plus a hot chocolate. She chooses a Big Mac meal for Eddie, with a Sprite. Can't really go wrong with that. She waits by the counter for the order, while Eddie sits at their usual table in the corner, by the window. It's the perfect seat. Wall behind, window and entrance to one side, the rest of the restaurant to the other – means it's the perfect place to observe everything that's going on.

It's six years since she met Eddie that first time, in this same McDonald's, both sneaking in a McMuffin breakfast before work. It was a bit embarrassing at the time, her a rookie DC and him a time-served DS that she had only seen in passing. But that breakfast had helped to form their very first bond, and now it's become their regular meeting point for when they need to discuss anything that blurs the lines between work and leisure.

It was in here that she told Eddie that she was leaving her long-term boyfriend, Gary, who, despite being very nice and totally devoted to her, was just not what she wanted anymore. It was also in here that Eddie had told her that despite his best attempts, he was unable to sort out his marriage to Carly, but as it turns out, both parties were fine with that. They've since broached the subject of dating – not each other, to be clear. Although there was a time when Becky had thought that might be on the cards, she'd pushed it out of her mind. It would be a complication she doesn't need. No, their dating chat has been mostly about the losers that Becky has met via dating apps, and the various attempts of Eddie's friends and colleagues to set him up. None of this has amounted to much for either of them, although Becky is starting to wonder if there might be something happening between her and Jonah, the CCTV whizz, but something is stopping her from sharing this with Eddie.

By all rights, this is the exact environment for Becky to tell Eddie about Juniper, and her conflicting feelings of having her mum back in her life, albeit in a coma that she is unlikely to wake from. But there's more to it than that. There's also

Allie, and how Becky has finally realised how much of her sister's life has been shaped by their mother's absence. How Becky survives by keeping it all in a little box, locked up in a part of her brain that she refuses to entertain opening.

She collects the tray of food, stopping off for a straw, a stirrer and some napkins and a few packets of salt, then sits down opposite Eddie. 'I went for the classic option,' she says, pushing his boxed burger towards him. 'But I can get you something else if you don't like it.'

Eddie opens the box and smiles. Picks up the burger and takes a bite. It doesn't look much like the ones on the billboards, but it looks decent enough. A few pieces of chopped lettuce fall into the box. He takes another bite and chews for a moment before speaking. 'So what have you been doing all day?'

Becky slides a clump of fries into her mouth. 'Is that us finished with the Helena chat?'

He nods. 'For the time being.'

She decides not to push it. Pushing things with Eddie rarely gets her anywhere. He'll tell her when he's ready. Besides, she can hardly push him when she's not exactly being forthright about her own life right now. 'Well... it was something Maria said that got me thinking, actually. I know it might be a while before we get any definitive tox results, but I'm going with a couple of theories here. One, she puts something in their drink. Enough to get them to be compliant...'

'They're horny blokes at Christmas parties, Becks. I hate to say it, but if she's showing even half an interest, it's not going to take much to persuade them.'

Becky rolls her eyes. 'Yes, I get that. Men are pigs, etcetera. I think we're all thinking that this feeds into her motive. But

I'm thinking still about how she kills them. Getting them to the room is easy. But assuming they're random, she doesn't know what they might be capable of... What if one of them was to turn on her?'

Eddie takes a sip of his drink. 'Maybe they have. Maybe there have been some thwarted attempts, where she's borne the brunt. She's hardly going to report them. Not if she was intending to try it again with other blokes.'

'Right. Agreed. I was thinking about what she might be injecting them with in the room. It might even be consensual. Maybe she's passing it off as a sex drug...'

'Andrew Morrison had bruising, suggesting the injection didn't go smoothly. No report of the same on Steve Bell.' Eddie takes a handful of fries and stuffs them into his mouth.

'So Andrew struggled. He wasn't up for it? Anyway... I was thinking, what would she use? How has it not been detected in any of the previous cases that Joe is digging into? Those were all accidental according to the coroner's reports. If that wasn't the case, why wasn't a drug picked up then?'

'Maybe there was no tox screen done. Maybe it got lost.' Eddie shrugs. 'Maybe they're still in a lab somewhere, waiting to be processed. If the PM looked like a heart attack, the tox wouldn't be marked as urgent... and we all know what happens to things not marked as urgent.'

'They disappear into the abyss.'

He noisily sucks up the last of his drink. 'Exactly.'

'I thought maybe it was an experimental drug. Something difficult to detect.' She takes the lid off her hot chocolate and sips it. Somewhere behind her, two youths are having an argument. She swivels around in her seat.

'Oi,' Eddie says, just the right level of loud. 'Pack it in, lads.'

They both turn to Eddie, puffing out their little chests. But they know who he is. Even in civvies he has that policeman air about him. One of them shoves the other and they mutter something about Feds before swaggering off outside to their gang at the door.

'Bring back National Service,' Eddie mutters. The corner of his mouth lifts into a smirk. It's one of his often rolled out 'daddism' clichés, along with 'were you born in a barn?' and 'you'll understand when you're older'.

'There's a company on the industrial estate just outside Woodham. It's called Innoxia Research. They have quite an interesting discovery and development pipeline, including something they are terming "ethical analgesics", which I've tried to make sense of but haven't got very far with yet. I wasn't aware that analgesics were unethical, but what do I know. Anyway, they're—'

'Drugs to knock you out for surgery. I see where you're going with this, Becks. It's a good theory. But—'

'Hear me out,' she says. 'I came across them the other day on a list of companies I'm digging into a bit. But then I came across them again. In the care home, actually...' She lets her sentence hang. Looks him in the eye. *Don't ask about my mum*, she says, non-verbally.

He nods. 'Go on.'

'There was some merch in there – water jugs, mugs, the pen that I signed myself in with. That sort of thing. Apparently they're running a trial at the clinic.' She takes another sip of her hot chocolate, and it is almost at non-palate burning level. 'You can look up all clinical trials on a website,' she says. 'They have to be listed on there, by law. What they're doing at the care home – testing drugs on some of the patients – is all legit, though I'm not sure how the consent part works in this case. I assume the relatives give it? Allowing the drug company to test their offerings alongside the standard care. Anyway, the security is pretty low level in this clinic. I left my mum's room to go to the toilet, and I got a bit lost. Wandered off and opened various doors. You get the picture. The point is that there aren't enough staff hanging around, and I'm sure it wouldn't be hard to take drugs from there, if you knew where to find them…'

Her personal mobile buzzes loudly and judders across the table. She lifts a finger up to her face and mouths, 'One sec.' It's an unknown mobile number, and she should probably ignore it, but she taps the screen anyway, answering the call.

'Hello?'

'Becks, it's me…'

Her sister's voice is flat. 'I dropped my phone. Had to get a burner while it's in getting fixed.'

Becky sighs. 'Can I call you later, Allie? I'm still at work.' She looks out of the window to avoid Eddie's hard stare. The gang from earlier are hanging around the bus stop across the road. One of them grabs a pair of sparkly reindeer antlers from a girl waiting for the bus, and some shrieking and arguing breaks out.

'I'll be back,' Eddie says.

She watches as he marches outside and crosses the road. There's some more arguing, some gesturing, and then the gang splits into its individual components and they all run off.

'I need you here with me, Becks. I can't do this on my own,' Allie says.

Becky bites her lip. Says nothing. A light pounding starts in her temple, above her left eye.

'Becky, are you there? When do you finish? Can you come up? I asked Dad but he says he's not coming in.' Her sister's voice breaks into sobs. Becky chokes back tears. Not for her mum, but for her sister. Who for all that travelling and happy-go-lucky attitude, is clearly vulnerable and need of her support.

'I'll call you back in a bit, Al.'

Becky ends the call. She's still staring out of the window. Across the road, Eddie picks up the antlers and hands them back to the girl, who smiles at him. He takes out his phone and taps out a message, frowning like he always does, still annoyed at himself for not getting to grips with the touch-screen keyboard since the death of his Blackberry. Then he lifts his head and clocks Becky watching him out of the window. Gives her a little smile and a wave. Becky's stomach does a little somersault.

As he sits back down opposite her, the musky remnants of his aftershave waft out from the neck of his shirt. Becky's breath hitches, and she gives herself a mental shake. *Not now, Becky. What the fuck is wrong with you?*

# 24

## The Party Girl

I give Mum a soft kiss on the back of her hand. It's hard to get close to her face now, with the tubes and the machines. Then I nip out of the room quietly and sneak past the manager's office. It's quiet in there now, the loud phone conversation over. I open the fire door carefully and close it again, rather than let it swing back itself and risk making a noise. I don't want to alert Mr Wade that I'm here.

Around the corner, in the next corridor, I can see the senior nurse on duty, sitting at the reception desk, scrolling through her phone.

The nurse, Lauren, is quite new; and like all of the staff here, she's very *nice*. But she's also incredibly indiscreet. I've heard her telling visitors private, personal things about some of the residents. It's like she forgets that just because the patients can't speak up to complain, that there is no one around to overhear what she says about them. Lauren doesn't realise that I often visit my mum out of hours. That I usually come in via the garden entrance, which is supposed to be locked and secured, but never is.

'Lauren, hey!'

She flinches, dropping her phone onto the counter in front of her. Then she laughs, and tries to gain some composure. 'Oh… I didn't realise anyone was here! I'm so sorry, I was miles away there. You know what it's like, just a bit of personal stuff to deal with before the shift officially starts.'

We both glance up at the clock. It's 8:17 a.m. I don't bother to ask what Lauren's official shift start time is. We both know that Lauren was slacking off because she honestly thinks that this is such a cushy job, what with her patients not being able to actually ask for any assistance. If I didn't already have my plans in place, I would be making a complaint about this place and taking Mum elsewhere. As it is, I will use Lauren's lax behaviour to my advantage.

'Can I help you with something?' Lauren's all sweet smiles now, trying to look like she cares. The staff here *are* nice, but it's mostly pretty fake. 'How's your mum today?'

I have to try very hard not to roll my eyes at this comment. How the hell is Lauren a senior nurse? Is there some sort of low-level entry programme for the people who staff these places? 'Oh you know,' I say, 'the same. She looks comfortable though.' I smile at Lauren, returning the fake grin. 'I was wondering if you could help me with something, actually?'

Lauren's smile widens. She likes to think she is a helpful person.

'I've had a bit of a mix-up at the bank, some of the standing orders not being paid on the correct dates, you know. That sort of annoying stuff.'

Lauren is still smiling.

'I wondered if you could just print out the statements for me for the last few months. Just so I can reconcile the dates and the amounts? I'm just trying to make it easier to sort it with the bank.' My face is starting to hurt a bit now. I'm not used to all this grinning.

'Ohhh...' She draws the word out like a sigh. Her first sign of hesitation. She might be new, but she will have been fully briefed on any unusual financial arrangements. After all, the main thing this place cares about is money. Mr Wade made that quite clear when he explained about the cost of the ventilator. How I should consider if we really wanted to continue down this route. This route... Like I was working out the quickest way to the airport from my house during rush hour. When actually what I was meant to be considering was whether I was going to let my mother die.

'I believe your mother's fees are paid by a third party? Perhaps you should talk to them about it.' She picks up the desk phone. 'Or, I can buzz Mr Wade. Maybe he can—'

I put my hand over hers, pushing the receiver back into the cradle. 'I'd rather not involve Mr Wade, if that's OK with you, Lauren? You know, I come in early quite a lot to see my mum. I hear things.' I pause, watching her face carefully for a reaction. 'I see things. Was that your boy-friend who left earlier, via the garden exit?'

Lauren's carefully made-up face blanches. 'You know, I need to go and get something from the storage cupboard around the back. You, um... You could come and sit round here and wait for me, if you like.' She smiles again, but it's darker. Less innocent. I think we understand one another. 'There's actually a Nespresso machine around here. You probably think that's quite appalling that we have it, given that the coffee machine in the visitors' lounge is so awful.'

Wow. She really does not want me to mention her extra-curricular activities to her boss. I knew she would be easy to persuade, but she's more of a pushover than I realised.

'That would be great. Thank you.' I give her another forced grin, then let it drop as soon as she slides out from behind the counter, giving me a little wink as she passes. No doubt she will use this little tête-à-tête we've had to embellish one of her inappropriate stories one day. Well, good. She can have it. Me and my mum will be long gone by then.

It takes about two minutes to find my files on the system. Absolutely no security needed. No password. Nothing. And everything neatly filed, exactly as you'd expect to find it. Probably Gloria's work. I wonder if *she* would have caved so easily if I'd asked her to show me the statements. She's been here the whole time I've been coming, and she seems almost apologetic every time she sees me. Like she knows that Wade and his pal O'Malley have been laughing behind my back all this time. I'm kicking myself now for not asking to see this before. But it didn't matter before – I was just glad someone was paying. A mysterious benefactor. Now I know why.

Client files>Accounts. My mother's name on the folder. Inside, thirteen years' worth of monthly statements, but I only need one to get the address.

***

I put the postcode into the maps app on my phone and then I find myself zoning out a bit as I drive the hire car across town. The night of the attack comes back to me in small, angry flashes. I was sixteen, in the middle of prep for exams but I was supposed to be at a friend's house, having pizza and staying over. We were going to watch *Monster* – that film about the female serial killer, Aileen Wournos. I'd been kind of fascinated by her for a while, and I was really intrigued to see how she might be portrayed by Charlize Theron. I think even then I knew something bad was going to happen to my mum.

It had started with waitressing at a few high end parties for a bit of extra cash, and then I know it had turned into something else. Something darker. She'd been bringing men home a lot since Dad died. Sometimes more than one. She was off her face half the time. Drinking, drugs, I don't know what. I kind of kept to myself, buried myself in my books in my room, wearing headphones to block out the noise of her *entertaining*.

I wish I'd done something to help her, but what could I do?

My friend… Sally Wood, her name was. She cancelled on me as I made my way across the other side of town on the bus. Said her dad had told her she wasn't allowed anyone round until the exams were over. She was fuming about it. But she was sorry… and I understood. I think if my dad had still been around he would also have been looking out for me, making sure I was studying and not wasting my time watching true-crime horror movies. So I got off the bus in town, and treated myself to dinner in Pizza Hut. They were running that buffet option. All you can eat for £4.99. Then I got the bus home, and that's when all hell broke loose. I saw it all, and they didn't even know I was there. I think staying hidden probably saved my life, but I will always wonder if I could have done something to save my mum from what happened to her. In fairness to them, I'm not sure they actually expected her to live.

By the time I arrive at the address, I'm literally boiling with rage. My skin feels hot to the touch, and my hands shake as I lift them off the steering wheel that I'd been gripping so tightly. *It's OK*, I tell myself. *It will all be over soon.* I pick up my bag and make my way up the path.

The house is in the posh part of town, as I expected. It's set back from the road by a sloped garden, filled with rockery shrubs and ornamental pine trees lining the borders. One of those double-bay fronted places with an oversized wooden door, painted a classy shade of emerald green. The front door is open into the tiled porch, and there are suitcases lined up in front of the half-glass inner door. There is a brass bell-pull outside the main door, and I yank it back with force, hearing the deep chimes ringing out inside the house.

'Just a minute,' Brendan calls out from behind the glass, 'you're twenty minutes early, you know.'

I hesitate then. He's expecting someone. This could be bad timing. But then I look down at the suitcases and deduce that he is probably waiting for a taxi. And there is twenty minutes to go. Knowing the cabs around here, it will be late.

I still have time. I yank the bell-pull again, and the clanging repeats.

The door opens swiftly, and there he is in front of me. He's aged since I saw him last. We all have, but his is the ageing of someone with money who likes the finer things in life. His face is puffy, cheeks red. He looks like he drinks too much, eats too much, and tries to fix it with surgical fillers. He is disgusting.

He looks annoyed for a moment, then confused, then his face settles into something else. Recognition.

'Ah,' he says. 'Hello, there. I guess I knew this day would come, but I'm sorry, love. I'm just on my way out. I'd invite you in but the taxi will be here any minute.' He shrugs, in a 'what can you do?' kind of way.

'Off somewhere nice are you, Mr O'Malley?' I step into the porch.

'Florida, actually. For a couple of months. I'm one of those Snow Birds, you know. Fly south for the winter. Get away from this awful weather.'

*Oh, well this is just perfect.*

'Really, I only need a few minutes of your time. I'm sure you can spare me that... after all these years. I wanted to thank you, really.' I take another step towards him.

He frowns, looking over my shoulder, as if he's expecting the taxi to pull up at any minute. 'Sure, OK then. Five minutes though, that's all I've got.'

I follow him into the house. *You've less time than that.* I smile to myself. The best part about all this is that no one will be looking for him. Everyone will just assume he's gone off on his winter holidays.

*Serendipity, Mr O'Malley*, I think, as I close the door behind me and slide the syringe out of my bag.

# 25

# Harry

It had been bittersweet, getting ready for the party. In some ways, he'd got what he wanted – he'd got the costume, and the tickets, and here he was at his table with all the people he considered to be his friends at work... Luke, who showed incredible restraint in not saying 'I told you so' about Heather not being that into him. Lorraine, who is a lot of fun and who Luke might actually like more than he makes out. And, of course, Joanne, everyone's favourite new girl, who apparently had fancied Harry since the day she started. Who knew?

So he's pleased with all that. But he still can't stop thinking about Heather. There was something much deeper about her than the other girls he'd dated. Problem was, it was so deep, it would have taken an extended excavation with a lot of machinery to get to the bottom of it.

Joanne isn't really that much of a slag, once you get to know her. All a front, Harry thinks – that over-the-top flirting thing she has going on. She's actually very sweet, and she's fun. And she looks incredible in her Poison Ivy costume. He's hoping he might get a chance to take it off her later. This party is kind of their first date, but they have been spending a lot of time together since Heather basically dumped him via text after #burntdinnergate. What a fool he'd been. His eyes scan the room, taking in all the superhero décor, and across to the bar, where one of the many Catwomen sits on a stool, facing away from him. He spotted a couple of women he recognised earlier, dressed in this costume. Sandra from accounts, who must've had to grease herself to slide into it, and Margaret from the canteen, who looked so uncomfortable he thought she might burst into tears. He's not sure who the one at the bar is, but something about the curve of her back, the shape of her shoulders, looks a little familiar. He thinks it might be Kirsty from reception. He hasn't spotted her elsewhere.

He takes a swig of red wine, glances around the table, and then realises that Joanne is actually talking to him, and the others are laughing, although not unkindly. 'Earth to Harry? Bloody hell, I thought you'd had a stroke or something.'

More laughter, mainly from Luke.

Harry smiles and squeezes Joanne's hand. 'Sorry... I was miles away!'

Luke rolls his eyes. 'So as I was saying...' Luke is dressed up as one of the many Batmans of the night, but his costume is a good quality, well fitted one that makes him look very muscular, and Harry has a feeling he didn't buy it just for this. 'I thought about booking a room for the night, but I'm not that keen on getting myself murdered by a hooker...'

Lorraine slaps him on the arm. 'It's "sex worker", and I didn't think you were planning to pay for it tonight?'

Luke throws his head back and guffaws. 'You offering me a freebie tonight, love? I did always wonder what you did in the evenings… Explains all those expensive hand-bags.'

Lorraine glares at him, but then joins in with his laughter. Luke's humour leaves a lot to be desired but for some reason, he's popular. Harry needs to loosen up sometimes, he realises. Maybe that's what put Heather off too.

*Stop thinking about her!* he shouts to himself, internally.

'You haven't got any fancy designer handbags, have you?' Joanne says, leaning over towards Lorraine and slopping a bit of white wine out of her glass and onto the white tablecloth. She's had a few tonight. They all have, in fairness. Luke noticed that the table next to them weren't drinking their free wine, so he swiped their bottles too.

'Oh god,' Lorraine says, her face displaying mock horror. 'That was on the news, wasn't it? They think the woman who killed those two men has a rare, posh bag… she must earn plenty in tips to afford one of them.' The two women laugh, and the other two across the table join in. Miranda and Laura. He doesn't know them that well but they seem like good fun.

'What bags?' Luke says. He doesn't like it when other people know things that he doesn't. Harry has no idea what they are talking about either, and he's not really that interested. He's just glad this event didn't get cancelled because of it. The police reports have been quite vague, but it seems like a sex worker might have killed a couple of clients. They're not saying if it's murder or accidental, just that they need to talk to her. *Obviously* they need to talk to her, especially if it's the same woman behind both. But it's not something that Harry is too worried about. He has no intention of hooking up with a hooker. He laughs at his own joke, though not out loud.

'These bags, you idiot.' Joanne holds out her phone and shows it around the table. One by one, people look at it. Some raise an eyebrow or nod.

'I'd love a bag like that,' Miranda says. 'I would never spend that on myself though, even if I could afford it.'

Luke snatches the phone. 'Five grand?' he booms. 'For that stupid little bag? Get yourself down to Hastings this summer, ladies. Plenty of knock-offs to be had down by the beach.' He laughs again, tips more wine into his glass, finishing the bottle. 'Time for another mine-sweep. We're all out, and those accountants are clearly not going to drink theirs. Boring fuckers.'

He tosses the phone back to Joanne, who catches it deftly and lays it on the table. She turns to Harry and mouths, '*He is such a twat*', then sticks her spoon into her dessert, shoving the last piece of cheesecake into her mouth and licking her lips seductively at him. But Harry's not really paying attention. Because out of the corner of his eye, he can see her phone screen, with the picture of the handbag still on it.

'May I...?' He doesn't wait for her to answer, just picks up the phone and looks at it more closely. Taps on the image to enlarge it to full screen. It's a coincidence, he's sure, but it feels like someone has tipped ice down the back of his rubber suit.

This is the bag he saw in Heather's room. The one he thought was a bit ostentatious. Not her kind of thing. Shiny red crocodile skin? Like, where would she use it? She never went anywhere. At least... she never went anywhere with him. He took a photo of that bag, didn't he? He thinks about taking out his phone and showing the others, but something about the whole situation makes him feel sick to his stomach.

He looks down at his untouched dessert, pushes it away. He's had too much to drink. He's being stupid. Heather is secretive, yes. Or just private, you could argue. It doesn't mean she's hiding anything. It makes no sense. She always said she liked to stay in, didn't like attention, didn't like big gatherings. He thought she was shy.

She can't be an... escort? She can't have... killed people?

So many thoughts whizz around his head, and he takes a sip of water to try and stop them. He's vaguely aware of Joanne beside him, saying something, but it sounds like it's coming from far away, or from underwater. He can hear blood pumping around inside his own head, if that's even possible. The music and clatter and chatter of the party is all zoned out. That woman at the bar. The mystery Cat-woman. She had looked over at him earlier, just briefly, and there was something familiar about her. He looks over at the bar now, but she is long gone. He would have spotted such a distinctive bag, wouldn't he?

Coincidence. That's all. Loads of women must have handbags like that. The bag on the photo that Joanne showed them all was Hermès. That's crazy designer, right? Probably cost a lot more than the police have esti-mated, especially if it's vintage. Heather couldn't have a bag like that. It probably *was* just a cheap knock-off from the beach. He's jumping to crazy conclusions because he wants to justify his own hurt. Yes, he might have Joanne now, and yes, he is definitely on a promise... He's vaguely aware of the heat of her hand on his leg, her breath in his ear.

But something about the bag has set off his Spidey-senses. He's wearing the wrong costume because the feel-ing is real. He's too hot, now. Far too hot.

He stands up, takes Joanne by the hand. 'Let's get some fresh air.'

# 26

# The Party Girl

I'm feeling quite psyched up after seeing Brendan. That had turned out to be a very cathartic experience. He'd barely closed the door when I'd leapt on him from behind, and stabbed the syringe into his neck. I think the shock helped accelerate the effects of that particular administration. On my way to his house, I'd thought about all the questions I wanted to ask him, about why he'd let Dad take the fall. About why he'd then 'helped' my mum by setting her up with his twisted cronies. I'd wanted him to look me in the eye and apologise. I'd wanted him to look me in the eye as I squeezed the life out of him.

But in the end, I'd acted on impulse. I didn't want to hear his excuses and lies. It's his fault that my mum is going to die. It's not the fault of the men that I'm targeting – but I will never know who Brendan's friends were, and I need to finish this my own way. So I've had to use proxies. Representatives of the type of creeps that my mum was forced to entertain. It's not like I don't give them a chance... Be *nice*, and you'll walk away. Be *naughty*, and I will make sure you never get that opportunity again.

Perhaps that's why I'm feeling ready to take the biggest risk of all. I'm *escalating*. That's what the profilers call it, isn't it? Do they even have those over here or are they only in America? Anyway, I'm sure the police work things out just the same. The last snippet of news had shown a photo of my 'distinctive handbag' and it's lucky I had the TV on at Mum's while I was getting ready or I'd have fucked myself up in a minute in here. I'm not sure who saw it and has made the owner the primary 'person of interest' but it doesn't really matter now. There is another option in Mum's wardrobe, an understated black Chanel number. I don't think she ever used it. It was still in the protective cotton pouch and the leather looks like it has never been touched. Like the red croc Hermès that is now splattered over the news, I suspect one of the men must've given it to her, and thus it's only fitting that I take them with me while on my mission.

I'm becoming a little bored with the hotel bars now too. Bored with the whole thing, in fact. It's exhausting. Dressing up, finding new clothes and wigs – having to find new places to buy them so that it doesn't look strange. I have managed to get most of what I need online but it's easier when you can see it all in one place, and for that, charity shops are my friends. But it all just takes time. I'm running out of that. I've been collecting things for years, because I've been thinking about doing this for years. I just hadn't worked up the courage until they told me that Mum was almost out of time. But I'm in control of that now too. Brendan's hold on us was severed the moment he made the financial decision to pull the plug.

I'm glad he won't get the satisfaction.

Dealing with Brendan wasn't something I'd envisaged. I wonder what would have happened if I hadn't overheard that phone call. I assume he would have stopped paying, and I would have had to make the decision to take Mum off the machines. Mum would have died, and Brendan would have got away with it all, and I wouldn't have had any closure at all. It was a bonus finding out about him like that. I could just stop now. Walk away. I reckon I still have a little time before the police finish putting all the pieces together.

But I feel like I need one more party. The finale, as it were. Brendan was an added bonus, but he wasn't part of my plan.

This big multi-office party is absolutely the best choice. There are three different groups sharing this space tonight, and the largest of them is Innoxia Research – and they are in fancy dress. It's a bold move, and not without its risks. But what do I have to lose?

I don't really like superheroes. I never have. But I did enjoy putting this outfit together. I did a bit of research and I really wanted to be Black Widow, but I needed a mask and I needed to blend in, so Catwoman it is. I managed to hire a great costume online. I don't imagine I'll find the time to return it.

I sip my drink, keeping an eye on the room. It's warm inside the mask, given that it covers a large part of my face. There are people here that would recognise me easily, so I can't stay long. Luckily there are two other bars for me to visit in here, and the Innoxia lot will more than likely just stick to the one nearest their own function. But I will have to be careful.

'Can I get you another one?' The barman has sidled into my space without me noticing. I'm distracted. I need to stay focussed. I quite like the look of this one though. He has kind eyes. In another life, I might have tried to have a proper conversation with him, but tonight is not that night, and I am not myself. I lean over and lift his name badge, and he steps closer – probably scared I'm going to rip it off his shirt. 'No thank you, *Simon*,' I say, emphasising his name, pretending I give a shit. 'But I'm sure I'll be back for more later.'

He picks up my empty glass and gives me a bemused smile. No salacious wink.

*Nice*, I think. *Well done, Simon.*

I swivel around in my seat, so I'm facing out into the room. Harry is still at his table. He was easy to spot. Ant Man is quite distinctive, and although I've seen more than one of them, he has chosen to take his mask off. His table is at the furthest corner from the bar, and it is laden with bottles of wine. The bar is not near the toilets, so I don't see any need for him to come over here. Harry is the type to stick with the freebies as long as they can be drawn out. He's in a lively-looking group, all waving arms and loud laughter, and I spot that new girl – Joanne – the one who everyone seems to adore. She's wearing the Poison Ivy costume that Harry got for me. It was that hanging on the wardrobe door that was enough for me to flee. Harry was only ever a distraction. He was a good cook, and a reasonably good shag, but he was starting to ask too many questions. He always thought the relationship was going somewhere, and I can't keep stringing him along. I'm not a bad person.

Just a really fucking angry one.

A man in a cheap, ill-fitting Batman suit starts to make a beeline for me, so I slide off my stool and spirit myself out of the room. That's enough, for now.

The bar in the function room at the other end of the wide, carpeted hall is designed with a 1930s vibe, the lights dimmed, lots of shiny Art Deco fittings. The people in here are mostly dressed in cocktail dresses and dinner jackets, but I see a couple of other superhero escapees over in the corner, so I think I can get away with it. I sidle up to the bar, resting my chin on my elbow…

And I'm shocked to see a familiar face.

I manage to hide it well as he comes sauntering towards me.

'Well, hello, Kitty,' he says, his mouth raised in a smirk. 'Of all the bars in all the towns…'

I give him a wry smile. 'Save it. What are you doing here?'

'I had to get a new job, babe. Have you not seen the news? The Woodham Hotel and Conference Centre is closed. They found a body in one of the bedrooms. You know'—he puts his hand on his chin and looks up, pretends to think—'I think you were there that night.'

'I think you have me mixed up with someone else.'

His expression changes. 'I don't think so.'

He turns away, starts fixing me a drink, even though I haven't asked him for anything. I'm trying to decide what to do. I did not expect to run into the barman from that night where I dealt with the lawyer. I could just leave right now. I can be out of the door and gone before anyone has a chance to stop me. My bag is in the stairwell near the fire exit, just down the hall. I can whip off my mask, pull on the baggy tracksuit and cap I've got in there. It doesn't have to end like this. But… He turns around, places a glass of something clear and fizzy in front of me, with a giant ball of ice and a couple of slices of fancy dried fruits jammed into the top. 'Sparkling water,' he says, his eyes as cold as my drink looks.

'I'm not really thirsty, actually.' He had his back to me, obscuring the drink as he added the various decorations, and I have no idea what else he might have put in there. He looks like the type to put things in girls' drinks. I've met his kind before. Good looking and charming, think they can have who they want. But they like to make sure.

He leans over the bar, his face close to mine. He smells sharp and peppery. 'I reckon you owe me a freebie, babe,' he sneers. 'Or I could just call the police right now. Should've called them last time. We don't really like escorts fleecing our guests.' He takes my chin in his rough hand and pulls me in closer. 'What happened with that bloke then? Sex game gone wrong?' I grab his hand and pull it off my face. Take a step back. I think I'm going to vomit, but I gulp in a couple of breaths of air, keeping it at bay. I would love a drink right now, but I'm not touching that one he made me. The fact that he thinks I killed someone and is not in the least bit concerned about it confirms my thoughts about him.

He is definitely not *nice*.

'I'll have a can of Coke, please. I'll open it myself.'

He smirks again, but he gets me the drink from the fridge. There are a couple of other customers waiting now, so he goes to serve them but I know he's keeping an eye on me. The Coke is icy cold and it burns down my throat, pushing my nausea away. The promise of the sugar rush hits me shortly afterwards, and suddenly I am alert once more.

I place the can on the bar, gesture to him with a finger. He hands over two bottles of beer to a customer, then walks slowly back to my end of the bar. He's enjoying this.

So am I.

'I'd be more than happy to provide you with my Gold Star service. What time do you finish? Can you get a room key? I've never stayed here before. Looks decent.'

He bites his lip. I think I've thrown him off guard. I don't think he was really expecting me to oblige. He knows he should call the police, but he's a risk taker. Like me.

'I'm on an early tomorrow. Need to get home. Meet me at midnight, at the car park entrance.'

I give him a wink. I'll find some way to amuse myself until then.

Perhaps I'll go and seek out Harry after all.

•

# 27

# Harry

Now that he's outside, the frosty night air on his face, resting his chin atop Joanne's coconut scented hair as she hugs him close, Harry is not sure he wants to go back in. If he's honest, the party is not as much fun as he'd thought it would be. Like most of these things, the build-up is way more exciting than the reality. The food has been disappointing, which to some wouldn't matter, but as someone who likes to cook, it actually offends him that people are expected to pay for crap food. The tickets weren't cheap, either, because the company is too tight to pay for them all to have a party, despite them bleating on about the profits. There has been plenty of wine though. Luke has made sure of that. But to be honest, Luke is being a massive, loud bore, and the wine is poor quality. Harry's got the beginnings of a headache already, and he's not even pissed.

He doesn't say any of this out loud though. Joanne has been very happy all evening and seems to genuinely like him, so he's not going to jeopardise that. He actually came outside because of the photo on her phone, but now that he's here in the chill air, he wonders if maybe he's being ridiculous. He was going to mention it. Maybe ask Joanne if she knew if people commonly had copies of that particular bag. But now he thinks he might leave it. He has a bottle of prosecco at home, and some nice nibbles – a tangy cheddar he picked up at a farmers' market, some fancy seeded crackers. Red grapes. He loves red grapes.

Joanne pulls away from him, but keeps her hands on the tops of his arms. She looks up at his face and smiles, opens her mouth slightly as she gently tugs on his sleeves, drawing him in.

The kiss starts softly. She tastes of vanilla and raspberry cheesecake. Then she presses her lips against him harder, and he starts to tingle in all the right places. He takes a step back, breaking it off.

She looks alarmed. 'Sorry, I—'

'No. No...' He pulls her in close again, hugging her. 'I don't want to do this here. We're in the bloody car park. I can actually smell the bins.'

Joanne laughs. 'You're right. Let's go back inside. I'm sure we can find a hidden corner somewhere a bit nicer than this. There's a 1930s themed bar along the other end of the corridor. I saw it earlier when I went for a wander. Maybe we could have a quiet drink in there?' She pauses. 'I know he's your mate, but Luke is a bit much tonight.'

'Well, he's not actually my *mate*. I only really see him at work. And yeah, he is a bit much tonight. Even more than usual, but I suspect that multiple bottles of wine might be playing a part in that.'

She takes his hand. 'Come on then—'

He shakes his head. 'I was thinking maybe we should just ditch it altogether? I've got some nice drinks and nibbles at home. We could have our own little party.'

Joanne raises an eyebrow. 'Can we keep the costumes on?'

Harry laughs. 'Absolutely. If we walk around the side of the car park, I can get an Uber to collect us on Seaford Road. It'll probably be easier than at the main entrance anyway.' He pulls her away from the fire exit. He'd expected it to be alarmed when he shoved the metal bar earlier as he hurried out, desperate for air, feeling like he was on the verge of a panic attack. But it wasn't alarmed, and it also didn't actually close properly, so they could easily go back inside that way, if they wanted. He doesn't. He just wants to leave, right now, and take Joanne home. Kick the ghost of Heather to the kerb for good.

She slides her hand out of his. 'Well I'm glad that Ant Man carries all that he needs on his person, but I'm afraid that Poison Ivy has a coat. And a bag. And her phone is in that bag, and her money and her keys.' She stands on tiptoe and leans in to kiss him quickly on the lips. 'Wait here for me. I'll be right back.'

A waft of distant noise leaches out as the door opens and he smiles to himself as she disappears along the corridor. *I'll be right back.* Isn't that immortal line in all horror movies, when one character leaves another one alone to go and check on a mysterious noise?

He wishes that Ant Man had thought to bring a coat, but he hadn't really expected to be hanging around in the freezing cold car park at nearly half past ten. How had it even got so late? Everything was a bit delayed, and the disco had already started before the food was cleared, but he's glad to be out of it now, despite freezing his nuts off outside this door. A wind has picked up too, bringing a blast of frigid air into his corner and he knows he can't wait here any longer.

There is a little shelter over by the bins, which he thinks might be the staff smoking hut. There's no one in there at the moment, not that he can see anyway. They're all too busy for a break, it seems. He wraps his arms around himself as he walks over to the three-sided wooden box. As he'd hoped, there is one of those outside heaters, and he presses the button – immediately warming up as the bars glow red above him. He holds his hand up to the heat, tilts his face upwards like a sunflower. It's just what he needs, despite the smell of stale cigarettes that haunts the little cabin.

A noise startles him, and he whirls around but he can't see anything. It sounds like breaking glass and someone walking on top of shards. A shattered, splintered, crunching sound.

Then it stops.

He imagines he can hear breathing. Someone close by, but out of sight. Or is it just his own breath? It's very quiet in this car park at this time of night, away from the traffic of the main road. And there are no sounds coming out of the hotel because all the windows are double-glazed and the fire door, despite being unlatched, is closed.

Despite the heat on the back of his head now, he feels a chill.

'Hello? Anyone there?'

No answer. That breathing again. He holds his breath, hoping the sound will stop, but it carries on. He exhales, and his breath puffs out in icy little clouds.

'You can come out, you know. I'm not going to bite.' He tries to inject some lightness and humour into his tone, but his voice shakes a little, and hearing that from his own mouth makes him more scared.

*You are being ridiculous*, he tells himself. But is he?

Someone is out there, he's sure of it. Why aren't they answering him?

Again, too many thoughts whizz around his head. He imagines who might be lurking in the darkness. One of the youths from the nearby estate, broken bottle in hand, ready to pounce and mug him? *Don't be stupid.*

Another crunching footstep over by the bins.

It must be one of the staff. 'Would you say something? You're freaking me out, here! I'm just one of the guests from the function. I'm not going to tell anyone if you're out here taking a sneaky break…' No answer.

*Fuck this.*

He should just go back inside. Grab Joanne. Get a taxi from the front door, and go home and enjoy what's left of the night. And the morning too, if all goes well. The heater clicks off, bathing him in darkness again, the cold instantly returning to his bones.

He steps out of the shelter, and starts to walk towards the door.

# 28

# Eddie

The morning briefing is frustrating, and Eddie knows that the team are getting fed up with the slow progress. They have pretty much nothing on the Andrew Morrison and Steve Bell murders. They are still combing through CCTV, hoping to find something. The toxicology results are still outstanding. There are no leads from the victims' families – the team who had followed up with Andrew Morrison's wife again, probing further into the possibility of him having a mistress, came back with nothing, and even the neighbour that Eddie had thought might know more, turned out to be basically just a busy-body.

It's just a bunch of dead ends. Even Joe is getting nowhere with his cold case checks, and it now seems that Helena might not be much use to them after all. Thankfully, Wild Bill has stayed away and left Eddie to do his job, but he's called for updates so many times that Eddie wonders if he might get away with blocking his number.

He catches Becky on his way back into the office, just as she returns from the kitchen carrying a pint glass filled with tap water.

'Got time for a chat?'

'Sure.'

She follows him to his office and partially closes the door. He's about to say something about that, but the main room is almost full today, and Eddie is more grateful than ever to have his own little sanctuary. There's all of the detectives working on this case, plus the ones covering everything else. There was a potential unexplained death found at one of the houses in the nice part of town, which is something that always warrants further investigation, because it's where the DCI lives and he doesn't like any mess in his manor. Turned out the guy had a heart condition, so it was a false alarm. Shame for him though. He had his suitcases at the door ready for a holiday in the sun. It was the traumatised taxi driver who had raised the alarm.

There's a lot of chatter. Everyone is trying to get things wrapped up for Christmas, and Eddie is getting worried the hotel murders are going to drag on into the new year, which they will, unless something else happens soon to break it open. Becky shoves the door fully closed, and the noise from the open-plan desks diminishes to a quiet burbling in the background. He lets out a long, slow sigh as Becky sits down in the chair opposite him and puts her glass on his desk.

'This case is pissing me off,' Eddie says. 'It feels like everything we need is just taking too long. There are too many assumptions being made. I'm starting to feel like I haven't a clue what I'm doing anymore.' He doesn't know why he's saying this. But something about this case is making him tired. He's lacking in energy to handle a serial killer case again, and he's not convinced that's what's going on. Not yet.

'It's not just you,' Becky says, sipping her water. 'But I have some good news, I spoke to a jeweller about the hair-clip. I didn't have time to go in and see him, but I emailed him a photo and he got back to me quickly. He's calling me about it in...' She stops, when her phone plays one of those annoying beep-boop ringtones. She grins at Eddie, then taps on her screen to answer, mouthing 'video call' to Eddie as she quickly smooths her hair with her free hand.

'Mr Wilson,' she says, smiling at the screen. 'Just give me a minute to set this up on the desk – I have my boss here with me too, DI Eddie Carmine.' She walks around to the other side of his desk and props the phone up against Eddie's monitor. Then she sits down.

Eddie screws up his face. He hates video calls. Of course they had been all the rage during the pandemic, but it was one of those annoying technological advances that had now rooted itself into everyday life. Like parking apps and bloody QR codes instead of menus.

'It's Alex, please,' the man says. 'I'm really glad you sent me such good photographs, DS Greene—'

'Becky is fine,' she says, 'and you can thank our scene of crime photographers for that – they are very skilled.'

Eddie is still on the other side of the desk, and Becky scribbles on a Post-it and slaps it down in front of him.

GET ON CAMERA. NOW!!!

Alex Wilson is talking again. 'This is really a very distinctive piece...'

Eddie rolls his eyes. *Really?* he thinks. *How many pieces of jewellery does this man see every day? Every week? It's just a hairclip. Is it really that distinctive?*

He drags his chair round and shoves it up next to Becky's. The man on the screen is about forty, with a mop of dark curly hair and a small pointed beard. *Elf*, Eddie thinks. One of Santa's Little Helpers.

'This is no ordinary hairclip,' the elf says. 'In basic terms, it's a very fancy vintage one...' Alex's cheeks glow pink with his obvious excitement. '... and get this. It's one of a pair.'

Eddie leans forward. 'Go on.'

'I keep a note of all unusual pieces, who brings them in and when, what I've valued them at, outcome of the consultation, etcetera. Sadly I didn't get to buy these hairclips, because the person who had them valued didn't come back. I tried to contact her, because she'd seemed keen to sell, given their worth...'

'Which was?' Becky asks.

'Around ten grand,' Alex says, 'for the pair.'

Eddie blows out a breath. 'Woah.'

Alex nods. 'Exactly. Except she was torn, because they'd belonged to her mother. They were original sixties costume jewellery but their uniqueness makes them valuable. They're Van Cleef & Arpels, signed and numbered. I couldn't quite believe they might be back on the market. They would have cost a bit when they were originally purchased, as they were limited edition, but they are now *very* rare. Only a few left in circulation.' He shrugs. 'Anyway, I tried to contact the woman a couple of times, but there was no reply, so eventually I gave up.'

'Finally,' Eddie mutters. 'Something.'

'Alex,' Becky says, 'do you have the full name of this woman?'

'Yes, of course. It's Karyn Latimer.'

'Thank you,' Becky says. 'This has been really helpful. Is it OK if I call you back if we need anything further?'

Alex nods enthusiastically. 'More than happy to help.'

Becky disconnects the call.

'Well,' Eddie says.

Becky is grinning. 'One of a pair…'

There's a knock at the door, and then it opens, and Joe comes bursting in carrying a sheaf of papers. 'Sorry, boss,' he says. Then he frowns. 'You never close your door.'

'Blame Becky. What have you got?'

He fans the papers out on Eddie's desk. 'Fast-tracked medical notes from all of those potential cold cases.'

'Nice,' Becky says. 'Anything interesting?'

'Do you want the good news or the bad news?' Joe says.

'Get on with it, please.' Eddie is not really in the mood for Joe's dramatics.

'Fine. The good news is that the cause of death is clear in all cases. They all had pre-existing medical conditions, and their heart attacks were exactly that. I don't think anyone is going to authorise re-opening them…'

'And?' Eddie says.

'Right, well, it means we can score off that line of enquiry and focus on the two live cases.' Joe bites his lip. 'Also… I have another bit of good news…' He grins, pleased with himself.

Eddie blinks, awaiting the punchline.

'There is no bad news!'

Eddie contemplates throwing a pen at him like a dart, but catches himself just in time. 'Thank you, Joe. Excellent work. Keep us updated on whatever else it is you're doing out there.'

Joe tuts, then scoops up the papers and marches out. The inflatable snowman has somehow wobbled itself around close to the door, and Joe gives it a little kick as he walks past.

Becky snorts. 'Don't upset Joe, boss. He's one of the good guys.' She gives him a hard look. 'Also, he's right. We can score that off. I wasn't buying the serial killer theory anyway.'

'Me neither. Kept Joe busy though.' Eddie leans back into his chair. 'How are you, Becks? I know you're avoiding telling me more about what's going on with your mum. Have you been back to Ivybridge yet?'

Becky examines her nails. 'Not yet. Allie is doing my head in with the constant texts and voice notes though.' She looks up again. 'Anyway, I'm still waiting for more from you on the mysterious Helena...'

He shakes his head. 'I'm not budging on that right now, but I'll tell you something else interesting though.' He pulls out his desk drawer.

She looks at him, eyebrows raised, waiting.

'The Photographer has been sending me letters.'

'What? When? What do they say?'

He frowns. 'Once a year, for the past six years. Always around this time.' He slides the envelopes across the desk, the open one on top. 'This is the only one I've read. Wants me to visit.' Eddie shrugs. 'Still trying to say that we got it wrong about one of the cases.'

Becky bites her lip. 'We got a confession. For all of it.'

'Apparently to shut us up.'

'Are you buying it?'

Eddie crosses his arms. 'I wasn't completely sure before. Ninety-nine per cent, maybe. But I think the letters might just be a way to pass the time. I'm sure it's all meaningless...'

'Can I read them?'

He nods. 'If you want. But not now. It's got nothing to do with this case. I just thought I should probably tell someone. Just in case anything happens. He sent a visiting order too. Obviously I'm not going.'

Becky takes a sip of her water. 'OK. Back to Helena first though. Could we get more from her now, do you think? I'm worried we're missing something obvious on our potential attacker. The profile is flimsy, at best.'

Eddie tries not to show his irritation. He'd rather Helena wasn't involved at all. 'It's a safe bet that it's the woman from the CCTV. She's seen heading to the room with Andrew Morrison. She's seen leaving the bar with Steve Bell... it's very likely we can join this all up via that Herman handbag.'

'It's *Hermès*, you idiot... and stop being so smug,' Becky says. 'It doesn't suit you.'

She presses a button on Eddie's keyboard and wakes his computer up from its sleep. She clicks and points and within moments, she has the CCTV open. She's much quicker than him at all this stuff. She opens up the footage from both cases, zooms in on the woman in each hotel.

'Both women look very different,' she says. 'We didn't get much from Connor Temple, the barman at the first hotel. He seems to have engaged with her a little, but although his description matches the woman on the CCTV there, it doesn't help us with the woman who may have killed Steve Bell.' She pauses. 'I'm still keen on the disguise theory, though. I mean... look at her walking. Similar gait. I think you're right that it's the same woman. We need to bring Temple in. He was *supposed* to have come in on his day off, but there's no record of him speaking to anyone. He's slipped through the net, and as useless as he will no doubt be, we need to get him to look at this. See if he might notice any similarities that we're missing. Other than the handbag, of course.'

Eddie nods. 'Connor Temple was fairly useless, but you're right – we definitely need to have another word with him. As for the bar staff from the second hotel – they were worse than useless. Three of them on and none of them remembers Steve or the woman he might have gone off with.'

'In fairness, you can see here from the CCTV that the bar is much busier that night. Something like that, you just get on with your work; you take the orders and fire out the drinks. You barely notice the faces.'

'I didn't realise you were such an expert on bar tending.'

She shrugs. 'Worked in the students' union a bit when I was at uni. It was hectic at times, like the night that Steve Bell died—'

Eddie's desk phone rings, and he leans over to check the caller ID. It's internal, from the call handling service, which is basically Miriam from the other side of the office. He hits the speakerphone button.

'Eddie. I've just had a call come in that I think you should take.'

'Go ahead,' Eddie says. He looks over at her through his open office door, but she is facing away from him in the far corner. He's not sure why she didn't just walk over, but maybe he spooked her with the closed door earlier. He'll make sure and talk to her later. Add another shit Christmas joke into the charity sweep. He hasn't told Becky, but he fully intends to win this with one of his five entries so far.

'We got a call from the Blackwood Hotel. They had a couple of functions on last night. One of the few hotels who decided not to cancel. Anyway, they said it's probably nothing, but given the current situation, and the request for them all to be vigilant... they have a barman who was on shift last night that was due in this morning, and he hasn't turned up.'

'I'm not surprised,' Becky says. 'He's probably knackered, doing a late and then an early.'

Eddie's stomach does a little flip. Wasn't that the hotel that Simon was doing his extra shift at last night? Did he come home? He has no idea, because his son's bedroom door was shut when Eddie left this morning, and if he'd been on a late he'd have been dead to the world at seven anyway.

'Right. Yes,' Miriam says, 'and I did ask if this was something he had done before or if it was unusual… but they said he's quite new, so they're not sure. Sorry, I know those are your questions to ask, but I was trying to help.'

Eddie sighs. This could well be nothing. People don't turn up for work all the time, especially in hospitality jobs, when they're overworked and underpaid. He knows that Simon has skived off a few times, although saying that, he has taught his son to be respectful, even when he's being lazy. He always calls in sick.

He'd known they might end up with loads of these waste of time calls, given that they'd put out an alert to all hotels and told them to keep an eye on things, and let the police know if anything unusual happened. He'll have to call Simon now though. Make sure he's OK. He has to be. Eddie is not equipped to deal with another dramatic incident at Christmas featuring one of his family members.

'I assume they've already tried calling him,' Eddie says.

'Yes… several times. I think they want someone to pop round and do a welfare check.'

Eddie barks out a laugh. 'Do they think we've got nothing better to do?'

'Of course, yes... I know.'

Miriam is achingly polite, as always, but Eddie feels like she is working up to something and enjoying the suspense. He is *not* enjoying it, and wants her to get to the point so that he can get on with his day. He was about to ask Becky to go and get them both some breakfast.

'Give us the contact details, please,' Becky says. 'We'll call and get some more info.'

'Oh great, thanks.' Miriam is smiling now – Eddie can hear it in her voice – and he can see it for himself as she swivels around in her chair to face him. She gives him a little wave from across the room. 'The manager is Anja Greenside at the Blackwood Hotel.' She pauses, and Becky scribbles it down on a Post-it from the small stack on Eddie's desk.

'Miriam?' Eddie is getting impatient now.

'Yeah, there's one more thing... and maybe I should have mentioned this at the start.'

Eddie closes his eyes and clamps his mouth shut for a moment before replying.

'What is it, Miriam?'

'Well, it's just that you know I mentioned he only started a couple of days ago? He was working in another hotel before that. The Woodham Hotel and Conference Centre...'

Becky and Eddie lock eyes.

'His name is Connor Temple.'

# 29

## Becky

Becky heads down the stairs first, while Eddie stops off to talk to Miriam and to check what the others are working on. They need to go round to Connor Temple's flat. It's more than likely that he's just overslept, or can't be arsed working his shift, but given his link to the Andrew Morrison case, it's definitely something they need to check out. Besides, given the chat they just had about the woman or *women* on the CCTV, they really need some more information from him. She's annoyed at herself for not chasing this up sooner.

She hears voices before she pushes through the doors into the small reception area. This is not unusual, but it's early in the day for the madness to start. She buzzes herself out through the security door that separates the main station facilities from the baying public and finds herself in the wake of a panicked, dishevelled brunette's screeching.

They have civilian operatives manning the front desk now. There are a couple of them on rotation, and today Matt Bennett has the pleasure of fielding the enquiries from the members of the public who prefer to talk to a real person, rather than submitting their queries online. There is a room at the back where those queries come in, and Becky, on downtime, enjoys popping in to talk to the staff in there to hear about some of the more ludicrous enquiries and reports that pop up. It is a special skill of those in that team, to be able to quickly sift through the detritus and pull out the items that actually need police attention.

Matt is wearing his *I am very patient* face, as the woman carries on with her babbling diatribe. She has her hands laid out flat on the counter and she is very close to invading Matt's personal space. Becky catches Matt's eye as she takes a small step back, and watches as Matt subtly does the same.

'... No,' she says, exasperated. 'It's my boyfriend's *ex* I'm talking about. She hasn't been at work for the last couple of days, and I know he was trying to protect her by not saying anything bad, but her behaviour is definitely weird... and it's not like her to be weird, because she's actually one of those brainy science types, and she mostly keeps to herself, but Harry's definitely been worried, and after the things I've learned about her now...' She lets her sentence trail off, and her shoulders slump. She's exhausted herself.

Becky steps in. This is not her job. Not really. She has no idea yet what is going on. But the woman is clearly distressed and needs to be calmed down before she works herself up any further. 'Would you like to take a seat? I can get you a glass of water, and then maybe we can start from the beginning?'

Eddie won't be pleased about this, but he's not here yet so he's clearly been held up talking to the others. Becky might as well make herself useful.

Matt flashes Becky a grateful smile as the woman turns to face her, finally noticing that there is someone behind her. She's pretty, but looks tired, with dark circles under her eyes and the remnants of smeared eyeliner. Becky casts her eyes quickly over the woman's clothing, noticing that her cotton joggers and fleece seem a little too big for her. She is wearing low-heeled sparkly pumps and is carrying a small black clutch. She smells slightly stale, like old perfume and the remnants of metabolising alcohol, but mixed with the fresh tang of clean clothes.

Becky suspects that the woman did not sleep at her own place last night. This is walk-of-shame in a man's leisurewear. Some alcohol fuelled drama that hopefully can be resolved once the hangover wears off. Becky gestures to the seating area, which is an L-shaped industrial grey sofa, with a laminate table at the join. Various leaflets are scattered across it, but other than that the place is quite tidy.

'Sit down there. I'll be back in a second.'

She watches as the woman sits down on the sofa and leans her arms on her knees. She glances at the entrance, then drops her head.

There is a water cooler in the room that leads off from the reception desk, and Becky hurries in and fills up a paper cup.

When she comes back, Eddie is standing at the end of the counter, talking to Matt about football. She's sure Eddie isn't particularly interested in the sport, but it's the universal language of men making small talk.

'There you are,' he says. 'We'll have to grab something to eat on the way. I'm starving.'

Becky cocks her head towards the woman on the sofa. 'Just give me a few minutes, will you?' She hands her the water and sits down on the other sofa. The woman takes it and gulps it down in one. 'Big night?'

The woman blows out a breath. Smiles painfully. 'Work Christmas party. You know what it's like…'

Becky nods, remembering her last major hangover and feeling strong sympathy for this woman. 'Did something happen? Sorry, maybe you could tell me your name? I'm Becky, I'm one of the detectives here.'

'Joanne. And yes, I guess you could say that something happened. It's my boyfriend. Harry was at the party with me last night, and he's—'

*Oh god,* Becky thinks. *Don't tell me he's gone missing…* It was only a matter of time before someone was reported missing or another body was found during this increasingly un-festive period.

Joanne stops talking as the doors to the entrance swish open, bringing with them a blast of cold air from outside. 'Oh thank god! Here he is. Maybe he should tell you what's been going on?'

Becky tries to remain patient, now that it seems that this is nothing urgent at all. She smiles patiently as the man walks into the station.

Harry is good looking in a slightly geeky kind of way, a tall man in similar casual sports gear to his companion. Becky looks down at Joanne's joggers and sees that they are rolled up at the bottom, which now confirms her earlier suspicion that these are not Joanne's clothes. 'Sorry,' he says. 'Couldn't find a parking space. All the visitor slots were full, so I had to go around the corner.'

The station has limited the visitors' car parking slots on purpose. It's not ideal, but the whole point of the online reporting thing is to avoid visitors so that they can all get on with their work in peace. Becky is regretting getting involved in this now, but feels like she can't just walk away until she knows what's happened. Eddie is looking over at her, arms crossed and brows knitted in his characteristic impatient stance.

'It's about my ex-girlfriend,' Harry says. He glances at Joanne, who gives him a small nod.

'I think she's got one of those bags... like the one on the news report about the man who died in the hotel?'

Becky feels the hair on the back of her neck stand up. Joanne had been going on about this woman acting strangely, hadn't she?

Eddie has clearly overheard, and he walks over to join them. 'Why don't we go through to one of the interview rooms? Do this properly?' He turns to Matt at the desk, who is now looking considerably more interested too. 'Call DC Dickson and get him to send a car round to check on Connor Temple, please. Then bring us some teas, Matt. Is that OK?'

Matt nods, quickly checking how everyone takes it, before Eddie swipes his fob to open the security door and Becky ushers Harry and Joanne through in front of her. This could all be nothing, of course. As she had mentioned before when the topic was discussed, plenty of women own fake designer bags. It didn't mean anything on its own, but something about Joanne's distress has definitely piqued Becky's interest.

They go into the nicest of the interview rooms, not that any of them are particularly luxurious, but this one at least has been painted in the last decade and the seats have slightly padded bottoms, instead of the plastic ones used in the other rooms.

Harry and Joanne sit on one side of the desk, and Becky notices that Joanne slips her hand into his. 'Are you arresting us?' she says, her face pale.

'Of course not,' Becky says. 'Now… why don't you start from the beginning?'

# 30
# Eddie

Eddie lets Becky take the lead on questioning the couple. He sits back in his seat, observing their body language. The lad is calm, but the woman seems on edge. But as they have mentioned already, they were at a party last night. Eddie suspects that she might have partied a bit harder than her boyfriend did.

'If we could just start with some basic details,' Becky says, a clean notepad in front of her, 'just to put everything into context. Then we can go into a bit more detail about why it is that you've decided to come in this morning?'

The man shuffles in his seat. 'Sure. I'm Harry Finch. I work with Joanne'—he glances around at his companion—'Joanne Reid... over at Innoxia Research. We had the office Christmas party in the Blackwood Hotel last night. It was superhero themed—'

'Which is why I currently look like a homeless person,' Joanne says, with a brief, nervous giggle. 'I stayed over at Harry's last night, and I, er, I forgot to take anything to change into.'

Eddie watches as Becky underlines, and then double-underlines the name of the company they work at. He recognises the name – it had come up already in Becky's searches. Also, the Blackwood is the hotel that Connor – presumed sleeping – and Simon – also presumed sleeping – were working at last night. It was all go in that place then, but when too much alcohol is involved, there is inevitably drama.

'So I'm guessing this is a fairly new relationship?' Becky looks from Harry to Joanne, and they both blush. 'Given you didn't have any of your stuff round at Harry's?'

Joanne nods. Bites her lip. 'It was my first time round there…'

'… and where is there, exactly?'

Harry states his address and Becky writes it down. 'Do you live alone, Harry?'

He nods. 'I was lucky to get the place as a new build. Ten years ago now. Prices have rocketed.'

Becky nods. 'So tell me about this ex-girlfriend.'

Harry steals a glance at Joanne. 'Just tell them everything you told me.' She pats his leg under the table.

Harry sucks in a breath. 'Her name is Heather Brody. I've known her for about two years. We were friends for quite a while before we started going out, and, well, she's always been quite a private person. Mainly liked to just come round mine, and I'd cook for us—'

Becky writes the name down, circling the surname. 'Did you spend time at her place at all?'

He shakes his head. 'No. In fact, until last week, I hadn't been round to hers at all. Well…' He pauses, and the blush from earlier creeps further across his face, making his ears glow red. 'I did sometimes drive round there and sit outside her flat.'

Joanne pulls her hand away from his knee. Her mouth falls open a little. Becky writes this down, staying casual, but Eddie knows she will be thinking the same as he is right now.

'That could be seen as unwanted attention you know, Harry…' she says, keeping her voice level.

He looks utterly mortified. 'I know.' He turns to Joanne, who looks like she is regretting her night spent with her potentially obsessive paramour. 'It's not like that.' He turns back to face Becky, then shifts his gaze between her and Eddie. 'We'd been together for six months! Luke said—'

'Who's Luke?' Eddie leans a little closer. This lad is starting to annoy him now. The door opens and Matt hands Eddie a tray, with four beige cups of brown sludge in them. He puts it on the table, but no one takes one.

Harry shifts his gaze to Eddie now. 'He's a friend from work. He… reckoned that Heather was messing me about. Thought maybe she had another boyfriend. That maybe she lived with him or something.'

Becky puts her pen down. 'And does she? Have another boyfriend, I mean? What happened when you went around there last week? I assume she invited you round, at last? That she maybe had her reasons for not doing so before?'

Harry puffs up his cheeks then breathes out. 'No, she didn't invite me, as such. She's been off work, and I was worried, so I went round…'

He pauses, but Becky says nothing, letting him speak. Eddie taps his fingers on the table in front of him.

'Her flat isn't that nice. I think maybe that was why she hadn't invited me before. I, um, I had a look around when she went in the shower. I didn't see any suggestion that anyone else lived there.'

Joanne makes a sound in her throat that Eddie interprets, based on her pinched face, as *disgusted*.

Becky picks up her pen again. 'I'm guessing this is how you came across the handbag?'

Harry nods. He looks absolutely gutted at the way the questioning has gone. Eddie imagines him and Joanne battling over this in bed this morning, debating about whether to tell the police about this Heather Brody because of one tiny little thing – a handbag that many women might own. Maybe Joanne thinking it was significant. Maybe Harry thinking he would end up revealing his underhand behaviour and worrying that she might not like it. He was right about that. Eddie didn't much like it either. But the handbag thing was worth delving into a bit further. Plus the company name had clearly set off Becky's radar, and he wanted to talk to her about this after he'd got rid of this unfortunately hungover pair.

'What was it about the bag that made it stick in your mind?' Becky says.

'It just wasn't her sort of thing. Red crocodile skin? I mean, I assumed it was fake... I hoped.' He crosses his arms. 'It was ostentatious. She was a fairly basic dresser. She didn't go anywhere flash, I wondered why she had it.'

'A gift, maybe? Something for special occasions.'

Harry shrugs. 'Sure. To be honest, I'd kind of forgotten about it, until it got mentioned last night and I saw a photo of it, and matched it up with the photo I took of hers. I'd thought maybe I could buy her a Christmas present to match it, but then I realised I couldn't...'

'Because then she would know you'd been poking about in her room?' Eddie says, keeping his voice level.

Harry glances at Joanne, whose face is thunderous now. 'Yes,' he mutters. Joanne moves her chair slightly away from him.

'How did it come up last night?' Becky raises her voice a little, re-focussing them all on the reason they're here.

Harry shifts in his chair. 'Like I said, we were at a Christmas party in a hotel. It kind of came up during conversation. You know… that there might be someone in there looking for their next victim?'

Joanne finds something interesting to look at on her lap.

'Was it you who mentioned the bag, Joanne?' Eddie asks her.

She looks at him. Nods. 'I saw it on the news. I mentioned it at the table, and most of the guys didn't know what the bag looked like, so I showed it around… and then Harry said he needed some air.' She side-eyes him. 'He didn't mention it to me again until later. Back at his.'

'I just wanted to go home,' Harry says. 'I waited for Joanne in the car park and got myself a bit spooked.'

'Right,' Becky says, 'and Heather… was she at this party?'

Harry shakes his head. 'That's why we broke up. I wanted her to come, kept asking her and she kept saying no. Said she hated parties. I bought tickets anyway, thought I could change her mind. She saw the costume hanging up before I had a chance to explain, to try and persuade her.'

Joanne is throwing Harry daggers now. 'You got that Poison Ivy costume for her? The one that I was wearing last night…?'

Harry nods. He looks utterly miserable. Like someone who's about to lose his second girlfriend in a week.

Becky taps her work phone, opens an app and taps a few more times. Eddie watches as Harry and Joanne look increasingly uncomfortable. This is going to be a very awkward drive home for them.

'Does Heather ever clip her hair up using one of these?'

She turns her phone around and lays it on the table. It's opened on one of the exhibits pages, showing the small, curled diamond hairclip that they picked up from Andrew Morrison's bedside.

Harry peers down at the phone. 'Well, not that I recall. Again, it looks a bit too fancy for her.' He looks away again. 'She did have a velvet jewellery box on her dressing table though. It was pretty old looking, and the catch was stiff and I couldn't open it.'

Joanne shoots him another dagger. 'You had a right old rummage in her things, didn't you?'

Becky puts a hand under the table beside Eddie, sticks her thumb up.

'Well,' Eddie says, giving the couple a wide grin. 'This has been very helpful. Both of you. Thanks so much for coming in. If you wouldn't mind giving us Heather's address, and if you could both also leave your contact details with Matt, at the desk, we'll be in touch again if we need anything else.'

Joanne's eyebrows shoot up. Her hand reaches towards Harry again, and he grabs it. She might be annoyed with him, but she is also loving being involved in this potential bit of drama. 'So you think Heather might be involved in this? I mean, I kind of thought we were being over-cautious, mentioning the bag...'

'You did exactly the right thing.' Becky stands up. 'Heather is definitely someone we'd like to talk to.'

She waits until the couple have left the interrogation room before she turns to Eddie, her eyes questioning. 'Well?'

'Well,' he says back. 'I think we might have a busy morning, and it's sadly not going to involve any breakfast.'

# 31

# Becky

'I've messaged Joe,' Becky says, as they walk along the first floor corridor towards the lair of the analysts. 'Told him to call that manager from the Woodham Hotel and Conference Centre...'

'Keith Walters.'

'That's him. Thought as Connor had been working there for a while there might be someone on the staff who could pop round, see if he's OK.'

Eddie nods. 'Good idea – although I also told Matt at the desk to get Joe on the case himself – we need a welfare check.'

'Agreed. Joe is also checking on that name from the jewellers – Karyn Latimer. It was years ago that she visited him, and it might be nothing, but it's worth running it, right?'

'Of course,' Eddie says. 'You circled the name of that drugs company too. You mentioned it before, too. Care to elaborate?'

'Yes,' she says. 'After this.'

They stop outside the large, open-plan IT room, which has as many desks as the CID office, but twice as many

231

people crammed into it. There are various sub-departments in here, but Becky doesn't need to check with Eddie about where they're headed.

Jonah Abboud and Julie Peters have commandeered a section in the far corner of the room, with their desks in an L-shape and their bank of monitors forming a partition down both sides. Becky can just see the tops of their heads, both adorned with oversized headphones.

Julie looks up first, sensing their arrival. 'The dream team.' She takes off her headphones and lays them on the desk in front of her, clicking her mouse to pause or shut down whatever it was she was looking at. Jonah notices them too, and slides his headphones off, draping them around his neck. He gives Becky a slow smile, and she feels her heart rate do a little bounce. She looks away for a moment, regaining her composure. Jonah really does have an effect on people.

She turns back to the tail end of Eddie's scowl.

'We need to look at the Andrew Morrison CCTV again. Pretty please.' She feels the weight of Eddie's stare, and gives herself a mental shake. *Stop. Flirting.*

'Of course.' Julie slides a couple of seats over from the wall and positions them next to her and Jonah.

'Cheers.' Eddie wedges himself in between the two analysts, even though there is less space there than on the seat at the other side of Julie.

Becky can see amusement in Julie's eyes, and Becky gives her a small eye roll. 'I want to compare some of the stills against this woman, if we can.' She's looked up Heather Brody on the PNC and found nothing, which is not a surprise. She's popped up on LinkedIn though, and although Becky's not sure how current the profile picture is, it's a start. Once they've decided if this is a lead worth pursuing, they can get another photograph.

'Ping that over, will you?' Julie says.

Becky shares it via Bluetooth, then taps out a message to Joe: *Talk to Matt at the desk. Follow up with Harry Finch. Request recent photographs of Heather Brody. Works at Innoxia Research. No luck on quick search other than basic LinkedIn. See what you can find? And let me know about hairclip woman too, please.*

Joe is the resident social media and search engine whizz in the department, and although there is an actual department for this, Becky doesn't want this info going any wider than CID and this corner of the room. Not just yet.

Both Jonah and Julie pull up the case notes and link into the system. 'Any idea what timeframe you're after?' Jonah starts flicking through various timestamped stills. 'Is it the bar to elevator part, or the person sneaking out later?'

'Let's start with the bar,' Eddie says. 'We need to go through this frame by frame, for every second that you have this woman on screen.'

'Sure thing, boss.' Jonah starts tapping away.

Meanwhile, Julie starts with some of the stills of the woman's partial face, and tries to increase the quality. She saves the LinkedIn photo, and clicks on a few options, before a timer wheel pops up and then she leans back in her seat.

'I'm still playing around with this system, but remember that work that Ashlie Long kicked off? The national crime scene photo matching thing?'

'Of course,' Becky says. It had been instrumental in them solving a major case. It was meant to be the next big thing, but budget cuts meant the project went unfinished.

233

'I think Ashlie got whipped off to bigger and better things. She was really very good at tracking people down via electronic means.'

'Something spooky?'

Julie laughs. 'I could tell you, but I'd have to kill you. Anyway, she left one hell of a legacy. Honestly, this facial recognition stuff is pure geek ecstasy.'

'Will it find us a match?'

Julie shrugs. 'Sadly we're at the mercy of the CCTV quality, and quite frankly, this stuff is quite bad.'

Becky sighs. She knew it was too good to be true, but when a carrot gets dangled in front of you, it's hard not to want to snatch it. The on-screen timer is still running, only a quarter way through.

'I think we should leave you to it… Can you let me know if you get anything? Even if it's just a partial match, or whatever. However that thing works.'

'Sure.'

She stands up to leave, waits for Eddie to take the hint. He is sitting very close to Jonah, and she's starting to think she might pass out from the stench of testosterone in the air in this small space.

'He absolutely reeks of cheap aftershave,' Eddie says, as they walk down the corridor towards the exit. Becky says nothing, but she laughs quietly to herself.

'Let's go and have a word with the elusive Ms Brody, shall we? We can call it a welfare check.'

Eddie has decided to drive, which is his way of exerting his manliness after an alpha-male battle like the one she just witnessed. She quite enjoyed it, but it's also left her feeling confused about how she feels about both men. Jonah is nice, and clearly available and interested. He's a civilian too, which makes things a lot less complex. Eddie is her boss. Also, he's too old for her, in years and in *baggage*, and he's definitely not interested in her as anything except a working partner. Right? She's going to have to debate this with Joe and Maria in the pub sometime soon, when they all actually have time to do anything leisurely. Maria has dropped hints before about Eddie but Becky always changes the subject. Perhaps it was finally time to stop doing that.

They pull up outside Heather's flat, but it looks from the road as though there is no one home. The rooms are all in darkness, and at this time of the year, with the natural light fairly low most of the day, you'd expect to see a glow. It also just feels empty, like no one has opened the curtains for a few days. They park the car anyway and go and press the buzzer. Eddie holds it down for longer than is necessary, but no one answers. No one opens the door.

Becky frowns and steps back a bit on the path to look upstairs again. Heather's is the upstairs flat in the two storey block, but there is no sign of life in the whole building. 'We should've asked Harry if there's anywhere else she was likely to be. Parent? Friends?'

Eddie pushes his hands into his pockets. 'Or maybe she just went to work today? Or is staying somewhere else to avoid her persistent borderline stalker of an ex?'

'Do you think he was that bad?'

Eddie shrugs. 'Weird energy, as the kids say. I'm sure he's harmless. But he's made quite the leap, practically accusing his ex of being a murderer, just because she didn't want to dress up in a rubber suit and drink cheap wine with him in a hotel function room.'

'You're right. All that sitting around outside her house smacks of desperate rather than dangerous. He knew very little about her, by the sounds of things. Private is one thing, but when you're seeing someone, you should kind of know them well enough to be invited around to their flat after six months.'

'Agreed. Neurotic ex overreaction. That poor girl he was with today. Not only did she clearly feel as rough as a badger's arse after their night out, she's just found out her new boyfriend is actually a bit of a shit. All that devotion he claims, but then he hooks up with the next available female who could fit into the Poison Ivy suit? Urgh.' He pauses. 'Incidentally... who is Poison Ivy?'

Becky laughs. 'Therein lies the irony. The character is a botanist and biochemist. She's like the superhero world's "hand of god" – she only kills those who deserve it.'

'With plants?'

'Yes... poisonous plants.'

'Interesting. Maybe Harry knows more than he realises. Let's keep her on the radar. See what we can dig up. Get it? See what I did there?'

'Dig up. Cool joke, Dad.'

A message comes in from Joe as they climb back into the car. *No luck on the barman. Didn't have any workmates, apparently. Reading between the lines, I don't think he was very well liked at that hotel. Keith sounded quite pleased that he'd moved on elsewhere before they re-opened. Sent a car round too, but they got called away to something more urgent. Let me know if you want me to follow up myself? Also, still looking for Brody. Will report back on that and the jeweller thing ASAP.*

Becky reads the message out to Eddie. 'I think we need to swing around there. Do this welfare check ourselves.'

As Eddie drives she opens up the list of pharmaceutical and biotechnology companies she'd started showing him in the office the day before. She scans through her list of notes, the names and the drugs, the pipelines. The medical conditions they were all hoping to treat. She stops, re-reads one of the names. 'Harry said he worked at Innoxia Research.' She clicks onto their website, and the same page comes up from before.

She recognises the logo straight away.

From the merchandise at the care home.

This was the company that was running the clinical trials. Ethical analgesics. Just the thing to knock someone out. Kill them, in fact. Naturally. And because the drugs weren't yet widely available, it would be almost impossible to find them via a tox screen.

# 32

# The Party Girl

I'm glad that Lauren's not on shift this morning. Hopefully she's taken some time off work to have a good think to herself about what she really wants from this job. She calls herself a nurse, but does she really want to help anyone? She works in a facility where most of the residents don't even know she's there. If it hadn't been for her help, I might consider getting rid of her, but truth is, she's not worth it.

I come in the side door as I usually do early on, and I bump into Gloria in the visitors' lounge while I'm getting myself a coffee.

'Oh, morning,' she says, that sweet fake smile on her face.

I used to think she was one of the better ones, but honestly now that I know the truth about what they've all been hiding from me all this time, I'm really not so sure.

'Hey,' I say, not sounding particularly friendly.

'Listen... I'm glad I bumped into you. I was hoping you might be in early. I... um... I spoke to Lauren.'

I huff out a breath. 'You know what I know then. About my mysterious benefactor. Guess what, Gloria? He's not a very nice man. I don't think your Mr Wade is either. Not if he's friends with that waste of air. You know he was the one who messed up everything for my dad at work? The destruction that led to his suicide? The suicide that led to my mum having to do what she had to do...' I let my sentence trail off. There's no point in this. I don't know how much of any of it Gloria knows. She's a nobody, in the grand scheme of things.

She swallows hard. 'Actually I wanted to talk to you about something else...' She sits down on one of the sofas, gestures for me to do the same. I don't really like this room. It's all a bit twee, with the florals and the nice carpet, the fresh flowers on the coffee table next to the glossy magazines. I come in here for coffee, and always found it to be adequate, but obviously now I know about the secret staff Nespresso machine behind the reception desk, I think this stuff tastes like pond water.

Not that I intend to be drinking it for too much longer.

'It's about what Mr Wade said, about there being no hope that...' She clears her throat. 'You know, what he said about your mum not getting better.'

'Go on.'

'Well, as you know, I've worked here as long as you've been coming here to visit your mum... and while, yes, usually, there's very little hope because most people don't wake up... well, some do. Someone just woke up this week.'

I sit up straighter. 'Who? How long had they been under? Did they have the same prognosis as my mum?'

Gloria shifts in her seat. 'They've been under for six years. I'm probably not meant to say, but I thought it was important that you know so that you can make the right decision for Karyn, you know? Maybe get a second opinion or something...'

'Who woke up, Gloria?'

She bites her lip. 'I can't tell you who. They're kind of famous. Anyway, it's really early days, but—'

'Someone famous has been in *here*? For six years?' I'm not convinced about this. Wouldn't there have been paparazzi and whatnot, trying to weasel their way in? Celeb friends coming to visit?

Gloria nods. 'Pretty much. Since the hospital released her a few months after the accident. She's in the last room down the opposite corridor from Karyn. I know you come in via the garden entrance mostly, so you'd never have any reason to pass her room…and, well, the family have asked us to keep it quiet. You know what it's like. We'd have reporters sneaking in, pretending to be visitors. We try very hard to be discreet here.'

I laugh at that. 'You're definitely that. You managed to keep the secret of who was paying my mum's bills for long enough… until he decided he didn't want to pay anymore.'

'I'm so sorry. I just thought you should know. I thought it might help.' She pauses. 'Also, I don't know why you've never requested one of the paid trial places from Innoxia. They gave one to someone just last week.'

'Busy times,' I say. 'I've been kind of pre-occupied.' I don't tell her that I've never thought to ask about a paid trial place, because I didn't realise that my own 'free' place had an expiry date.

I stand up, smile at her. 'This has helped a lot, actually. Thank you.'

She stays in the visitors' room, watching me leave. I'm glad she's told me, but I'm a realist. All of the doctors told me from the start that the longer the patient stays under, the less chance of them waking up. Plus, my mum's injuries were severe. By rights, she shouldn't have survived.

Sometimes I wish she hadn't. Especially now that I know that it's Brendan's filthy money that's been keeping her alive.

Back in Mum's room, things are just as I'd left them the day before, and the day before that, and the day before that too. And all the days before that. The only change of recent note is the ventilator, of course. I knew we were nearing the end when that became the only option. But it's hard, after coming here for all these years, to imagine what I might do with myself when I've got no reason to visit. I can't see myself as anything other than what I am now: a grieving daughter, visiting her hopeless mother. I just hope I've done enough payback to help my mum move on to whatever comes after this earthly life – if anything.

I've told her about all the parties. Of course I have. I know that mostly they say she can't hear me, but I'm not so sure about that. I watch all the machines that monitor her. I watch how there is the tiniest blip of activity when I tell her the things I've done. She hasn't moved at all. Not even a reflex. Believe me, I watch very closely. But when I close my eyes, sometimes I imagine that her mouth curls up into the tiniest of smiles. That maybe she whispers to me, her voice a wisp in the wind: *you did good, my girl.*

Things took an interesting turn with Brendan and then Connor. Brendan in many ways was the most important of them all. Connor... well, he was mostly collateral damage. If only he hadn't been so greedy. He could have pretended not to recognise me. But after I found what was in his bathroom cabinet, I feel like I've just done another favour for the females of Woodham. Another sleazy creep off the streets. Did he really think I was going to fall for his pathetic Rohypnol game? Flunitrazepam is the chemical name for it. He actually had the proper prescription type in his cabinet, his name on it and everything. Although the writing on the packaging wasn't in English, other than the label. Portuguese, I think. I'd love to know which GPs are still actually prescribing it for severe insomnia, given how it's mostly used now. And giving it to someone like him? It's a shame I don't have time to check out the prescribing GP. Pay them a little visit. Ask them why they're prescribing the water-soluble date-rape friendly tablet that the UK does not legally allow. I look over at Mum. Her skin is paler than before. It's almost translucent now. She's slipping away, and I know I need to let her go.

I'm going to be so lonely without her, but I have to release us both from Brendan's hold.

My phone buzzes and I take it out of my pocket. I've no idea who can be sending me a message as I rarely get messages from anyone these days. I haven't been at work, and they keep sending me emails, which are easy to ignore. I blocked most of my contacts the other day. I've had enough of the fake friends.

There is a message from a number I don't recognise. Several missed calls too. I don't have alerts for unknown calls. I open the message: *I'm so sorry, I've been trying to call you. I fucked up… I told the police about that fake designer bag of yours. I saw it in your room when I came round the other day. I'M SO SORRY! I was mad at you. I'll help you. Tell me where you are? Please? The police are looking for you too. Hx*

Oh Harry, you stupid little prick. I don't know what I was thinking getting involved with him. He was a distraction, nothing more. He made me nice food sometimes, but

243

he was too needy and I let things go too far with him. Let him get too close, although really, I didn't let him close at all. Except the once. I shouldn't have let him in that day. I should've known he was the type to snoop through my things.

I thought I had a bit more time. Enough time for one more party. There are two options tonight. A standard one, at the Garden Suites Lodge, where it will be easy to blend in, and then there's the big one, at the Cedars Hotel. Grand and flash and a perfect end to my campaign. Of course I knew I wouldn't be able to do it forever. And this place has a roof garden. I'm considering a very dramatic finale for myself. Like I said – there's nothing for me without Mum.

But can I still go ahead now? If the police are on to me, they'll either find me, or they'll stop me. They'll get the hotel to cancel the party, like they did after I dealt with that lawyer. Typical arrogant bastard. If only these men were polite. If only they saw me as more than a body with holes they wanted to explore. If they were just *nice*, then I wouldn't have to be *naughty*.

You fucking idiot, Harry. I should have dealt with him in the car park when I had the chance. They will be closing in on me soon.

I pick up the old velvet jewellery box that I'd brought in from my flat. I want to brush Mum's hair, put the hairclips in to make her look nice, this one last time. I open the box. The hairclip sparkles under the harsh overhead light, and I gasp. My head swims.

There is only one clip in the box.

I close my eyes, thinking back to that night I last wore it. In the room with the lawyer. His hands grappling for my head, trying to yank my hair as he flailed on the bed, eyes

244

wide with terror and confusion. The police have had the hairclip the whole time. Probably with my hair in it too. They haven't found me yet, because there was no way to trace me with it. But when they do find me, the forensic evidence will help seal my fate. That, plus the handbag that Harry has kindly let them know about. It's not fake though. Mum's clients were the real deal.

*Well, Harry, I guess you just forced my hand.*

I don't want Mum here for this. I can't have her around when they catch me. The staff have told me over the years that she is unaware of me being there with her, but I don't believe them. She knows. I've told her everything.

I am free… and the best thing I can do now is free her too.

I don't stop to think anymore. To wallow. I walk around the bed and unplug every single plug. There are a few beeps, and then the horrible wheezing whine stops. Then I lean over my mum and fasten the hairclip on one side. Her hair is thin, and the hairclip sparkles brightly against her delicate scalp. Then I take a step back, and gently remove the breathing-machine that is clamped to her face. I kiss her on the cheek. Her skin is so soft. A tear rolls down my face and lands on her, and I carefully wipe it away.

'Bye, Mum,' I whisper. 'I love you.'

I close my eyes, and I hear her saying: *I love you too.*

# 33
## Becky

'I definitely think there's something in my unlicensed experimental drug theory.' Becky is still reading the website for Innoxia Research.

Eddie takes a roundabout too fast, and she slides across the seat, banging her head against the window. 'Alright, Lewis Hamilton. Might want to ease up on the gas a bit there.'

'Sorry.' The car slows down as he takes them off the main road and along the quieter street towards Connor's flat. 'Just can't wait to visit this lovely part of town again.' He pulls up outside the building. It looks dead and grey, as it did before. 'Sounds like you're on to something, Becks. Do you want to message Joe, get him on the case? Or wait until we check this out and get back to the station.'

She frowns. It's a dilemma. She wants the glory, obviously, but also, Joe is in the office today and could be following up on this. Calling Innoxia Research and finding out who they might need to talk to. She decides that expediency is the right call, taps him another message. 'I can pick it up when we get back. We can work together on it.'

'Cool.' Eddie is already out of the car. 'Put your coat on,' he says, 'it's Baltic out here.'

She's glad of the coat as they stand outside Connor's flat, pressing the buzzer and getting no answer. Sleet is drifting at them sideways, hitting her cheeks with a soft, wet flutter. She shoves her hands deep into her pockets. 'Are we just going to waste time pressing buzzers this week, standing out in the cold? I want to know why the patrol from earlier buggered off without checking this out properly.'

Eddie laughs. 'You and me both, Becks. If it wasn't a life or death emergency, I'll have someone's bollocks for baubles. And yes, before you say anything, no we do not have enough patrol cars. Cuts, Becks. Those were the first things to be *streamlined*. Which is incredibly useful, obviously.' He presses the buzzer again. 'No wonder the public hate us.'

Becky pushes the door and it springs open. 'Security, eh?'

Eddie follows her inside, and they make their way to Connor's front door. Then Becky stops, turns to him with a hand raised out in front. 'Hang on. Didn't he say he was planning to ditch the hotel work and do a ski season? Maybe that's where he is. He's probably got his phone switched off to avoid roaming charges, if he's in Europe.'

'So, what… just like that? After a late shift last night? He's packed up and left?'

'Maybe he had an early flight. Some of those budget airlines fly out at the crack of dawn. Especially at this time of year.'

'You might well be right. But let's check out the flat first, just in case.'

Eddie holds up a hand to knock on the door, then turns back to Becky, who spots it at the same time. This door is open too.

'Okaaaay,' she says. 'Should we call this in?'

Eddie is wearing his dilemma face. She knows it well. It's a kind of pinched mouth, scrunched up to one side. Eyebrows slightly raised. 'He might not be here. Don't want to waste anyone else's time when we're literally on the doorstep, do we?'

She shrugs. 'You're the boss.'

He pushes the door open with his elbow. The flat is cloaked in semi-darkness, suggesting closed curtains. He takes a step inside, and she follows, sniffing the air. It smells stale, but nothing alarming has entered her nostrils yet – and she's usually the first one to sniff out a scent of death. She's almost as good as the police dogs, but it can be annoying as she's always convinced that something in her fridge has gone off. One time, there was a tiny sliver of camembert in there that had not been well-wrapped. It smelled worse than a two-day-old corpse. She's smelling very little in this flat though. She wonders if maybe she's coming down with a cold. Or worse. That bloody COVID seems to have got worse again since people have mostly stopped worrying about it.

'Connor? Are you awake? It's Eddie Carmine and Becky Greene. We spoke a few days ago?' He takes a few more steps into the hall. 'Sorry to wake you...'

Eddie walks down towards the living room, while Becky takes a look in the kitchen. It's quite neat and tidy, but there are two wine bottles and two glasses on the counter by the sink. So he did come home last night, it seems. There's a prescription packet lying on the table, and she takes a pen out of her pocket, uses it to poke the box, flipping it over so she can read the label. It's made out to Connor, but the rest of the wording on the box is not written in English.

She takes a photo of it with her phone, so she can check what it is later.

The kitchen clock ticks loudly in the quiet room.

'Eddie – anything?' She walks back into the hall. Eddie is standing at the entrance to what she assumes is a bedroom. His face is different now. His eyes are steely. His mouth drawn into a tight line. He gestures towards the room with a tiny nod of his head.

Becky feels that familiar fizzing burst of adrenaline, the nausea kicking in as she walks towards Eddie. Then she turns to look into the bedroom, and sees that Connor is still in bed, like they first suspected. The big fluffy robe that he'd been wearing last time they saw him is lying crumpled on the floor, like a skinned bear. The steps that she's been trained to take in these instances scroll across her brain like a newsflash ticker.

*Preservation of life.*

*Check if the victim is still alive.*

She takes a few steps into the room, leans down to the bed where Connor is lying, facing out towards the door. She can smell it now. What she should have been able to smell outside.

Death.

She puts her fingers to his neck, searching for a pulse that she knows is not there.

His blank staring eyes were the first giveaway.

The bloody mess that used to be the back of his head, is the second.

# 34
## Eddie

They'd had to leave the flat and wait in the car after they'd called it in, but luckily the crime scene officers had arrived fairly quickly, along with Stuart and Keir, and a couple of uniforms who'd come to assist. Becky had spent the waiting time on the phone talking to Joe, who was looking into her Innoxia Research theory.

Eddie had gone round the other flats in the building to see if there was anyone there who had seen or heard anything unusual, but there was no one in. A proper door-to-door would be done, but once they'd handed over to forensics, their part here was done and they had to hand it over to another team. It couldn't be helped that they'd already potentially contaminated the crime scene. Eddie knows he'll have a shit tonne of paperwork to deal with on that – but he maintains that it was the right move to check on Connor themselves.

It's just a pity they were several hours too late.

Dr Maria – one of the first to arrive at the scene after they had called it in – had given an estimated time of death of around four to six hours ago, and from what they had seen in the bed, initial suggestions were that he had died in it given the blood spatter behind him on the bed and the walls, and the baseball bat that had been tucked into bed beside him. A quick search from Becky had revealed that the prescription drugs in the kitchen were generic branded Rohypnol. Hopefully not enough time had passed for this to be eliminated from his bloodstream, assuming he'd taken, or been given any. They were his drugs, and he may legitimately have them for insomnia, but as Becky had discovered, this particular brand is not prescribed routinely in the UK, due to the tablets being breakable and water soluble... and perfect for spiking drinks with.

He'd asked the technicians to check how many were still in the box. He had a feeling that the person who did this might have taken some away with them.

Now, back at the station, in the meeting room that smells of Miriam's freshly baked cinnamon rolls, Eddie is updating the wider team on this latest development.

'We know from the CCTV footage that it's highly likely Connor saw and spoke to Andrew Morrison's killer on Sunday night at the Woodham Hotel and Conference Centre. We now suspect that he came across her again last night, at the Blackwood Hotel, though whether she sought him out or it was simply that he ended up working in the wrong bar, at the wrong time, we can't be sure.' He pauses, checks his notes. 'What we do have now, is a strong lead.' He clicks on the pointer and a slide appears. Eddie doesn't usually piss about making slides for his updates, but he wants to get this face out there for everyone to see.

'This is Dr Heather Brody. She's a research scientist at Innoxia Research. This small biotechnology company, as Becky and Joe have uncovered, specialises in analgesics and anaesthetics made from natural sources. They currently have no licensed drugs, but several are in their pipeline, many at advanced stages in the clinical trials process – one of which is being conducted at the Ivybridge Care Home.' He glances over at Becky, but she keeps her expression neutral.

'Heather's name came up because her ex-boyfriend was concerned about her not being at work much lately... and possibly because he's a bit over-attentive, but we won't worry about that for now. He was mostly concerned, because she has one of these.' He clicks again, and a photograph of the red crocodile skin handbag pops up on the screen. 'We're trying to track her down. So far, we've established that she's not at work, and she's not at home, and that she doesn't have many friends. But we will find her.'

The DCI is back in the station today, and he stands up to delight them all with one of his single claps. 'Great work, Eddie and team. I believe we're still searching through CCTV too – and that's now been expanded to cover all hotels in the area. Is that right, Jonah?'

'Yep. We're on it.'

'OK...' Eddie says, bristling slightly as he catches Jonah flicking one of his big grins at Becky. 'We also have a bit more on the cold cases, thanks to Joe...' He pauses. 'Basically, that's a dead end. All of the deaths were of natural causes and there's nothing to suggest otherwise. So, we're back to what's happening in the here and now: Andrew Morrison, Steve Bell. And now Connor Temple. We suspect this latest murder is likely to be connected to the first two, but the MO is different. He's covered in blood, for a start. Anyone got anything else to bring to the party? It is nearly Christmas after all...'

'The hairclip,' Joe says. 'It belonged to a woman called Karyn Latimer. I'm still looking into it.'

Wild Bill claps again. 'Good team work, Eddie. Now, while the main focus is tracking down Heather Brody and bringing her in for questioning as soon as possible, I'd also like you to hear a few more words from our resident expert, Dr Helena Summers, who has come up with an interesting plan. Helena?'

Helena stands up, her smiling gaze travelling around the room and resting briefly on Eddie. He takes a few deep breaths, trying not to think about why they haven't found time to talk to one another yet, one on one. Mostly this is his fault. He's seen her make moves to approach him. Always subtle – a light brush of a hand, an attempt to catch his eye, but he blanks it out and makes himself appear too busy. No one knows his history with her; even Becks only knows the basics. He's just not sure if he's built all this up in his head. For all he knows, she might just think of him as one of her love-sick teenage boyfriends.

Or worse... maybe she hasn't thought about him at all.

The slide with the handbag vanishes and is replaced with one of Helena's, titled 'Honeytrap' and written in big, bold letters.

Eddie glances over at Becky, who raises her eyebrows and squeezes her lips into a shape that he interprets as 'this could be interesting'.

'As you all know, the honeytrap is a commonly used technique by private investigators seeking to catch out cheating spouses.'

There are a few murmurs around the room. A, 'state the bleeding obvious, love,' from Keir Jameson, who Eddie shoots a glare.

'Our killer is escalating,' she says. 'If we continue to hold the assumption that these two cases are linked, my theory is that she is getting rid of predatory men. She's honeytrapping herself, in a way. She wants them to pick her up, and if they do, she kills them. It will be impossible to find via CCTV as we have hours and hours of footage, and she is clearly changing her appearance, but I think we have a lone female out there, and in most cases, this kind of pattern is based on revenge. Has something happened to her? A sexual assault that went unpunished? Perhaps not to her, but to someone she loves?' Helena pauses, letting her words sink in. 'Assuming she also killed the barman who could identify her, she has gone from careful, subtle kills – which would have gone undetected had she not left bruises on the first, along with trace evidence that proves she was there – to something infinitely more violent, with Connor. Something has triggered this change in behaviour. My theory is that she will not stop until she is caught or harmed in some way. It's possible she might want one of her victims to fight back.' She lowers her voice. 'This may be a woman who no longer wants to live.'

Her gaze rests on Eddie, and he has to admit he is grudgingly impressed. Maybe there is something in this profiling lark after all.

'It's not long until Christmas,' Helena says. 'The office parties are starting to dry up as people turn their focus to their family plans, or preparing to go away for the festive period. She is running out of time.' She pauses again, sucks in a breath. 'My theory is that she will want to go out with a bang. Thanks to some excellent searching by the team, we know that though there are a couple of parties happening tonight, there is really only one to be at – the party of all parties, at the Cedars Hotel. This is a big company, with a big budget. It's the plushest hotel in the area. Our lady killer is not going to want to miss out on this. So'—she grins—'we're going to send someone in to lure her out. DCI Wilde has been in touch with the covert ops team at Farndean station, and they are sending someone over to us right now.'

*Well*, Eddie thinks. Helena and Wild Bill have certainly been busy little bees, while he and the rest of the team have been running around like blue-arsed flies. He's still uncomfortable that his investigation has been used as a guinea pig for this criminology collaboration. He wonders about the timing, and if it's just a distraction to keep their minds off how Bill's involvement all started, with Jonty's cheerful slides about the threats of closure.

He will attempt to remain open-minded, but he would rather just keep searching for Heather Brody in the usual ways.

Helena crosses her arms and Eddie sees the glint of a diamond ring on her left hand, sparkling under the strip lights. He looks away. Catches Becky's eye She's been watching this interaction closely. Of course she has. It's probably about time he told her more about Helena, just so Becky can confirm that it's nothing and drop it. Because it *is* nothing, and it *was* nothing, and he has a job to do here. If this covert officer does his job, they'll have this wrapped up for Christmas... and then maybe Eddie can book himself a last minute escape as far away from happy families as possible.

# 35
## Becky

As she leaves the meeting room, she notices that Eddie is waiting behind, presumably to talk to Helena. She's desperate to know more about all *that*, but it will have to wait. She's thinking she'll invite Eddie round for Christmas. She's invited him every year since they started working together, and every year he hasn't turned up. Although she's not even sure why she's thinking about this right now – who knows what will be happening at Christmas, what with the unexpected arrival of her mum, and Allie already starting to disintegrate over it. She hasn't even spoken to her dad about it yet; it's been easy to use this case as a reason to not have to spend too much time talking to her family.

Helena's honeytrap idea is interesting, and her theory about 'one last party' is convincing. She'd like to talk to Helena herself, soon, before the investigation is over. Or maybe when it *is* over, because if things go to plan, they'll be celebrating before long.

She has a missed call on her phone, and the voicemail icon shows she has a message. She hits play.

'Becky? This is Gloria, the nurse you spoke to before at the Ivybridge Care Home? It's about your sister. I'm getting quite concerned. She hasn't left Juniper's bedside in days. She needs some support, and I know you're busy, but... She doesn't know I've called you, and I don't know all the background, so I understand if this is too hard, but maybe pop along and see her? Allie, I mean, if not your... If not Juniper. Anyway, call me back or just come in if you can. I'm on shift until ten tonight. There's, um, there's something else I wanted to mention to you too, actually. Speak soon.'

*Oh great*, Becky thinks. She dreads to think what the 'something else' might be. Joe is on his way to the kitchen, and she grabs his arm as he passes. 'I'm nipping out. Something I need to follow up on.'

He spins round, theatrically. 'I was going to ask if we were going over to Innoxia Research together? I've got an appointment to talk to the head honcho in an hour.'

Becky bites her lip. She should go with Joe. Allie can wait until later... Gloria sounded a little frantic, though, and Becky does want to find out what she wants.

'Can I meet you there? I don't think I'll be too long.'

Joe shrugs. 'Sure. I'm happy to get hold of all the info and take all the credit.' He winks and wiggles his hips as he walks away from her, throwing her a little wave over his shoulder. 'Later, girlfriend.' He says it in the faux-American twang that he has perfected. She laughs. He is obsessed with *RuPaul's Drag Race*.

Becky plays loud music in the car as she drives over to the care home alone. Eddie got her into nineties rock music, since that first year case together where they spent a lot of time in his car. She will never admit it, but she's been hooked on it ever since, with various Spotify playlists on the go, and Red Hot Chilli Peppers are wailing about giving it away as she pulls into the car park.

Gloria is waiting for her at the door. She looks frozen, standing there in her short-sleeved tunic. Her smile looks forced.

'Is everything OK?' Becky tries to usher her inside, but she shakes her head.

'I need to tell you something… It's confidential and I probably shouldn't say anything. But maybe we should go and see Allie first?'

Becky is intrigued. 'OK. But I have to let you know, if it's something criminal, I will have to report it.'

Gloria rubs her hands up and down her bare arms. 'Of course. I just want to explain it to you informally, first.' She leads Becky inside, grabbing a cardigan from behind the reception desk as they pass. 'I'm an idiot. I don't know what I was doing outside without this on.'

Becky follows the nurse down the corridor towards Juniper's room. 'Your sister is really *not* coping,' she says under her breath, before pushing the door open and walking inside.

The room is dim and stuffy – the windows and curtains tightly shut – and stale with that antiseptic smell mixed with sweat and boiled food. Even though she is unlikely to be eating for a long time, if ever again, Becky's mum is not going to be able to escape the unique aroma of hospital food. Juniper looks pretty much the same as last time Becky saw her. Asleep. Peaceful. Becky swallows down a lump in her throat. She has so many conflicting emotions about seeing her mum like this.

Allie is slumped in the seat next to the bed, her head in her hands.

'Al? I'm here. Are you OK? Shall we go and get some air?'

Allie raises her head. Her face is pale, her eyes ringed with dark shadows. 'Oh, *now* you turn up. *Now* you've got time for me.'

'I'm in the middle of a big case… You know what it's like. I can't just drop everything and sit in a darkened room all day when it suits me.'

Gloria's eyes widen, and Becky regrets her harsh words. Allie doesn't seem too bothered though. She just smirks, shakes her head. 'Can you get Dad to come in? Or even Christine? Surely someone must give a shit.'

Becky is not sure that their dad's latest girlfriend is likely to care too much about Juniper, but she might come for Allie. She's slightly surprised that her dad hasn't been in, but then also not surprised at all. Juniper treated him like crap then left him to bring up two children. He doesn't owe her anything.

What a mess this all is.

'I'll call them, Al. And I'll be back as soon as I can, OK?'

'Whatever.'

Becky follows Gloria out of the room. 'I'm sorry about that. Things are a bit tricky with our mum.'

'I gathered,' Gloria says, as they walk along the corridor. 'But you know, even if just for your sister's sake, now might be a good time for some reconciliation.' She lowers her voice, leading Becky down another corridor. 'In here is what I wanted to talk to you about.'

She leads her into another of the bedrooms. A woman is lying on the bed, blankets pulled up high on her chest, her arms resting on top of the covers. Her eyes are closed, and she looks peaceful. Next to her is a large piece of medical machinery, plus the usual monitors and controls. It takes Becky only a second to notice that the machines are switched off. And there is a faint but familiar smell in here, mixed with the usual stuffy smell of the place, the bodies, the disinfectant, the meals... even though most residents are unconscious. Not this one though.

This one is dead.

'Oh,' Becky says. 'I'm sorry. Have you already contacted the family?'

Gloria looks like she's about to burst into tears. She shakes her head. 'Not yet... I found her just a little while ago, but I think she might have been like this for a few hours. I tidied her up a little. Pulled her eyelids down. It's quite frightening when they have their eyes open and there's no light left behind them.'

Becky blinks, shaking off the image of Connor from earlier on.

'Was no one in to check on her?' Becky says it kindly, but she is curious and has no idea why Gloria is being so furtive about this. Residents must die in here on a regular basis. Given that they are all long-term sick, there's probably very little need to record any of their deaths as suspicious.

'Her daughter was here this morning. I spoke to her in the visitors' lounge. I think she left shortly after. I got caught up in something else... We're short staffed today and I had no real reason to check on Karyn until I did... and when I did, it was too late.'

'She'd already died? I understand that's very upsetting, but—'

'No, you don't understand.' Gloria shakes her head. 'I'm going to be in so much trouble for this. Mr Wade – the manager? – he's out all day today, and he doesn't know… And I was told to inform him straight away when anything changed with her, and…' She lets her sentence trail off, rubs her face. 'We put Karyn on a ventilator last week.' She points to the machine. 'That's it there. There is a mouthpiece that fits over her face. It helps her to breathe. Without it, she would die very quickly.'

'I understand—'

'When I came in to check on her, the mouthpiece was hanging off the side of the bed.'

Becky raises her eyebrows. 'Could it have fallen off?' A long shot, but had to be asked.

Gloria shakes her head. 'No chance of that. Impossible. Also, the monitor was unplugged.'

Becky blows out a long sigh. 'So someone did this deliberately?' She looks at the woman in the bed. Says a silent prayer for her, even though she's not religious. She just hopes that she is at peace now, wherever that might be. 'Who else is working today?'

'Just a couple of kitchen staff, but honestly, they never leave the kitchen. I know you'll need to talk to them, but I don't think they had anything to do with this.' She strokes the woman's hand. 'Karyn was going to die soon anyway, that's what Mr Wade told her daughter. I did suggest to her privately that she got a second opinion. Best to be sure before making such a big decision.'

'Switching off the machines?'

'Exactly. That poor girl has been coming here to visit her mum for thirteen years. I've watched her grow from a teenager to a woman. I've listened to her when she's sobbed tears of rage, vowing to make those men pay…'

Becky's heart skips a beat. 'Which men? What happened to this woman?'

'It's awful. She was violently attacked at home. Left for dead.'

Becky's work phone pings and buzzes with a notification.

'What's this woman's name?' she says, sucking in a deep breath.

'Karyn Latimer.'

Becky releases the breath. Tries to stay calm. Karyn Latimer is the woman who went to the jeweller to sell her expensive hairclips, but then never returned to the shop to go ahead with the sale.

Gloria is still talking. 'As I said, she's been here for thirteen years. Her care has been privately funded, but... well, that was due to end soon, with the increased costs. And I don't think Heather could afford it by herself.'

Becky's stomach flutters.

'Her daughter is called Heather? Heather Latimer? Do you have contact details for her, please?'

'Of course,' Gloria says. 'She doesn't go by Latimer, though. She decided to change to her mum's maiden name.'

Becky is suddenly very, very awake. 'Is it Brody? Is that her surname now?'

Gloria looks at her strangely. 'That's right... I know she stays at her mum's now and then. That's the address we have on file, but I can give you her mobile number too. But please... this is why I wanted to explain it all to you, before I made it official. Don't be too hard on her for this. The poor girl must've been desperate, to do something like this. She's a good girl. She's never stopped visiting. Never stopped caring... I told her she needed to think about herself for a change. Maybe now she can.'

Becky opens the message from Joe: *I finally got a chance to look up Karyn Latimer. Here's a link to the case. 2010. 'Woman gang raped and brutally assaulted at home believed to have been working as an escort.'*

*Shit.*

'Thank you,' Becky says, trying to stop her voice from shaking. 'I'm going to need to go now. But please, don't let anyone else into this room. It's a crime scene. I'll have a team come over as soon as possible. They'll need to interview you fully, take your clothes and fingerprints. The kitchen staff too. Don't let them go home, OK?'

Gloria is crying now, but she nods. 'I'll call Mr Wade.'

'Yes, do that. But don't let him into the room...and please, I will do what I can to help Heather, but I really need to ask you not to contact her now. I'll take it from here. I just need that phone number and address.'

Becky is trying to stay calm as she hurries along the corridor after Gloria. But the adrenaline is swirling around in her bloodstream like a bath fizzer. She needs to talk to Eddie straight away.

# 36

## The Party Girl

I've been feeling pretty jittery since I left Mum. I half expected Gloria to come running out behind me, discovering what I had done. But she didn't, which makes me think that no one in that place really cared enough. Not even her. In some ways it's a relief that I won't have to go there again. I can move on. Gloria always told me I should be thinking about myself, living my life for me. It's what my mum would have wanted.

I hate when people say that. How can anyone really know what she would have wanted? She was lost to me long before those men took her away. She was lost long before I pulled that stupid machine off her face. I feel clear headed about it now. In hindsight, I shouldn't have let them hook her up to that machine in the first place. Just let her slip away when she started to deteriorate. But I wanted that little bit more time. I think maybe I just wanted one last Christmas with her.

The house was cold today when I went in, but I enjoyed a scented bath, and used the little portable heater from Mum's wardrobe to warm up the bedroom while I got dressed.

I decided on vintage for tonight. I always knew the last party would be special. It's coming to the end of the season. People have had enough of their drunken colleagues. Time to do those last bits of shopping, drink a few mulled wines while wandering around the German market, buying expensive nativity ornaments and silly slogan placards.

She bought this dress in the Selfridges sale. I was with her. I was fourteen, and I was so excited to be heading *up west*, as she liked to call it. We shopped on Oxford Street, Regent Street, hung out at Piccadilly Circus for a bit, watching someone perform tricks with giant flaming hoops. We went to the Hard Rock Café, then we ended up in Covent Garden, where she pulled out a pair of tickets for the Opera House and I couldn't believe I was so lucky. I never asked where she got them from. How she could afford them. Or the dress. Because even in the sale, it was still a fortune. I realise now that one of her men must have given her the money for it all.

I was a bit naïve, I think. I didn't really understand the hostessing at the parties, or the men she entertained at home. Not then. I did soon, though. When things started to change, and she started to change, and no amount of fancy make-up could hide her dull skin and her dead eyes.

This hotel bar is stunning. Dark marble top, shiny gold fittings. The right kind of mood lighting and the perfect level of ambient music. I've had a look in the various function suites, and the same pattern follows. This is definitely the classiest venue that I've worked so far. I almost regret getting rid of that cute barman. He would have fitted in well in this place.

I catch a glance of myself in the long mirror behind the bar, the hexagonal tile breaking my face into many pieces. The dress is perfect. A dark, ruby velvet with spaghetti straps and a long slit up the thigh. I've brought a gold clutch, and the black velvet pumps have gold tipped kitten heels. I bought a new lipstick in a shade called Vampire's Kiss, which could not be more perfect if it tried. I'm also wigless. Deciding to go with my own honey blonde, given a neat demi-wave using my mum's old styling wand.

I'm having a Kir Royale. Because the colour matches my theme. And for once, a little alcohol boost is just what I need.

I haven't bothered with my getaway bag this time. I fully intend to leave this place exactly as I entered it. I'm on borrowed time as it is. I might as well look my best for the grand finale.

I sense him behind me as I sip my drink. There is a moment every time, when that body heat closes in. The scent. The change in the atmosphere around me as his breath tickles the back of my neck. That split second where I wonder if he will grab me and drag me away. Hurt me.

Kill me.

Or if he will move around to face me, stand too close to me. Smile. Wait expectantly for me to fall for his charms within an instant.

I don't smell the alluring scents of their aftershaves and colognes anymore. All I smell is what's underneath. Testosterone. Acidic notes of sweat. An underlying stench of the control they believe they possess.

I smile into the mirror, and his face, looking over my shoulder, smiles back.

'Hello,' he says. 'Can I get you another one of those?' He gestures towards my champagne flute, half-full now.

'Thank you.' I flutter my eyelashes a couple of times. Just enough. Signal received, loud and clear.

He hails the smartly dressed woman serving the bar, asks for two more. It's a common game. Mirror the drink, mirror the moves. We are in sync, this says. He slides himself onto the stool next to me. He's in a neatly fitted dinner suit. Not my favourite attire, but it's that kind of place. The women all look stunning. The men look like penguins.

'I'm David Addison,' he says. 'Are you new at Baker & Fraser? I don't think I've seen you around…' He pauses, sips his drink. 'I'm positive I would remember you.'

'Jodie.' I hold out a hand to shake his, but he lifts mine and kisses it instead. I can't help but smile. He's going all out, even though I've already left zero doubt that I'm a sure thing. If I didn't know better, I'd think he was playing me at my own game.

'Jodie…?' He cocks his head slightly, like a curious spaniel.

'Baker. Although I'm named after Foster. My mum loved her in *Bugsy Malone*.'

'She should've called you Tallulah,' he says.

Her theme song worms itself into my head and I have an urge to sing it. I should've adopted her persona long ago.

*I live till I die.*

'Are we going to ditch this place and have drinks in your suite, David?'

He looks slightly taken aback. But then he readjusts his expression. Re-joins the show. The moment is lost when his phone buzzes in his pocket.

He looks momentarily furious. 'I'm sorry. Please excuse me.' He turns away to fiddle around with it, switching it off, I hope, and I take the opportunity to try out my new toy.

I tip out the already crushed tablet I took from Connor's kitchen from its tiny plastic bag, and drop it into his drink, giving it a little swizzle with my finger. I watch in the mirror as I do this, just in case he is looking in there too. If there's a moment of doubt, I'll just knock the glass over the bar. My heart rate ratchets up a couple of notches as the drink fizzes, and then settles.

I don't usually use this sort of prop, but I got a bit spooked after the lawyer, who didn't get quite as drunk as I wanted, and didn't go along so easily with my plans for recreational drugs. I'd managed to inject him under the guise of some foot fetish carry on, but it had almost gone wrong and I was much more wary with the guy after that. Steve? Was that his name? Luckily he was more than up for any kind of chemical sexual activities I had in mind. I can't gauge it with Dinner-Jacket-Dave, so I'm being cautious. But I will have to act quickly once he drinks it. I'm sure there are people watching me tonight. I'd be disappointed if there weren't.

David returns, giving me his full attention once more.

'Was that your wife?'

He laughs, but there is a genuine glint of sadness in his eyes. 'No need to worry about anything like that.'

'Maybe we should drink these and head up? I'm sure you have some good champagne in the mini bar.' I pick up my first drink, knock it back in one. Barely a mouthful in there. I sip the other one, looking him in the eye.

He mirrors me, as I knew he would.

Two more sips, and we're both done. I lick my lips, tasting the sharp blackberry tang of the Crème de cassis at the bottom of the glass.

He looks in the mirror, then glances around, ever so briefly. Checking who is watching. No doubt wanting to show off what he's pulled and how quickly he's done it. Perhaps there was a bet. Maybe he's not yet sure if this is something he's going to have to pay for. Whichever it is, he's up for it. He looks me straight in the eye, licks his lips. Winks. I slide off the stool and take his hand.

Game on.

# 37
## Becky

She calls Eddie via the handsfree when she gets into the car, but it rings through. She sends a message – *where are you???* – then starts driving and calls Joe instead.

'Hey,' he says. 'I've literally just left Innoxia. Do you know where the name comes from, by the way? It's from the plant *Datura innoxia*. One of the deadly nightshades. Causes delirium. Poisonous in high doses, but just one of the many plants they are researching. Pulling out the best bits and leaving the dangerous bits alone, I guess. Anyway, they confirmed that Heather works there, and also that she's not been on form recently. Off sick a lot. Distracted. And wait... get this... they've been doing an audit, and they think that some stock has gone missing from their current clinical trial over at—'

'Ivybridge Care Home,' Becky says. 'I'm just leaving there, as it happens.'

Joe sighs. 'One step ahead as ever. Anyway, they were planning to deal with it rather than involve us. Wanted to do some more internal investigations first. The full HR due diligence process.'

'Well,' Becky says, pulling out of the car park, 'that's good employee care. Not so good for us. However, I do have a lot more news about her...'

'You saw the article I sent you?'

'I did. What a tragedy. I can completely understand why she wants to punish the men who did this to her mother.'

'Just unfortunate that she's gone for randoms instead.'

'Yeah... I want to know more about why that is. Luckily for us, I have another address. Eddie's not picking up, so do you want to come with me?'

Joe hesitates, and she thinks he must've been cut off.

'Joe? You still there?'

'I'm here. Sorry, was just getting into the car.' She hears the door slamming shut, the engine starting. 'Maybe we should call this in? Get some back-up?'

Becky had a feeling he would say that. Joe is by the book when it comes to this sort of thing, and she usually is too – but too much time with Eddie is rubbing off on her. She needs to act on this now. Besides, if their eminent profiler, Dr Helena Summers, is correct, Heather won't be at home. She'll be at the Cedars Hotel, for the biggest party of the season. Being baited by one officer, and watched by several others who've been asked to dress in their best party gear to carry out surveillance.

'I just want to check out the place, see if there's any sign of her. In theory, she should be out partying. Did Eddie go over to the Cedars, by the way? I saw the message asking for volunteers for the surveillance op.'

'Dunno. I was already in the meeting by then. But really... I can't see Eddie going voluntarily to any party. Especially one where you can only pretend to get drunk, and have to be on your guard the whole time.'

'True. OK, the address is 22 Midway Crescent. I'll probably be there in five.'

'See you there.' Joe hangs up.

She should call Eddie again, leave a proper message to tell him what they are doing. She could also call Stuart Fyfe, ask him to assist. But she doesn't want to spook Heather, if by some small chance she *is* at home. She runs through a few potential cover stories she can use for knocking on her door.

There is a pick-up truck turning out of the junction as she passes the old warehouses on the way to Heather's mum's address. A car sits on the back, burnt almost completely to its shell. They really need to sort out the security at that place. They've been called out before to investigate various criminal goings-on behind those buildings, and this is not the first burnt out car she's heard of being left in there. The local car scrapper usually goes on the hunt for them, hoping to salvage something. Cars never burn out completely. There is always something that can be used.

Joe's car is waiting at the address. He must have come from the other direction. Becky parks just a little further down the street. It's one of the nicer areas around here, filled with pretty, detached 1930s houses with well-kept gardens, in the most part. The pavements dotted with mature oaks, some with roots protruding over the walkway and towards the bottom of the drives. A couple of kids' bikes on lawns, glistening with frost. Warm light glimpsed through slatted blinds.

Number twenty-two stands out because it looks cold and empty. No lights on, that Becky can see. And while the front of the house is neat and tidy, there are no planters, no covered up furniture. It looks sad and lonely in a street where there is an abundance of life. They walk up the path together.

'I seem to spend my life ringing doorbells that nobody answers,' she says, pressing the button.

Joe pulls up his collar, zipping his wind jacket right up to the top. 'That's very profound, Becks. Shall we try around the back?'

The side gate is unlocked, so they go around to have a look, and it's the same story around there. A bare garden and the house in darkness.

'Well,' Joe says. 'At least we can confirm she is *not* here.' He cups his hands around the front bay window and peers inside. 'It looks like no one's sat in there for years.'

Becky's phone buzzes. It's a message from Eddie: *Beck come here please, cant see what doing can you now? Head hurts…pls xwhiwodp*

She reads it again. Shows it to Joe. 'What the fuck? That's like a butt-dial from a pocket full of vodka. Call him.'

This is not like Eddie at all. He's a stickler for proper messages, with punctuation. This is barely legible. She dials his number, and it rings three times then is cut off and goes to answer machine. She calls again, and it goes straight to answer machine.

It's been switched off.

She has a very bad feeling about this. 'Did you say Eddie had gone to the Cedars?' she says. 'When that message said they were looking for volunteers, I thought they meant to hang around sipping mocktails… they do have an actual trained undercover ops officer doing the main part, right?'

'We need to call someone,' Joe says. His eyes are wide with alarm.

Becky makes a quick decision. She calls DS Stuart Fyfe, who picks up straight away, but answers in a hushed tone. 'Becky… everything OK?'

'Where's Eddie? He just sent me a really strange message, and now his phone is switched off. Is he with you?'

'Didn't he tell you?' He sounds a little wary now. Unsure of himself. This makes her bad feeling increase ten-fold.

'Tell me what, Stuart? I'm getting worried now—'

'The covert officer they sent wasn't suitable. The surveillance team spotted Heather Brody entering the Cedars. We had to make a quick decision…'

Panic hits her like a cold shower of hailstones.

'Please don't tell me…'

'Yes, Becky…' Stuart says. 'Eddie is the honeytrap.'

# 38

## Eddie

His phone rings again, and as he tries to slide the button on the screen, it drops from his hand onto the carpet. He leans forward from the seat of the padded armchair to try and pick it up, but just as his finger makes contact, it slides away and he lurches towards the floor. He puts both hands out to steady himself, manages to push himself back up again. His vision swims, the room swirling in a mass of shapes and colours. His head feels like it's been split with an axe. He slumps back into the seat, his head dropping to his chest. He tries to pinch himself on his thigh, but his fingers don't seem to be working properly.

'You don't look like a David,' the woman says. 'And definitely not a Dave.'

He lifts his head towards the direction of her voice, sees the shimmering outline of her sitting on the bed.

'I think someone's been telling porkies.' She gets up and walks towards him, and he tries to push himself further back in the seat. 'What's your real name? Tell you what, I'll go first. I'm not Jodie. I'm Heather.'

He swallows, and it feels like a lump of air has solidified and is trying to block his throat. He blinks, trying to focus.

'Eddie...'

'OK. I recognised the name you gave, by the way. David Addison. Bruce Willis in *Moonlighting*, wasn't it? I loved watching that with my mum. She had the boxset on DVD. We watched a lot of things together. Lots of re-watches too. *Rentaghost*. Remember that? Mum gave me a little soft toy cat with a jester's hat on, and I named it Claypole. After Timothy. The cute little jester. Do you remember?'

Eddie grunts.

'Such a shame he was dead. Timothy, I mean. *Moonlighting*, though. That was a great series. Cybill Shepherd was just so beautiful. Did you know that the will-they-won't-they element was the biggest driver of that show when it first aired? Viewing figures plummeted when they finally got it on... Just shows you, doesn't it? People love the suspense. The thrill of the chase is so much sweeter than the kill, don't you think?'

She picks up his phone.

'I'll turn this off for you, shall I? We don't need any interruptions.'

'What are you going to do?' he manages, although the words feel slow and thick, like they are being dredged from a tin of syrup.

She drags over another chair and places it in front of him. Sits down, leans in close, her breath warm on his face. 'I haven't decided yet, Eddie. You see, I'm not going to be able to do this sort of thing anymore. Yours might be the last hotel room I'm in for a while. Ever, in fact. I'm debating whether to carry on as normal, or do things a bit differently.'

'What. Things.' The more he forces out words, the more in control he feels. He tries to sit up straighter, but he's just so tired. What was he doing drinking that drink with her at the bar? She's opened a bottle of champagne from the mini bar, but neither of them have drunk any of it. He'd started to get woozy not long after they'd come into the room, and she'd seemed a bit surprised by that.

'To be honest, I kind of thought you'd be trying a bit harder to have sex with me, Eddie. But look at you…still fully clothed, and barely able to move your own arms. I don't think your hands will be up to much. Or any other part of your anatomy.'

'Please…' he says, the word long and drawn out, his head swimming again. He tries to grip onto the arms of the chair, but his hands don't have any strength.

'You don't need to plead. It won't make any difference. Whatever I'm doing, I'm going to do it. That's how it works, right? That's how your lot conduct yourself.' She stands up, starts pacing the room, and her ruby coloured dress smears across his vision like a blossoming stain. 'You *men*. You think you can just take what you want, don't you? You command, we follow. That's what those men who killed my mum did, Eddie. She might not have officially died that night, but she was dead to me. They treated her like a piece of meat. A plaything. They broke her. Her body couldn't stand it so it shut down. Thirteen years, Eddie. Do you know what that did to me? A young girl, in her formative years… Do you know what it made me think of men?' She runs towards him then, a blur of red. Shouts into his face. 'You disgust me.'

'Police,' Eddie says again. This time more clearly. 'I'm police.'

She pulls back as if she's been slapped. Then her face looms in closer again, a slow smile spreading across it. 'You might well be, Eddie. But you're still a *man*.'

# 39

## Becky

Becky parks in a space close to the front entrance that clearly states 'Reserved', and quickly shows the top-hatted doorman her ID before he can open his mouth. She hears a car door slam, and Joe is there behind her, jogging across the car park.

DS Stuart Fyfe is waiting for them in the hotel lobby. He's dressed in a dinner jacket that looks a little too tight across his shoulders, the sleeves slightly too short. He clocks her expression and holds up a placatory hand. 'All under control here, DS Greene. Eddie stepped in at the last minute and we've watched him the whole time. They've only just gone up to the room, and we have people up on each floor. We've given him a panic button inside his jacket, but the plan is to send in "room service" in about'—he checks his watch—'ten minutes.'

'I think you need to do something now, Stuart.' She holds up her phone, showing him the garbled message. 'His phone is off, and this message is not up to his usual standard of lucidity.' She sucks in a breath, the cold night air catching in her throat. 'Was there someone at the bar monitoring his drinks?'

'They only had one, downed it and left… both drinks were completely visible on the bar, and we don't think she's been spiking anyway, it's—'

'She took Rohypnol from Connor Temple's flat. I'm certain of it. I think she knows she's on borrowed time, and it's an insurance policy. She can't have any fuck-ups on her last day, can she? We need to get someone into that room now, Stuart. I don't think he's safe.'

All the time she is saying this she is thinking to herself what a stupid, reckless idiot Eddie is for doing this. When the trained undercover officer was no good, they should have cancelled this plan. People think just anyone can go undercover, when actually, it's a highly trained role. You can't just shove on a dinner suit and put on a charm offensive and hope for the best. As soon as he's out of there, she intends to give Eddie a bollocking.

'Let's go then,' he says. 'We have Keir set up for room service duties. He won that role as he convinced us all that he worked in a hotel for a summer before he started police training. Also, no one else wanted to do it.'

Becky rolls her eyes. 'All of that figures.'

They travel up together in the lift. She and Joe sticking out like a pair of sore thumbs in their normal work gear, amongst all the black tie and cocktail dresses they'd passed in the lobby. But no one seemed to care too much. They were too busy getting drunk and deciding who to snog under the mistletoe – that festive justification for cheating. Another poisonous plant to add to the theme of this case.

Poison Ivy. *Datura innoxia*. Mistletoe… It's turning into quite the botanical murder mystery.

DC Keir Jameson is standing by the lift, dressed in black trousers and a sickly golden-toned shirt with 'Cedars' written across the breast pocket. He's standing behind one of those giant room service trolleys, a silver dome atop a cream dinner plate, an ice bucket with a bottle of champagne sticking out of it, and a white linen napkin draped over the side.

'Good evening, madam,' he says to Becky. 'I hope you're enjoying your stay.'

She gives him a hard look. 'We need to do this. Now.'

'Oh right, OK.' Keir straightens up and smooths back his thick black hair. 'Let's go.'

'What do we do if they won't let him in?' Becky says to Stuart.

He holds up a room keycard. 'Then we go in anyway.'

They follow a short distance behind Keir. Becky sees now that there are others ready and waiting up here, sitting at the other end of the long hallway, on a couple of couches, pretending to look at their phones. One of them nods when he spots Stuart, and Becky recognises him as one of the uniforms that had worked that first morning when Andrew Morrison was found.

Becky feels that fizz of excitement she gets when things are close to being over, but there is still a big bit of action to happen before they get to that point. If they are right about all of this, then they will soon have Heather Brody in custody, and they can hope that she tells them exactly who she has killed and why. Perhaps Andrew Morrison and Steve Bell's families will have some closure for Christmas. Connor Temple's too. Not that it will make anything better, but at least knowing that the person responsible for destroying their lives is behind bars has to help a little. If they are wrong about this… She gives herself a little shake. *We are not wrong.*

283

The three of them stay out of sight in case someone looks through the peephole as Keir knocks loudly on the door. 'Room service.' No answer. He looks at Becky, his eyes questioning. Becky nods.

'Room service.' Louder this time.

Still no answer.

Keir leans in beneath the peephole, his ear pressed against the door. 'Nothing,' he mouths. He knocks again. 'Do you want me to leave it outside?'

Becky touches Stuart's elbow. 'We need to go in,' she hisses. 'Now.'

Stuart hands Becky the keycard. Keir pulls the trolley to the other side of the door, and Becky steps in close. She knocks on the door twice. Pauses. They all listen, but there is not a sound coming from the other side. Becky gives them the thumbs up, before holding the keycard against the access plate. It flashes green, and there is a click. She pushes the door open and walks in to the bedroom, Stuart hot on her heels, Joe and Keir close behind.

'This is Detective Sergeant Becky Greene from Woodham CID. We are entering this room as we have reason to believe that someone inside may be in distress or danger...'

The room is ice cold. The doors to the balcony are open wide, the thin, gauzy inner drapes blowing in the breeze. It's dark there, no balcony lighting. It's not that bright in the bedroom, either – just one small lamp on over by the bed, and the glow of the light coming from under the partially closed bathroom door. Now that they're inside, they can hear the sounds that they couldn't hear from outside. They must have spent a fortune on sound-proofing here. There's the sound of traffic on the main road outside...

and another sound, coming from the bathroom. Running water.

There is no sound of Eddie. Or Heather.

'They can't have left,' Keir says. 'We've got people at both ends of the corridor. At the lifts, at the stairwell...'

'Heather?' Stuart says, his voice loud in the empty space.

'Eddie?' Becky walks further into the large L-shaped room. There are two puffy mustard coloured armchairs, facing each other, but one is upturned. A king-sized bed with too many pillows, a mustard throw draped along the bottom. It appears untouched, except for a light indentation where it looks like someone might have been sitting. A bottle of champagne is open on the dresser, some poured into two glasses. The bathroom door is ajar, on the other side of the bed.

Joe walks over to the balcony doors. Turns back to them. 'She's outside,' he says. 'Alone.'

Becky walks over to the doors and sticks her head around the corner, just enough to see where she is. She's sitting on one of the patio-style chairs, knees drawn up to her chest, arms clasped tightly around her legs. Her face is pale, her lips turning blue. Her eyes huge and scared.

'Bathroom,' she says.

Stuart pushes his way past Becky, rattling off commands to Joe. 'Get her inside and warmed up. Heather, do you have any weapons?'

Becky doesn't hear what they say in response. She's already in the bathroom, as is Keir... and he's already found Eddie.

'Oh Jesus Christ.' Becky grabs the biggest towel and moves in to help Keir as he holds on to Eddie, manoeuvring him out of the shower. He manages to get him onto the floor, where Eddie starts shivering. She reaches in to turn off the water. It's freezing. Eddie is fully clothed, and drenched. His eyes reach hers, but they struggle to focus.

'You need to get him warmed up, Keir. Get him stripped and in a hot shower.'

'Was. Trying. To. Wake. Up,' Eddie manages, through chattering teeth. 'Am. OK.'

Becky leans down and pulls him close, hugs him tightly, the cold water from his suit soaking into her jumper. 'It's just as well you are, you idiot. Because if anything happened to you, I'd kill you.'

# 40

## The Party Girl

I'd like to say it was fun while it lasted, but I didn't do it for fun. Now that it's all over, I just feel numb. They took my dress and my shoes, even my underwear. Put them all in evidence bags. But I'm not sure what they'll get from them. I didn't really do anything *naughty*, did I? Not this time. I actually slept last night. Even on that tiny, narrow cot with the slightly scratchy blankets, wearing the grey tracksuit they have provided me with – none of my home comforts, is what I mean – and yet I slept better than ever. I think my mind is free, at last, from all the rage and the demons that have inhabited it since I was fourteen. Because yes, it all started when I lost my dad, and then two years later, I lost my mum too.

Thirteen years after that, and I've lost her all over again. But now we are both free.

Of course, I know I will never be *physically* free. I'm going to prison for this. I'm not going to let them convince me to try for a plea of insanity or diminished responsibility. I knew exactly what I was doing when I started all this, and I know exactly what I'm doing now.

The detective who told me his name was David Addison is sitting opposite me now, no longer in his dinner suit, but in another, plainer one, with a white shirt underneath that still has the lines from where it was folded inside the packaging. I must admit, I'm a little surprised he's here now, in the interview room with me. But I only gave him a quarter of a tablet, and it looks like it has fully worn off after a good night's sleep and no doubt copious amounts of water. Sitting beside him is the younger female detective. Very pretty. Kind eyes. Despite her fear for her partner, she treated me with compassion in that hotel room.

I zone out a little as they go through the details. Detective Inspector Eddie Carmine, Detective Sergeant Becky Greene. Reading me my rights, blah blah blah. They have provided me with a solicitor, who took the basic details from me before this and instructed me to say as little as possible. Well, I'm not sure I'm going to adhere to that. I actually want to tell them what happened.

Detective Carmine starts reading out a couple of names. They don't mean a lot to me because I didn't pay a lot of attention to the names the men gave me – like me, they were probably lying. But then the detective slides photographs across the table towards me, the names written underneath, and I touch each one gently, nodding as I go. Andrew Morrison. Steve Bell. Connor Temple. That one wasn't part of the plan, but here we are. He took a battering because I'd had enough of men like him. He thought he could drug *me*? Do what he wanted to me? He made a big mistake that night.

'Yes. I killed these men.' I lean back in the seat. 'I'm not trying to be cocky, just factual. I'd like to get this over with as soon as possible.'

Detective Greene shifts in her seat. 'Don't you want to explain, Heather? Tell us why?'

'What's the point? I want to confess. I can write it all down, if you like.'

'It's probably better if we do that, Heather,' Carmine says. 'We'll use the transcript from the recording. Then we'll print it out, and you can sign it. After that – assuming this is the route you want to take – we'll hold you in custody until you can see a judge, probably tomorrow, and they'll inform you of next steps.'

'Sentencing?'

'Well, yes,' he says. 'If you do plead guilty, we don't need to go through the lengthy trial process, but there is still a process. It takes time... and also, this time of year'—he shrugs—'things tend to take a lot longer.'

'I expect you'll want to hold me on remand.'

Carmine sighs. 'Yes. I expect that we will.'

I'm not making this very exciting for them, I know. I will in a minute though. I decide to wait it out, see what else they want to mention.

'We've looked into what happened to your mum,' Greene says, her voice gentle. 'Karyn Latimer was attacked by multiple men, at your home, in 2010. None of them were ever caught. They subjected her to a sustained and violent sexual assault. There were no witnesses, but the post mortem revealed four separate semen profiles. Four sets of DNA. None of them on our database back then... but we are requesting to re-test these now. We'd like to catch these men, Heather. This won't be the only time they've hurt someone.'

Well, this is unexpected. 'Thank you,' I say, I feel a small smile threatening the corners of my lips. 'I can help you with that, I think. One of them was called Brendan O'Malley. The Kingpin, if you like. His friends may think he's flown to Florida for some winter sun, but you'll find him on the floor of his front hallway. It would have looked like a heart attack, but it wasn't.'

Both detectives do a good job of keeping their faces neutral.

'Thank you for telling us, Heather,' Carmine says, cool as you like. He glances at his colleague. 'We already found Mr O'Malley, actually. The taxi driver called it in.'

I shrug. Hardly matters now, does it? Greene taps something into her phone, no doubt alerting the rest of their team that they have to look into this straight away. I hope they haven't buried him already.

I carry on with my miserable story. 'I saw the whole thing, detectives. I was meant to be staying with a friend that night, but the plans changed. I came home early...' I pause, checking that they want me to continue. The solicitor, Valerie Shaw, does not. She shoots me a look of exasperation, whispers that I should stop talking now. But I ignore her. It's time to get all of this out in the open.

'I heard the noises coming from her room. It wasn't that unusual by then. She'd been attending parties. Hostessing, I think you call it. She was an escort. My dad died in 2008, leaving us with horrendous debt. He killed himself. And then Brendan O'Malley, his old work colleague, offered my mum a job. I think at first, it actually was just a bit of sexy waitressing. But I'm sure you know how these things go. Men can be very persuasive, when it comes to money and sex.' I take a sip of water from the beige plastic cup on the table in front of me. 'Long story short, she started bringing her punters home. She was high most of the time. Whatever got her through it, I guess. That night I heard several voices, mixed in with the music, and her shrieks, and honestly? It wasn't anything I hadn't seen before. Usually when it happened, I'd go to my room and put on headphones, drown it out. In the morning I'd take her breakfast in bed, and we'd pretend it never happened.'

Detective Greene looks up from the notes she has been furiously scribbling. 'Had you witnessed any of the men being violent before?'

'Now and then. The odd slap, mainly. Nothing she couldn't cover with make-up.'

'But this night was different?' Carmine leans forward. 'Did you hear or see anything unusual while this was going on?'

I shake my head, then remember I have to talk, for the recording. 'There were always drugs. Drinks. I think they just went too far. I didn't see it all. I went to my room and put on my headphones like usual, and when I went through in the morning, I couldn't wake her up. I honestly thought she was dead.' I look down at the table. 'I know this is an awful thing to say, but I wish she had died then.' I raise my head again. Look from Detective Carmine to Detective Greene. 'If she had, then I don't think any of the rest of this would have happened.' It's only when a tear rolls down my face, leaving a little dark stain on my sweatshirt, that I realise I am crying. I close my eyes, and I can see Mum's face. She's smiling.

*Sleep peacefully now, Mum. It's over, at last.*

# 41

## Eddie

Eddie is not keen on neatly wrapped up endings. He doesn't quite believe them, somehow. But this is not like before. This is not the same as the Photographer case.

Thankfully, Brendan O'Malley is still in the fridge, awaiting his funeral date. Like everything else, the festive period is a total bugger for getting things done. Dr Maria will perform a post mortem, searching for the puncture wound in O'Malley's neck that Heather had added to her confession. None of the tox screens have come back anyway, but when they do, Eddie is sure that they will all match up.

The manager of the Ivybridge Care Home admitted that he'd known that O'Malley had something to do with Karyn Latimer's attack, but he'd chosen to take the money because, clearly, he was an amoral bastard. Even O'Malley hadn't been aware of how much he was paying over the usual rate for that room. It was only when the ventilator cost had been factored in, that it had flagged up in his accounts. Wade would be tried for his part in it all, and Eddie hoped to personally see to it that the weaselly creep got what was coming to him.

O'Malley, at least, had already got that.

He isn't going to waste any time mourning a man like that. He shudders, thinking of him, and all that poor Karyn Latimer had gone through. As for Heather, she was full of remorse, and they would be pushing for a lenient sentence of some sort. Though there was essentially no possibility of her getting out of prison ever again, there were a couple of different options of where she could be incarcerated, and Eddie hoped the judge would show some compassion on that front.

Ultimately, no matter how tragic her story was, there was no excuse for what she had done. She'd killed two innocent strangers in hotel rooms, purely because they wanted to have sex with her. That wasn't a crime in itself, but Eddie was fully aware of her twisted logic. The killing of barman Connor Temple came from a place of desperation – and, it seemed, he was no angel himself. Who knows how many women had fallen victim to his drinks spiking game?

Eddie, of course, was lucky to be alive too. Stepping into that honeytrap role had been stupid, in hindsight. But he'd gone along with the momentum of it, and thankfully, his colleagues had his back.

He takes a bite of the chocolate muffin that Miriam has thrust into his hand. She's made a tray of them, dusted with icing sugar to look like snow. Plus a tray of gingerbread men, and some sort of truffles rolled in coconut. They are all sipping festive punch, which appears to be apple juice with bits of cinnamon stick floating in it.

They've drawn the Christmas Dip, and Joe's incredibly shit joke has won him a festive hamper filled with more food than anyone could eat in a month. He says he's donating it to the food bank, and so he should because it's a bloody fix that he's won his own prize.

Eddie scans the room slowly, taking in the excited team of revellers. Some of them will be going to the pub after this, but he's not really up for it. He wants a quiet night in with Simon before he jets off in the morning to Madeira, to spend Christmas with his mum and his siblings and his grandparents. The invite was extended to Eddie too. But he's declined. As tempting as the lure of winter sunshine might be, not to mention being with all three of his children, he does not want to spend the holiday period with his ex-wife. And more than that, he does not want to spend it with her parents.

Becky is over in the other corner, deep in conversation with Jonah Abboud. Every time she laughs, she throws her head back, and Jonah looks increasingly smug. They'd make a nice couple, he thinks, and he doesn't know why this bothers him so much, but it does.

Stuart Fyfe and Keir Jameson are being bored to death by Jonty, over by the Christmas tree. Joe, who is working the room while sampling all of Miriam's baked goods, catches Eddie's eye and gives him a cake-filled grin. He nods towards Jonty, giving a little eye roll, and Eddie can't help but smile. They are quite a team, this hotch potch of people in his department.

Wild Bill is secretly drinking whisky from his plastic cup, and boring a couple of the junior team members with his crap poetry. He catches Eddie's eye, lifts his cup in a salute, mouths 'do you want some?', and Eddie smiles and shakes his head. He bloody hates the stuff.

The inflatable snowman is partially deflated, and it's floating around like a drunkard at closing time. Eddie looks forward to the moment where he can stick a pin in the thing and stamp it to death on the floor.

Bruce Springsteen is singing his smoky, croaky version of 'Santa Claus is Comin' to Town' and Eddie takes this as his cue to leave. He's about to slip out without telling anyone – it's always the easiest way – when a voice comes from his right, and a hand touches his arm.

'I hope you weren't planning a French exit,' Helena says.

Eddie turns. Her eyes are sparkling. Almost dancing with mischief. He remembers those eyes. Can it really be almost thirty years since he saw them last? They look just as he remembers. He recalls that Beautiful South song, about growing old, and the prettiest eyes being the constant over the years, and it's so accurate that he feels a jolt in his chest. His breath hitches in his throat.

It feels like only yesterday when the pair of them were madly in love. Before they had that stupid argument, which changed both of their lives forever.

'Well done,' he says. 'I have to admit I was sceptical, but that profiling was excellent work.'

She bites her lip. He's not sure if he's imagining it, but he thinks she looks disappointed. 'You really want to talk about work?'

He glances at her left hand. At the gold band she wears on her third finger. He still has a slight indentation from where his was for all that time. He wonders if the dent will ever fill out, or if it will always be there as a memory.

Helena follows his gaze then shakes her head. 'I wear this for work, Eddie. Stops unwanted attention in the workplace.'

Eddie's mouth falls open. 'Oh...'

'Come on,' she says. 'Let's ditch this joint. We've got a hell of a lot of catching up to do.'

He grabs his coat off the hook by the door, and just as he's pulling it on, he catches Becky's eye. She's listening to something that Jonah is saying, his face close to her ear. She's not quite laughing, but there's a hint of a smile on her face. She looks happy. She needs that right now. What with everything that's going on with her mum. He'll call her tomorrow, and they'll talk properly then. They have to be due another sausage and egg McMuffin debrief.

He slips one of Miriam's gingerbread men into his pocket.

'Ready?' Helena's voice asks from behind him.

He winks at Becky. Mouths, 'Merry Christmas.'

Then he turns back to Helena, and they walk out of the door.

Maybe *The Boss* was right. Maybe Santa Claus is coming to town after all.

# 42

## Harry

Heather has been all over the news. Victim or murderous bitch? Various headlines showing some leanings towards sympathy, Twitter threads filled with copious use of the #metoo and #timesup hashtags calling for leniency; others, of course, labelling her a monster. There are loads of articles about her mum too, and that O'Malley man and his part in it all.

While obviously Harry can't condone what Heather did to those innocent men in the hotel rooms, and the poor barman who was obviously only trying to have a nice time with her, Harry does have some empathy over why she did it. Things with Joanne cooled off a bit after their visit to the police station, and the things he said that had made him sound a bit... obsessive. However, it helped that the newspapers who wanted to talk to him – which was, and still is, basically all of them – have been very excited to get him to reveal all about dating a murderer. They've spun the obsession into something quite different, using the angle that he'd been suspicious about Heather's activities all along – had always known there was something not quite right about the shy, lonely scientist, who kept herself to herself but led a terrifying double-life as a femme fatale.

There was that one article, one of those long-form essays that people seem to like these days, and that had dismissed Harry's part in it all, suggesting that he was more of a sad loser than Heather. He doesn't share the link to that particular article on his socials.

His socials... now there's a thing. He wasn't really that bothered about any of them before. He had a Facebook account, where he shared holiday snaps and wished people he didn't talk to for 364 days a year a happy birthday. He had a Twitter (aka 'X') account because he liked to follow some of the live tweetalongs when there was something controversial happening, or when a new superhero film was released. But he'd gone from having 142 followers (most of them bots) to 25k, and it was growing every day. Joanne had set up an Instagram account for him, adding a photo of them in their superhero suits at the Christmas party, a blurred figure circled in the background – one of the many Catwomen who were there that night – captioned: 'Is this one Heather?' This had led to various spin-off clickbait articles with headlines like 'The chilling moment they realise a murderer is watching them'.

All in all, things have worked out well for Harry. He deserves it though, after everything Heather put him through. All her lies. She was really quite mean to him, he thinks, when he goes through it all, time after time, regaling all of his new friends. He's never been so popular, and he likes it.

He wonders what would have happened if he hadn't gone to the police about Heather's bag. Perhaps he should have tried to talk to her first, tried to understand. But he was upset about the party. All that effort he'd gone to, getting her tickets and a really cool costume to wear. She was so ungrateful! No doubt they would have caught her anyway. He does feel a little guilty about putting things in motion, but really, it's her fault, not his.

All he ever tried to do was be a good boyfriend.

Maybe if she'd just let him do that. If she'd just relaxed a bit, let herself be loved by someone, guided by someone, then maybe she wouldn't have had to do what she did.

She seemed to have tarred all men with that same horrible brush.

It's a shame Heather didn't understand that he was only trying to help her.

Her and all these bloody feminists with their ridiculous notions, ranting about the patriarchy. Harry smiles to himself, thinking of his own favourite hashtag.

*#NotAllMen*

# 43

## Eddie

ONE WEEK LATER

Eddie has been forced into some last minute Christmas shopping and he's spent the past two hours battling the crowds in the high street and the shopping centre, freezing his nuts off just for something that will be ripped open and eaten, or sprayed, or stuck on a shelf and set on fire. What is the actual point of scented candles anyway? He checks his phone in the car, as he sits there in the car park for a moment, getting the heaters up to full blast. He has a message from Becky, asking if she can have a week off. He says yes, even though it's last minute, because he can't even imagine how she is coping with her mum and her sister right now. Then he reads a message from Simon, with a picture of a cold beer and a ridiculously blue swimming pool, captioned, 'still time to fly over for Christmas lunch by the sea'. He'll think of a suitable reply to that later, although right now, inside his steamed-up car, the thought is tempting.

He also has a message from Helena, confirming their dinner date for this evening. They're taking things slow, and it might go nowhere, but at the moment, they are both enjoying one another's company – reminiscing one minute, trying to catch up on the last thirty years, the next. Helena is divorced, one son at university. She's only been back in Woodham for a year, which explains why he hasn't come across her until now.

Incredibly, he has Wild Bill to thank for it.

He heads back home, taking a diversion off the ring road, where road works have sprung up overnight. He slows down as he is diverted via a series of unfamiliar and not particularly pleasant residential streets. A scrawny, unkempt man in a Santa costume that looks three sizes too big for him appears from a side-alley, a black bin bag in one hand. He looks furtively up and down the street, and catches Eddie's eye, before giving him a toothy snarl, and hurrying off down the street with his sack. Is this the perfect cover for a burglar? The man definitely looks like a creep. He looks like the antithesis of a bloke that delivers presents to children. Eddie dislikes Santa. He always has. The whole concept of taking your kids to see a bloke in a cheap costume with a pillow stuffed up the front. Letting them sit on his knee... Eddie shudders.

Thankfully, the whole festive period is almost over for another year.

*Bah, humbug.*

# Acknowledgements

Avid readers of mine will know that this is not the first outing for Detectives Carmine and Greene... *The Deaths of December* was released in 2017, and I had always planned to write more, but for various reasons, that didn't happen, and I wrote quite a few other books instead. But I always knew I wanted to write more of these characters, and I actually had the idea for *The Party Season* all the way back then. But it wasn't until fellow author and good pal, Luca Veste, invited me to dinner with his editor, Jo Dickinson, in February 2022 that the idea became reality. Jo passed me over to Beth Wickington, who, as it turns out, has an equally gleeful love of murderous Christmas thrillers – and thus *The Party Season* was born. So thank you, Luca, for being the best Christmas elf – and thank you Jo, for gifting me an editor who actually came up with something so gruesome during brainstorming the *next* book, that I felt genuinely sick. A match made in heaven. HUGE thanks to Beth for sharing my vision, and for giving me the insightful editorial notes that made this book much better than when I first delivered it to her. Thanks to Laura, for a fantastic copyedit, and thank you to everyone at Hodder who has worked on this book to get it out there and into the hands of readers.

Thanks, as ever, to Phil Patterson – the agent who always has my back, who makes me laugh and keeps me sane through this torturous process we call publishing. Phil was very disturbed by one of the characters in this book, which made me confident that I had got it just right.

I'm very grateful to Stevie Curran, who generously bid for and won the Young Lives Vs Cancer auction to choose a character name for this book. Stevie kindly chose to include Polish tutor Maria Szczepańska, and I hope I have done her justice by making her a smart, wise-cracking pathologist. I have a feeling this won't be her only outing in the fictional community of Woodham.

Thank you to all of my author pals who keep me going when writing is hard and who amuse me at crime writing festivals. Special thanks to Steph Broadribb, who always reads the first chapter, and implores me to write the rest of the book.

Thank you to all the readers, reviewers, bloggers, influencers and general crime writing cheerleaders. I love your messages of support and encouragement over the years. Without all of you, there would be no point in doing this!

Massive thanks to my family and my friends, who shout about my books to whoever they meet, and buy them all even when I give them freebies.

And my final thanks, as is tradition, to JLOH – the twinkling star at the top of my tree.

★ ★ ★

If you'd like to receive my occasional updates and enter my giveaways, you can sign-up here: https://sjihollidayblog.wordpress.com/sign-up-here/

Read on for the first chapter of
*The Deaths of December*, Carmine
and Greene's first festive mystery

# 1

## BECKY

Becky's washing her hands in the sink, glad that it's one of those three-in-one things with no mirror above it so she can avoid seeing the bags under her eyes. She shakes her hands, waits for the dryer to come on, gets a sudden waft of something deeply unpleasant. She side-eyes the woman standing next to her, muttering away to herself, and can't work out if it's the mangy coat that smells like a dead animal or the woman inside it. She holds her breath. She's smelled three-day-old corpses less pungent than this.

She batters through the swing door out of the toilets, escapes into the sanctuary of the restaurant. Blinks at the too-bright lights, inhales the fried egg smell. 'Jingle Bell Rock' is playing on the sound system. The place is packed, as it always is just before ten thirty, when sausage and egg muffins get replaced by burgers and fries. It's a treat, this, she keeps telling herself. Not the surroundings, maybe, but the breakfast. Definitely. After the week she's had.

She's got her tray, head down – looking for a table – has to be at the side, with a seat at the back, facing into the room. Standard copper thing, that. Make sure you can see what's going on. Too busy, though, to notice that she's about to walk slap bang into someone.

A hand stops her.

'Morning.'

She looks up, blinks. Feels her heart slide into her stomach. She'd wanted to enjoy this food on her own. Have a bit of time before work, where it'd be full on as always, even though she was due a day off now, after the mad few days she's had.

'Eddie. You slumming it too?'

'Food of the Gods, this,' he says. He nods at a table where a bunch of schoolkids have departed, leaving an explosion of wrappers and cups and half-eaten hash browns. Last day of term. They don't care if they're late. Before she can say anything, a quiet woman in uniform and a sad little Santa hat appears and sweeps it all carefully away, leaving that damp cloth smell hovering just above the Formica. She can hardly say no. She slides along the plastic seat, and he follows her in. He unwraps his breakfast and starts eating, staring straight ahead. Savouring it. She does the same. Muffin. Hash brown. She uncaps the orange juice and drinks it in one.

'So,' he says. 'Tough week? Saw you were on DS Fyfe's team. The assault on campus. Nasty.'

She wipes her mouth on a napkin. 'Awful. But, you know. We got him. Jack was like a dog with a bone on that one.'

He nods. 'Good. Good. Can't say I've been so lucky. Still working on the Hollis murder. We've got nothing. No one saw anything. Victim had no enemies, no dodgy ex, no psycho neighbour. Nothing. Someone just swooped in, smashed her over the back of the head with a stone vase, and left her there. If it wasn't for the parcel delivery coming that afternoon, noticing that the door wasn't properly shut, we don't even know how long the poor woman might have been left lying on the carpet.'

'Just before Christmas, too,' Becky says. 'Horrible.'

Eddie's face crinkles into a frown. 'To be honest, anything that can distract me from the hell that's Christmas is a good thing. I can't be doing with it all. Never have done. Well, when the kids were small, I suppose. But now? Everyone spends too much money, eats too much, drinks too much, then moans about their credit card bills in January while they try to survive on a diet of avocado and squeezed lemon juice.'

She can't help but laugh. 'Are you finished, Mr Scrooge?'

'Oh come on. Don't tell me you like it, do you? All the crowds, the non-stop jingly music. Drunks wearing antlers throwing up in your garden?'

'I love Christmas, actually. We make quite a big thing of it at home. We don't spend too much money, but we make sure the whole family's there for lunch – turkey, sprouts, sherry – the lot. A small gift each, roaring fire. Christmas CD . . .'

'You're winding me up?'

'Nope. Nine more sleeps, I can't wait—' She's about to say more, when she sees the woman in the fur coat tottering across to a freshly departed table, mine-sweeping the remains. Jamming half a breakfast muffin into her mouth, wrapping up the other bits and shoving them into her pocket. She sighs.

'Lady Margaret,' Eddie says. 'Still going strong, it seems.'

'They'll throw her out in a minute.'

'She'll be gone before they get the chance. She's been doing this for years. You must've seen her before?'

Eddie slides out of the seat, walks up behind the woman, who's walking casually out of the restaurant as if she belongs there, just like everyone else.

'Morning, Ma'am,' he says.

'Oh, hello, Edward,' she says. Becky sees her row of blackened teeth and starts to breathe through her mouth again.

'Not making a nuisance of yourself, are you?' he says.

'Me?' She laughs. 'You know me, Edward.'

Eddie holds open the door for her and she disappears out into the frosty morning, pulling her coat around herself and bustling off up the street with a purpose, as if she has somewhere to go, somewhere to be, that isn't a bus shelter. Or, if she's lucky, a few hours in the community centre with the rest of her cronies.

'Come on,' Eddie says.

She matches his pace as they walk through the town centre, past the stallholders still setting up their wares – the hotdog stands, the towering tree with its twinkling silver lights. Someone has hung some sort of garland around the long-legged spaceship that is almost hidden on a side street until you nearly walk into it. The HG Wells legacy, more noticeable from the name of one of the popular chain pubs than the giant steel alien. War of the Worlds? That's just this town on a Saturday night.

She's momentarily transfixed by a group of solemn Chinese carol singers, and their sandwich board that reads: *John 3:16 For God so loved the world that he gave his one and only Son, that whoever believes in him shall not perish but have eternal life.*

If only it was that simple . . . Besides – is eternal life really such a good thing?

When they arrive at the station building, Eddie disappears, leaving her with a quick nod of his head. As she pauses next to the front desk, taking off her gloves and stuffing them into her pockets, a uniformed constable appears from a door to the side.

'Ah, perfect timing, Detective Constable Greene,' he says. 'You can take the mail up to CID.' He thrusts a pile into her arms. Brown envelopes. A few white ones that could be Christmas cards – or abuse – they quite often received abuse. And a large square envelope, addressed 'To A Detective who knows what to do'.

# It's shaping up to be a deadly little Christmas…

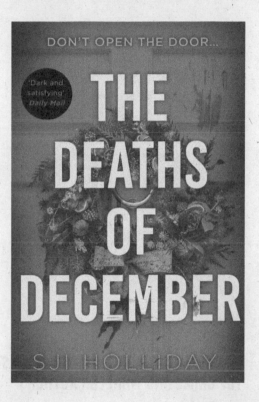

Meet Detectives Greene and Carmine as they work together to solve their first festive murder mystery.

Available now.

# THRILLINGLY GOOD BOOKS FROM CRIMINALLY GOOD WRITERS

CRIME FILES BRINGS YOU THE LATEST RELEASES FROM TOP CRIME AND THRILLER AUTHORS.

SIGN UP ONLINE FOR OUR MONTHLY NEWSLETTER AND BE THE FIRST TO KNOW ABOUT OUR COMPETITIONS, NEW BOOKS AND MORE.